He got out of a ⬚ mint-condition Corvette.

"Unusual transportation for a crossing guard," Valerie murmured. Stupid thing to say. But damn, there was a lot about this man that didn't add up.

"I haven't always been a crossing guard."

No kidding. "What did you used to be?"

"An unhappy member of the corporate world. Now I'm a happy crossing guard."

An explanation of sorts, if somewhat flippantly delivered. But no answer at all. How could someone with his drive and intelligence be satisfied not using his talents?

"You're going to be a crossing guard for the rest of your life?"

"You have a problem with that?" Kirk's tone was light.

"No." Maybe. It just seemed like such a waste.

"It's honorable work. And the kids—including your twins—deserve the best."

"Of course they do." But it didn't take a businessman successful enough to drive a mint-condition vintage Corvette to provide that at a low-traffic side street.

Valerie knew, without another word being said, that this particular conversation was over.

Dear Reader,

I want to tell you about something that happened to me when I was writing this book. I discovered that I've spent my entire life ignorant of the judicial system, which has been serving me diligently every single day. Of course, I knew it existed. I've been in a courtroom, seen hundreds of trials on television. I knew all about being a judge—I thought. I knew so much I missed the fact that I didn't know anything at all.

Every day while we go about our business there are, in every county in the nation, people who carry the pressure of making life-determining decisions. As I was doing research for this book, I sat in a juvenile courtroom, to the side of the judge's bench, and saw what she saw—the kids out there in front of her, the attorneys and parents and witnesses and victims. I saw the fear in the eyes of teenage offenders whose lives might be forever changed that day. And the hope felt by those who might be given another chance. And I saw us. You and me. Out living our lives. Taking for granted that the judge is going to look into the eyes of a sixteen-year-old, see the hope and the fear, and still make the decision that will keep us all safe. Including that kid…

I could hardly handle a morning of that pressure. And I was experiencing it vicariously. I've always known that doctors did miraculous things—holding lives in their hands every day. And policemen. And firefighters and paramedics. I missed the fact that judges give their lives and hearts and minds to preserving *all* our lives. I, for one, will be aware and grateful that they're in those courtrooms, taking this challenge upon themselves so that the rest of us can raise our children and send them off to school and grocery shop and go to church without worrying too much that the person next to us is a criminal. A heartfelt thank-you!

I love to hear from readers. You can reach me at P.O. Box 15065, Scottsdale, AZ 85267 or visit me at www.tarataylorquinn.com.

Tara Taylor Quinn

For the Children
Tara Taylor Quinn

HARLEQUIN®

TORONTO • NEW YORK • LONDON
AMSTERDAM • PARIS • SYDNEY • HAMBURG
STOCKHOLM • ATHENS • TOKYO • MILAN • MADRID
PRAGUE • WARSAW • BUDAPEST • AUCKLAND

ISBN 0-373-71171-9

FOR THE CHILDREN

To Sherry. You've enriched my life beyond measure.

ACKNOWLEDGMENTS

Heartfelt thanks to Judge Sherry Stephens
and her staff for their generous assistance
with technical aspects of this story. Any liberties taken—
and all mistakes made—are mine.

CHAPTER ONE

"TOUGH MORNING, Valerie?"

The black silk robe flowing around her, Superior Court juvenile judge Valerie Simms smiled and nodded at Judge Hal Collins Wednesday morning. She stopped briefly in the hall on the short trek from the courtroom to her quiet high-ceilinged sanctuary. "How about you, Hal? A piece of cake as usual?"

"It wasn't bad," he said, still smiling. With a little wave, he disappeared into his office.

It wasn't that Hal didn't care about the kids they tried to help after parents and schools had failed to make a difference. But he didn't let any of it get to him.

Someday, when she grew up, she was going to be just like him.

Trying to pretend she already was, Valerie shook off the Billings case and thought, instead, about the lunch date she had ahead of her—with her in-line skates and the new concrete jogging trail not far from the Mesa, Arizona, Juvenile Court Division. She'd have just enough time to get in ten miles and a quick shower before she was due back in court. She'd already reviewed her afternoon calendar, which left the entire hour-and-a-half lunch break free.

"How'd it go?" Valerie's supportive and energetic judicial assistant met her at the door of her office.

Valerie grimaced. Unsnapped her robe.

"That bad, huh?" Leah Carmichael followed her inside the large, peaceful room.

"Not really." Hanging up her robe, sinking into the plush maroon leather of her desk chair, Valerie continued, "I released Sam Marsden. I think he's ready."

"He spent a lot of time on the report you asked him to write about his community service."

He had. She'd been pleased with his work. And, for this boy, she was honestly hopeful.

Leah sat in one of the two maple chairs across from Valerie's desk, crossing her legs as though settling in for a long chat. In her taupe slacks and jacket with perfectly matched shoes, she looked every bit the professional Valerie knew her to be.

Attention to detail was among the many strong points Valerie appreciated about Leah. She'd chosen well when she'd hired her first J.A.

"The Marcos kid was as unbending as ever. I told him that if I see him again, I'm going to detain him."

Signing a request to issue a warrant for truancy, Valerie gave Leah a brief rundown on the rest of the morning's calendar.

"What about Abraham Billings?" Her assistant fingered a few strands of her light brown hair. The top of her head bore several intricate and perfectly ordered braids that day, with the rest of her hair hanging straight to midback. Val wondered how early Leah had to get up to achieve such an elaborate style.

And whether or not she felt the result was worth the time and effort.

"Judge Simms?"

"I let him stay with his mom."

Leah stood. "Well if you think that's where he should be then that's good. I'll bet he was happy."

"Yeah. He was." She met Leah's clear blue and damnably trusting eyes. "I wanted to remove him."

"You did?"

She nodded.

"Then why didn't you?" Sinking back to the chair, Leah's glistening lips hung open.

"Diane Smith recommended removal. She's a darn good probation officer. She's been to the boy's home. I haven't."

And the boy's mother...

"You knew that before you went in."

Carla Billings, in spite of her many shortcomings, had been so in tune with her son she'd seemed to have felt every breath he took. A person had to be pretty insensitive to rent apart a bond that close.

Valerie didn't think she'd survive if Blake and Brian were ever taken away from her...

"I did know it, you're right," Valerie answered belatedly when Leah continued to silently appraise her.

"C.P.S. moved for removal."

And Diane had spent more time with the boy.

"Abraham put up a good fight for himself. He was willing to do whatever he had to do to stay home."

"So what does he have to do?"

"He's on probation with community service." It was the strongest penalty she could give for truancy.

"I want to keep as close an eye on that boy as possible," she said. "And I want him busy, out of his home participating in a good cause, for as many of his waking hours as we can manage."

She wanted him away from the mother she'd just allowed to retain custody. Though nothing had been proven yet, no official filing, Abraham's mother was most likely prostituting out of her home—although there'd been a vague claim that she was some sort of bookkeeper.

That was all speculation at this point, however. Right now, her biggest concern was Carla's incorrigible twelve-year-old son. A young man who'd attended only nineteen of the first forty days of his seventh-grade year. The middle of October, and already the kid was in jeopardy of having to repeat the grade.

A grade he'd barely reached due to absenteeism in his last year of elementary school.

His probation required thirty-two hours of commitment weekly. And just as important, constant communication with a probation officer. It was a harsh disposition. And Abraham had signed the requisite contract without hesitation. Most of his thirty-two hours had to be fulfilled by attending his classes at Menlo Ranch Junior High.

"They tried CUTS, right?" Leah asked, frowning, referring to the Court Unified Truancy Suppression program.

Judicial assistants reviewed all files. Valerie's J.A. remembered everything she read. "A requisite component of the program is parental participation.'' The implication was clear.

Valerie also remembered everything in the files she read. Including the name of Abraham's school. Menlo Ranch. Which her own sons attended.

"You want me to send your robe out for dry cleaning?" Leah got to her feet.

Valerie shook her head. As her assistant left, closing the door behind her, she slouched back in her chair, hands linked across her stomach, and stared at the ceiling. Her job was to make decisions. She'd made one.

So why was she doubting that she'd done her job?

In her mind's eye, she suddenly pictured a man. The new crossing guard at the boy's school. He'd only been around since the start of the semester, replacing old Mr. Grimble who'd been working the corner in front of the elementary/junior-high complex since Blake and Brian had started kindergarten. The new guy wasn't old—mid-thirties, Valerie guessed. Younger than her own thirty-seven years.

He was about medium height for a man. Five-eleven maybe. And although he wasn't skinny, he was slim. Clean-shaven. With brown hair cut in a businesslike style above his ears. But what Valerie remembered most about him was the way his mouth quirked to the right when he smiled.

And he'd been smiling at her—and everyone else approaching his crosswalk—since the first day of school eight weeks before. Every morning when she dropped the boys at his corner. He waved, too. And she'd heard him call her boys by name—their right names. An unusual feat for someone who wasn't intimately acquainted with them. Blake and Brian were identical twins.

Standing, Valerie grabbed her clothes out of the canvas bag she carried back and forth to work, locked her office door and quickly changed. She'd never spoken to the crosswalk man. Didn't even know his name. But thinking about him calmed her, anyway.

She put on her in-line skates at the trunk of her car, skated a full twelve miles in less than an hour, showered, and still had time for a bowl of soup with crackers.

By the time she was seated for her Wednesday-afternoon calendar, she felt whole again. Confident. Ready to determine new directions for the lives of her troubled kids.

"Hi, Cindy, got your lunch money today?" Kirk smiled at the pint-size redhead standing at the corner with him on the fourth Thursday in October.

"Yep, see?" she said, holding it up for him.

He glanced quickly at the couple of dollars she held, returning his attention immediately to the goings-on around him. There would be no children in his street unless he said so. "Good," he told the fourth-grader. "Now, be sure you put it someplace you can find it at lunchtime."

"I will." The girl giggled, and skipped across the street as he stepped out, raising his sign to stop traffic.

Several other kids had gathered, as well. Kirk greeted each of them by name as they passed. Steve and Kaitlin and little Jimmy Granger. Jake and Josh and Melissa and...

The day, the job, continued. When school had started in August, he'd given himself a week to learn the names of the kids. Since then, he'd paid close attention to the children themselves.

As soon as he stepped back to the curb, a car pulled up on the west corner. Abraham Billings. That made six days in a row.

Kirk was impressed.

Until the past week and a half, Abraham had missed school more often than he'd come. But when he did show, his mother always dropped him off. She kissed him on the cheek, then sat in her car watching until he'd disappeared inside the school.

Kirk could imagine Susan there, doing the same with Alicia.

"Hey, buddy," Kirk said as the boy approached his corner.

"Hi." The word was barely uttered.

At the moment Abraham was the only one waiting there to cross. Which meant that Kirk could hold him there for a second, have a chance to talk with him.

"You okay?" Kirk had known for months that this agile young man had problems.

"Yeah."

He waved to the boy's mom, who waved back. Abraham scowled.

"You mad at her?" Kirk asked.

"No." The tone was almost belligerent.

Abraham was probably one of the best-looking kids in his class. Tanned and lithe, he had perfectly proportioned features and big brown eyes. He wasn't looking particularly attractive at the moment, however.

Deciding to leave well enough alone for that day, Kirk adjusted the edge of his bright orange vest and waited for enough kids to warrant stopping traffic. He didn't see any children coming down the street. He'd wait another thirty seconds and then halt traffic anyway.

"Do you hafta wave at her like that?" The question seemed to burst from Abraham.

"Like what?"

"Like she's a piece of meat or something."

Whoa. Kirk frowned, framing his next words carefully around something he sensed was there but hadn't yet identified.

"I wave at all the mothers," he said easily. "And fathers, too. Every day."

"Why?"

"To let them know they can trust their kids to me."

"Oh."

Another car was approaching. The Smith boys. They were good kids. Kirk knew several Smiths, including the business professor in college who'd mentored him during his undergrad years and then grad school—and guided him through his first multimillion-dollar deal.

Glad that Smith was such a common name, Kirk kept hoping that the more decent Smiths he knew, like his professor, the less pain he'd feel at the thought of the one bastard he'd never met—the Smith who'd changed his life forever.

"That's dumb." Abraham was staring out at the street, but didn't seem to be focusing on much.

"Why?"

"I don't know, man, it just is."

The Smith boys had stopped halfway out of their car, apparently listening to some last-minute instruction from their mother. According to her sons, she had a different name—Simms. And apparently she was a juvenile court judge.

"Basketball tryouts are next Tuesday," Kirk said casually.

"So?"

"I'm the coach." Steve McDonald, principal of Menlo Ranch and the one person who'd remained a friend to Kirk all his life, had included the coaching position in the package he'd presented last spring. It was intended to save Kirk from himself. And it seemed to be working.

"So?"

"I'd like you to try out."

"I'm too short."

"You're quick. And I've seen you at lunch, tossing trash in the can from eight feet away. You never miss."

Kirk served as lunchroom monitor during the middle part of the day.

Shoving his hands in the pockets of his freshly laundered jeans, Abraham shrugged his backpack higher on to his shoulders. "I don't have time."

"It's only for an hour or two after school."

"What is?"

The Smith twins had arrived. Kirk looked up and

waved as their classic blond beauty of a mother pulled past them. He waited for her to go and then stepped off the curb.

"Basketball tryouts," he answered Blake. "They're next Tuesday."

Abraham had already left them.

"Cool," Brian said. "Can anyone try out?"

"Of course."

The boys were walking slowly across the street, seemingly oblivious to the traffic they were holding up.

"You coaching?" Blake asked.

"Yeah."

"We'll be there," Brian called as they raced the last few yards to the opposite curb.

Kirk watched them go, his forehead creased.

Something wasn't quite right with Brian Smith. He shuffled when he walked. Like he was too lethargic to pick up his feet.

That was as far as Kirk had gotten with his analysis, however. Those two were hard to get to know. They were cheerful and friendly on the surface, but didn't reveal much about their inner thoughts and feelings. They covered for each other, looked out for each other—almost as though they didn't need anyone else. As though they had one identity instead of two.

Kirk was no psychiatrist, but he didn't think that could be good for them.

"HEY, BOY, you want to see how babies are made?"

Coming in from school late Thursday afternoon,

Abe didn't recognize the male voice that had called out to him from the end of the hall. He glanced sideways at the guy standing in the trailer Abe shared with his mother. He didn't recognize the man.

Except that they all looked alike. Too tall. Too fat. Too bald—or too gray. Too dressed up. Too slick. And always, always too sickening.

Reaching his room at the opposite end of the hall, Abe ignored the man. He'd been doing his community service work at the old folks home since class got out and he wanted to change clothes.

"'Cause I've got some great pictures of your mom I can show ya…"

Abe shut his bedroom door. Put on his headphones. And waited for his mother to call him to dinner.

"HI, MOM."

Blake and Brian were in the kitchen, leaning on the counter in front of the small television set mounted above the countertop, when Valerie came in with dinner on Thursday night.

"What're we having?"

The question was from Blake. Brian wouldn't care.

"Chinese."

"Cool."

Blake turned back to some basketball game they'd been watching on one of the cable sports stations.

"Basketball season hasn't started yet."

Brian glanced at her. "It's a rerun."

"We do have a large-screen television set in the family room."

"We were waiting for you."

Valerie set the bags of food on the counter, going to a cupboard for glasses and paper plates. She dropped a kiss on each boy's head as she passed.

Every day without fail, since their father's death, she'd found the boys waiting for her when she came into the house through the garage door that led to the kitchen.

They were good boys. She paused, hand in midair over the shelf of glassware, as Brian leaned his shoulder into his brother. Blake accepted the extra weight.

They were the best.

Which didn't mean that raising them alone was an easy task.

"How was your day at school?" she asked them five minutes later. Television off, they sat together at the breakfast bar in the kitchen. Takeout was always eaten there.

"Good," Brian told her. "We're trying out—"

"For basketball," Blake finished. "Tryouts are—"

"Next week." Brian jumped in as his twin took another bite of egg roll. Brian didn't have to deal with the problem of a full mouth. He wasn't eating much.

The boys talked more about the tryouts and Valerie delighted in their enthusiasm.

"How was your day in court?" Brian again. Her little nurturer.

"Fine," she told them, making herself think about the great job Leah was doing so she wouldn't be telling them a lie.

Before she was sworn in as one of the youngest female Superior Court judges in the state of Arizona, she'd promised herself that she would not bring her work home.

Her day in court. The hostile teenager who'd spit at her when she'd given her ruling, committing him to a secure facility due to his repeated failures to follow the terms of his probation; the fifteen-year-old girl seeking an abortion against the will of her parents—these were not things that belonged in the home she'd built for her boys.

"Come on, Bry, eat up," she said. "There's still enough light to shoot some baskets before you do your homework." And before she tackled the load of jeans that was waiting for her, the bills she'd been putting off for almost a week, a call to the landscaper to tend to the sprinkler head that was spraying wide and a return call to her parents back home in Indiana. At some point she had to get to the grocery store, too. This was the third night that week for fast food.

"I'm not hungry."

Brian's reply was not a surprise. "Did you guys have a snack when you got home?" she asked. *Please let his lack of appetite be because he's full.*

"Naw. There's nothing here to snack on," Brian said, pushing rice around on his paper plate.

Valerie's appetite suddenly matched her son's. "Did you have a big lunch?"

Blake dropped his fork with a sigh. Refusing to look at his twin, he pinned her with green eyes that were so like their father's. "He hasn't eaten lunch all week, Mom."

Brian continued to arrange little mounds of rice.

"Is this true?" she asked him, the tension gathering in every nerve.

Blake looked at Brian, who finally lifted his head and stared back at his brother. "I guess."

"Brian Alan Smith, do you mean to tell me you've been going without meals again?"

The boy opened his mouth, but she didn't wait to hear what he had to say.

"You looked me in the eye and promised me you'd eat!" Her voice, trembling with disappointment, had almost reached shouting volume.

He tried again to speak.

"You lied to me!" Her throat hurt with the force of her yell.

Both boys stared at her. Silent. Their eyes wide. And sad.

"Don't you have anything to say for yourself?" she asked her youngest—by six and a half minutes—son.

"I'm sorry."

"Do you want to die, Brian?" She wasn't yet capable of sounding calm.

He shook his head.

"*Do* you?" she yelled at him.

"No!" A healthy dose of life accompanied the declaration.

"Well, you're going to," she told him, hating the derision she heard in her voice. Hating even more the sense of panic that was driving her to treat her son so abominably. Hated the fact that there were times when the weight of raising these two all alone overwhelmed her.

"No, I'm not, Mom," Brian said, his tone soothing.

His twin sat silent, face straight, eyes revealing a hint of fear.

"You heard the doctor, Brian," Valerie said, forcing herself to speak at a normal level. "Three times in six months, you've heard the doctor. You're borderline anorexic and if you don't eat you're going to kill yourself."

"I'll eat."

"Then do it."

"Okay."

"Now."

"Mom…"

"Now! Brian." Her voice started to rise again. And then, as though she'd used up all her anger, her heart softened. She looked at the young boy who'd needlessly burdened himself with an adult's concerns—with the responsibilities he believed his father had held.

"You're going to stunt your growth, Bry," she said gently. "You and Blake are just entering your biggest growth years. He already weighs ten pounds more than you do. And if this keeps up, he'll spring right up—but you won't."

With pinched cheeks Blake turned to his brother. "Eat a couple of egg rolls, Bry, and then we can go shoot some hoops."

Giving a troubled nod, Brian did as he was told.

CHAPTER TWO

KIRK HATED Friday nights. They meant a whole weekend ahead with nothing to do but lecture himself.

He particularly hated this Friday night.

Letting himself into his plush Ahwatukee home, in a secluded Phoenix neighborhood set into the base of South Mountain, he tossed his keys on the antique cherry-wood table by the door, caught the alarm before it went off and headed straight for the phone.

He ignored the blinking red dot that signified messages. Saw on the LED screen attached to the blinking machine that there were twelve calls waiting for him and still ignored it. It was the same every day.

He'd push the playback button sometime that evening. And half listen to the messages. It was a form of treatment—to listen and remain calm, unaffected.

Sometimes he needed a drink first.

Tonight, he needed the phone.

Corporate attorney Troy Winston always picked up Kirk's calls immediately. Even now.

"What's up, buddy?" Kirk's right-hand man of ten years greeted him.

"Susan had a baby." Kirk could barely get the words past the stiffness in his face. He'd run into an acquaintance of theirs at the Corvette dealership when he'd gone in for an oil job that afternoon.

"Okay."

No surprise there. Kirk felt the stab of disappointment.

"You knew."

"Yeah. I ran into Bob Morrison a few months back."

A name from his past. His ex-brother-in-law. Kirk didn't respond.

"And you didn't bother to tell me."

"I didn't think it mattered."

Susan's gone on with her life, Troy's tone of voice told him. He stood, feet apart, the muscles of his thighs straining against the legs of his jeans.

"The baby's a month old."

"Let it go, buddy," his attorney, the only person still on Kirk's payroll, advised him. "Give up this idiotic plan you've locked yourself into and get on with your life. Go out. Call someone. Date. You could have a new kid, too."

"I have a kid."

"Kirk, you're really starting to worry me. I went along with this whole school guard thing because I thought you needed some time off. But I didn't think it would last a week, let alone three months. All this isolation is starting to get to you."

"I slept with Susan ten months ago."

"You guys weren't speaking to each other ten months ago. As a matter of fact, as I remember it, the woman freaked out anytime you were close enough to breathe the same air."

He could always count on Troy to tell him the truth. That was why the man had quickly risen to the seat right next to Kirk Chandler, CEO of one of the nation's most controversial, well-known and financially successful acquisitions firms.

Of course, all of that was over. Done. Kirk had closed the company almost a year ago. And Troy, while still handling Kirk's personal affairs, was enjoying the good life.

Kirk took a deep breath. And another. He concentrated on the fingers holding the phone, refusing to allow them to clamp the thing so tightly it bruised his hand.

"I ran into her one night at the cemetery. She didn't freak."

"Not freaking at a cemetery bears no resemblance to having sex. None. At all. Let me swing by, take you out for a beer. I know a couple of women who'd—"

"It was late. I was there when she came walking up. We were both too tired to make sense of anything...."

"Not good enough, Kirk. You forget who you're talking to. This was the woman who, after your divorce, not only had her own name changed, but changed your daughter's as well. Hell, I was there when Susan turned into a raving lunatic at the funeral just because your car was close by."

Sliding his free hand into the pocket of his jeans, Kirk flexed the muscles in his shoulders and down his back. The flannel shirt he was wearing still felt odd to skin more used to silk.

"I was crying. That night."

Silence hung on the line.

He'd left Troy Winston speechless. At a different moment, there'd be some satisfaction, maybe even humor, in that. Another moment in another lifetime.

"She walked straight into my arms, broken, needy. Hurting so bad she was craving death...."

Kirk knew he had to stop. To think about his fingers on the phone.

Loosen up, man. Loosen up. It's in the past. It can't be changed. The future can be changed.

They were the only words that kept him sane.

"The woman I'd married, planned to grow old with, was in my arms. I walked her home. And when she didn't want me to leave, I stayed."

"I'll make some calls."

Troy's voice was deadly serious as he rang off.

And Kirk was satisfied.

BY SUNDAY NIGHT, all the boys could talk about was the basketball tryouts coming up that week. There was a practice Monday after school and the actual tryouts were on Tuesday. Throughout the weekend they'd alternated between half killing themselves in the driveway, attempting to become shooting stars in two days, and driving her crazy with energy that only seemed to grow the more they expended it.

"Larry Bird flicked his wrist right as he threw the ball. That's the trick," Blake said, rolling the die but forgetting to move his little metal car along the Monopoly board.

"Dan Majerle was the best-three point shooter in

the league. I think he flicked his wrist, too," Brian added, staring at the board. "We need to flick our wrists…"

"And we didn't practice that at all."

Neither boy seemed to notice that the game in which they were currently engaged had stalled.

"Mom? Can we go shoot—"

"No!" Valerie laughed. "It's pitch black out there, guys. You have tomorrow's practice and you'll have time before dinner tomorrow, too."

"Do you think we'll have to do one-on-ones?" Blake asked his brother.

The die still lay, double sixes, on the Monopoly board. Valerie was quite proud of her six red hotels and twelve green houses.

Her boys, who were usually land magnates, owned the utilities and a few of the railroads.

"I'm sure," Brian said, frowning. "You don't have to worry, though. Just steal the ball and blow them away."

Picking up the Community Chest and Chance Cards, she put them in their storage slot on top of the one-dollar bills. Then she cleared off the rest of the board and folded it to fit inside the box.

The real estate didn't really mean that much. She'd had no competition.

The twins continued to discuss everything from shoes and socks to ways they could maintain control of the ball, completely oblivious to the game's disappearance.

"Let's go get some ice cream," Valerie finally suggested.

In tandem, the boys looked at her. At the empty table. And then back at her.

"Sorry, Mom." Brian spoke for both of them.

She grinned. "It's okay, guys. I'm glad to see you so jazzed about something."

And she was. Overjoyed, actually. Brian had been eating all weekend. She realized this was just a temporary fix, but it seemed pretty obvious that basketball could be the thing they'd been searching for to help her son with his flagging self-esteem.

Talk of basketball continued as all three ate their ice-cream cones, filled with the strangest concoctions of vanilla ice cream and mix-ins they could come up with, stopped by the store for the week's groceries, and then tried to focus on the boys' homework. Brian hauled out a disgusting-looking object he'd been hiding, unbeknownst to her, wrapped in a towel under his bed.

"It's my science project, Mom!" he'd protested when she insisted he throw it away immediately.

"What is it?" Valerie wasn't convinced.

"A piece of bread I dipped in fabric softener. There's another one dipped in diet soda."

"Yeah," Blake piped up from his spot on the living-room floor. "His theory is that one will be preserved and the other will be eaten away by the acid. Cool, huh?"

Yeah. Cool. She should've had girls.

"Mom?" Pen in his mouth, Blake was frowning as he looked up at her. "Dad would be really happy if he knew we were trying out for the team, huh?"

Valerie straightened the cushions on the couch. "Of course he would."

"And he'd come watch every single game, wouldn't he?" Brian asked, stopping on the way back to his room to return the experiment.

Blake chuckled. "Yeah, he'd be one of those dads who know every kid's name and stats and shout from the stands like a maniac."

It was clear the boy meant that as a compliment.

Valerie agreed with only one part. The shouting. But it wouldn't have been from the stands in a junior-high gym.

"He wouldn't have missed a single one," she told the boys, leaning over to pick up some lint from the off-white carpet.

She was saved from any further sojourns down fairy-tale lane when, apparently satisfied, they returned to more immediate concerns. Algebra problems that were due in the morning.

Thomas Smith was dead. Leaving behind a memory that was mostly not bad to his sons. Valerie knew that was because the boys' memories had become selective—the human mind protecting itself, she supposed. So wasn't it kinder to let the myth perpetuate itself?

Or was she just weak? Choosing the easier way of pretending all had been well, rather than being honest with the boys.

Some things could remain buried forever, but there were others the boys would eventually have to know....

Not now. Not yet. They were still children. Her little boys.

And Brian was already treading such dangerous ground.

KIRK TOSSED his cell phone from one hand to the other and then back, looking down at the elegant kitchen tile again; 6:00 a.m. Arizona time meant that it was eight o'clock in Virginia. He'd put off the call all weekend. Another hour and it would be time for him to head in to work. He liked to be on the corner long before the first kid arrived at school, and there was an early choir practice that morning.

Another hour and he'd make it. He could do this—follow through on his decision to abandon his old life as CEO of Chandler Acquisitions, the career that had consumed him to the point of heartlessness. He could outlast the temptation of making a final perfect deal. He was actually gaining a measure of peace in the job his old friend, Steve McDonald, had offered him during a painfully dark night several months before. Back then he'd been slowly killing himself—with hard truths and liquor. These days, taking care of the children as he'd promised Alicia he would, he actually slept at night.

He could put down the phone; the number implanted in his memory would eventually fade, along with the rest of Friday night's messages begging him to handle just one more deal.

Someday, maybe even his uncanny ability to remember them at all would disappear.

The Gandoyne company produced aluminum cans,

specifically for food products. Aster Sealants owned the patent on a material that would seal and reseal aluminum lids. This sealant had various uses, but if it was put together with food-product storage it could make both companies wealthy beyond their wildest dreams.

The caller who'd left the number was Gandoyne's son, who had no interest in taking over the business, who was worried about his father's health and who had heard of Kirk's win-at-all-costs reputation. He'd gone on to say that both companies were family-owned, headed by stereotypical patriarchs intent on doing business in the same way as their fathers and *their* fathers before them. They refused to sell stock options. Refused to let anyone else have any say in their businesses or give up the least measure of control.

"Leave them to it," Kirk told the cup of coffee he'd poured, which had grown cold. He dumped out the offensive liquid, rinsed the mug and put it back in the cupboard.

"You can't do that," Susan used to say. "It wasn't washed."

"My mouth never touched it," he'd tell her.

"But the coffee did."

"And coffee is just what it'll have in it the next time I use it."

"It's still wet," she'd say next.

There wasn't a lot Kirk managed to do right around the house. Of course, you couldn't blame him much on that score. He'd never spent enough time around a house to learn.

And he'd tell her, "It'll be dry by tomorrow morning when I need it again."

She'd quit arguing, but her eyes would be speaking loud disapproval. And he'd bet his living trust that she'd go back afterward and wash the mug. Probably the whole cupboard of mugs in case any of the others were contaminated by his inadequate sense of what was sanitary—and acceptable.

Leaning against the counter, staring at the cell phone on the tiled island across from him, Kirk felt satisfied that, at least in this imagined exchange between him and Susan, he'd had the last word.

Gandoyne and his family were going to lose his empire if he didn't reinvent his business practices. Aster Sealants would get an offer too good to refuse. Or if they said no, they'd lose out altogether when some young upshot fresh from Podunk College U.S.A. found a way to make the edges of an opened aluminum lid nonsharp and resealable. If Aster could do it, so would someone else.

And that someone would sell to another someone who made aluminum cans. Those two someones would get filthy rich while two old men went bankrupt.

The cell phone rang.

"Chandler." Some habits died hard.

"Douglas's name is on the birth certificate."

Alexander Douglas. Susan's new husband.

"I expected as much."

"In the state of Arizona, that makes him the kid's father."

Kirk lowered the hand holding the phone. Watched

the coffee in the pot. Put the phone back to his ear. "The bastard has my wife. I'll see him in hell before he gets my son, too."

"Arizona laws are pretty clear."

"File whatever you have to file to get me a paternity test."

"You aren't thinking straight, Kirk." Kirk knew Troy Winston only dared say the words because he couldn't see Kirk's face. That muscle in his jaw started to tic.

"I've never been thinking straighter," he said softly. "That child is mine, and I will do whatever it takes to be a part of his life. If I have to sue, I'll sue. Just get me that paternity test."

"Sure thing, boss."

Kirk was pleased as he disconnected the call—in spite of the offended tone he'd heard in the voice of his most trusted associate.

He was sorry he'd been rough on Troy. Maybe even sorry that this would rock Susan's world. But he was going to do this.

He was determined.

And he was Kirk Chandler.

Thumb on the keypad of his cell phone, Kirk dialed the direct line to Edgar Gandoyne. It was now almost eight-thirty in Virginia. And Kirk had half an hour to get to work.

"ALL RISE."

Valerie walked through the hall door leading from her office to the courtroom after a five-minute break, taking a deep breath as she went through the change from emotional woman to detached judge.

"You may be seated."

The six other people in the small room sat as she took her seat on the bench. Smiling at Ashley, the court clerk who usually worked with her, Valerie checked the day's files.

Mona, the bailiff working this morning's schedule, announced the first case in the same clear, unemotional voice Valerie had been hearing since her first day on the bench.

As Ben White's name was announced, Valerie glanced up, looking at the four people sitting on the dais eight feet in front of her and six feet below. Behind them was a hard wooden bench that could seat maybe four visitors. And an upholstered, sound-buffered wall.

An intimate setting for their little party.

The visitor's bench was empty.

Ben was looking down. She waited.

A couple of seconds later the twelve-year-old boy gave a surreptitious and very hesitant glance in her direction.

She smiled at him. And forced herself to ignore the catch in her lungs. Ben might be the same size as Blake and Brian, but his life was not theirs.

He was the most important person in that room and she wanted him to know it.

Those eyes were trained in her direction for only a second, but she read the fear there.

She called for those present to introduce themselves.

Debbie Malcolm, state prosecutor on the White case, went first.

"Gordon White, father to the juvenile." Ben's father had been in her courtroom before.

"Leslie White, mother." As had she.

Ben was next. He stated his name, looking at her briefly, and then lowering his eyes.

Ben's attorney, Tyson Hunter, a public defender Valerie saw often, was next. During the difficult first minutes of this proceeding, everyone in the room, with the exception of Ben, was occupied with whatever papers were in front of them.

There wasn't a lot of eye contact in Valerie's working life.

With a crease in his forehead that had grown more pronounced over the months Valerie had been seeing Ben, the boy was peering at the papers in his lawyer's hands. His papers.

The file was thick.

Valerie had a version of the same file in front of her.

Without looking at the boy again, she began with the legal protocol, turning Ben from a twelve-year-old child to a case number. For the record she asked if Ben's biographical information was correct. His attorney stated in the affirmative, both of them going through their notes during the exchange.

Detachment was critical to her. She was about to make a decision that was going to change, one way or another, the rest of this all-American-looking boy's life.

Debbie Malcolm, for the state, recommended, in

light of the evidence before them, that Ben be detained.

Valerie had known coming into the room that this would be the recommendation.

Ben's attorney spoke next, trying to explain away repeated truancies as no danger to the community. In great and passionate detail, he told the court about the boy's scholastic abilities, his remarkable IQ that was blamed for a boredom that drove him from classrooms. The misdemeanors the lawyer dismissed in much the same way, managing to assert more than once that detention was for those who were a danger to the community. He believed that there were other, more beneficial ways to handle the case before them and asked for a lesser sentence.

Six months ago, Valerie would have been swayed by the arguments. They were solid. Sound. As good as anything she'd ever done during her life on the other side of the bench.

Looking at the boy's parents, she asked, "How's he doing at home?"

Ben's father said fine.

His mother wiped away the tears that were sliding slowly down her face.

Valerie glanced at Ben. His face was impassive, which sent alarms to her nerve endings. At twelve years of age, the boy was unmoved by his mother's anguish. Anguish that he had caused.

His mother's statement was rife with confusion, helplessness, an engulfing desire to do what was best for her son and the honesty to admit she had no more ideas.

"Do you have anything to say?" she asked Ben, pinning him now with her most serious stare. Unless something happened in the next thirty seconds to convince her otherwise, Ben White had just sealed his fate.

"No, Your Honor."

"Okay." Valerie scanned the pages in front of her once more, making absolutely certain she'd seen everything—every note, date, justification, charge, recommendation and previous disposition. She was warm in her robe. Warmer than normal. She was aware of the heavy circular metal plaque on the wall behind her, almost as though it were radiating heat. Its words were emblazoned on her mind. Great Seal of the State of Arizona. 1912.

The state of Arizona had entrusted her with this decision.

"Ben, based on the number of times I've seen you in this court, and based on the fact that you've violated the terms of your intensive probation, I am going to have you detained, here at Juvenile Detention for a period of ninety days." In spite of the sharp intake of breath she heard from the dais, Valerie continued, explaining legalities, conditions. "Do you understand what that means?"

She gazed at the boy. Not at his parents. His mother's tears were not going to help Valerie do her job.

The boy was stone-faced, as usual. Until he opened his mouth to speak.

"No! Your Honor, no! Please don't send me there! I'll do everything just like you say, I promise." With tears streaming down his face, he looked frantically over to his parents. "Please, don't let them take me away from you...."

Basketball tryouts. Today Blake and Brian had basketball tryouts.

"Please!"

She read him the rest of the disposition.

Detention was this boy's only hope.

She believed that.

The thought carried her from the room and down the hall to her office, but it didn't erase the sight of that terrified face from her mind's eye. Or stop her from imagining the next hour and the way the boy's life was going to be drastically changed.

Ben had reason to be terrified. Juvenile detention stripped a kid not just of his freedom, but of any false pride he might retain. Her hope was that reducing Ben White to the most basic aspects of existence, he'd be able to begin again, to rebuild his life, to find a positive direction.

Her other hope was that neither of her sons ever had reason to look like that.

CHAPTER THREE

LEAH LOOKED UP from her desk outside Valerie's office when Valerie entered their suite. "Did you detain him?"

"Yes." She didn't stop to chat.

In her office, hanging up her robe, Valerie concentrated on detaching herself from the image of Ben White. She couldn't do her job if she didn't. Nor could she be a good mother outside the job....

"What's the little smile for?" Leah asked, walking into Valerie's office a couple of minutes later.

She told her J.A. about the boys' basketball tryouts that afternoon. And how their enthusiasm had completely consumed them. They just *had* to make that team.

"Do you know who the coach is?"

"Yeah, he's that crossing guard I told you about."

"The one who looks far too sexy to be a crossing guard?"

"I never said that!"

"Not in words, maybe!" Leah grinned, dropping into the chair in front of Valerie's desk.

"What I've said is that it's hard to believe someone who moves with his confidence is content standing on a street corner with a stop sign."

"Do you have any idea how many times you've said it, though?"

Was she really talking about the man that much? She made a mental note to stop.

"It's just that something about him strikes me, you know?" she said now, thoughts of the smile he'd given her that morning starting to replace the memory of the look in Ben's eyes.

"Yeah, I *know*," Leah said, her grin growing wider.

"Not like that." Valerie picked up a pen, drew some lines on the top of a small pad of sticky notes. "He represents everything I haven't known in a man," she continued slowly. She and Leah had never spoken about anything like this before. "He sees the incredible value in children. He gives his time to them."

"Isn't that what Hal and the other male judges and probation officers and C.P.S. workers and attorneys do every day?"

"Of course." Valerie glanced up. She couldn't explain what made the guard different. He just was.

"So you think the boys will make the team?"

"I pray that they do." She'd been offering up little prayers for days. "Neither of them is particularly tall or talented at handling the ball, but Brian's a great shooter." She chuckled. "I can vouch for that. We spent more time on the driveway this weekend than we did in the house.

"Besides, it's just a junior-high team. At that age they let everyone who tries out have a place on the team, don't they?"

Leah didn't know.

Valerie didn't, either. She just hoped to God the boys were chosen. Basketball was going to be Brian's lifeline.

"You had a call from someone named Susan Douglas." Leah passed a note she'd been holding across the desk. "Said she's a friend of yours and needs to speak with you today. She was hoping before your morning calendar."

Susan Douglas. It was turning out to be a day for difficult situations. She reached for the note. "I'll call now."

Leah stood. "I've never heard you mention her before."

"I told you my husband died two years ago, in a car accident...."

"Yeah." Her eyes filled with compassion, Leah sat down again.

"The accident was his fault."

"I'd heard that."

"Did you also hear that he was drunk?"

"No!"

Valerie nodded, fighting other mental visions she'd spend a lifetime trying to erase. "I'm friends with a couple of reporters who wanted to protect me and the boys, so the accident didn't get much press coverage. Also, it happened shortly after 9/11...." She paused. "He hit a little girl...."

She stopped abruptly. The morning she'd had, the life she was having, had briefly gotten the better of her. She would not cry.

Tears didn't help. She'd already shed so many and they never eased the pain.

They couldn't change the past. They couldn't bring that little girl back.

Leah was staring at her, an odd mixture of horror, shock and compassion on her face.

"Was she badly hurt?" she asked hoarsely.

Valerie nodded. Scrambled frantically for the detachment that would see her through. "She lived for almost a week, but there was never really any hope...."

"Oh, God, Val, I heard there was some kind of tragedy involved, but I never guessed... I'm sorry— I had no idea... I'm so sorry."

And this was one reason Valerie didn't talk about that part of her life. People had no idea what to do or say. After the accident, even though the tragedy had been kept out of the papers, Valerie had found that the friends she and Thomas had shared slowly stopped calling. And she understood why. No one knew what to say.

Because there was nothing to say.

A year later, she'd received her appointment to the bench. She'd started a new job, a new life and was trying desperately to let go of the most painful parts of the old one.

"Susan is the little girl's mother."

"You know her?"

"I got in touch with her after...I'd seen Alicia's obituary. It listed her mother's name, said she was survived by a loving family and friends, and that was all. But there'd been this picture...."

She drew some more lines. Evenly spaced, even in length and thickness. Parallel in every way. Perfectly balanced.

"I knew there was nothing I could do, but I had to try to help."

"Why am I not surprised?" Leah's smile was sad. And full of love.

"She was so kind," Valerie told her assistant. "Even in the face of her own grief, she was concerned about me and my widowhood. As we talked, we found we had something else in common—our poor choice in husbands. Apparently, the little girl's father was out of the same mold as my husband. Except that Susan and her husband had already been divorced when Alicia was killed."

"Oh my gosh! That poor woman!"

"Yeah. She had it pretty rough for a while there. She'll never completely recover from her daughter's death, but..." Valerie paused, feeling again that horrible stab of guilt about all the things she hadn't done that might have prevented the senseless tragedy. "She remarried shortly after the accident and although I haven't spoken with her, I heard not too long ago that she's had a new baby. I sent a little outfit."

"Maybe that's why she's calling, then," Leah said, standing again. "To thank you."

Valerie hoped so, thinking of the nearly broken woman she'd known. God, she hoped so.

SUSAN DOUGLAS COULDN'T think straight. Alex had been so good to her. The only good thing in her life at a time when she'd thought she'd never be capable of feeling good again. He'd saved her life. Literally.

And then spent many, many months slowly putting that life back together. Handing her the pieces as she was ready to receive them.

And never once, during all of that, had he made her feel as though she couldn't do it without him. He'd never diminished her. He'd nurtured her.

She owed him everything.

She'd chewed the nails of both hands by midmorning that last Tuesday in October. She'd left the message for Valerie at eight, hoping the judge would call before her morning session started. And now it was ten-thirty.

The baby had been up, eaten, had his bath, occupying her for several hours. But now he was asleep again, leaving her alone with her thoughts. Far too alone...

The phone rang and she jumped, knocking it off its cradle. With a glance at herself in the mirror, she grabbed the mobile receiver from the floor.

She looked fine. Her shoulder-length dark hair was perfectly styled, her makeup exquisite, her slacks and sweater the epitome of fashion on a body that was model-slim just a month after her baby's birth. If one overlooked the bleeding cuticle on her right index finger, she could easily pass for the rich socialite she'd always wanted to be.

"Hello?" She caught it on the fifth ring.

"Susan?"

"Valerie, hi!" Susan lifted her middle finger to her teeth. "Thanks for calling back so soon."

"Of course! I'm always here for you, you know that."

Tears filled Susan's eyes. It happened a lot.

"I need your opinion." If she hoped to get through this, she'd have to make it quick. She could read the warning signs.

"Sure, what about?"

How did Valerie always manage to sound cheerful? She'd suffered a hell of a lot, too. In some ways more than Susan had. Yet, try as she might, Susan couldn't find the pure goodwill that infused Valerie Simms's voice.

"It's complicated."

"Okay, shoot."

"I just had a baby."

"I know! Congratulations! Did you get the outfit I sent?"

"Yes." Susan paced the kitchen floor, stepping only on the diamond-shaped markings in the pattern. "I'm late with thank-you notes and I'm really sorry. Alex mailed the last of them this morning."

"Then you're way ahead of where I was!" Valerie laughed. "The twins were six months old before I got around to even *thinking* about thank-you notes."

Susan didn't feel "ahead." As a matter of fact, she was sliding back so fast she was terrified. Everything confused her.

Except that she had to protect Alex. And baby Colton.

"My ex-husband is trying to challenge Colton's paternity."

"*What!*"

"He says the baby is his and not Alex's."

"Is the man insane?" Valerie asked, and then continued, "No, wait, we know he's insane. But he can't be *that* insane! You've been divorced for three years!"

"I know." She was blowing it. Wasn't putting enough indignation into her voice. Valerie was her only hope of winning this.

"Is there some reason for him to think the child is his?"

"Colton is Alex's son."

"But is there some reason your ex might think otherwise?"

"No, of course not," Susan said, trying to collect herself. "We slept together once, after the divorce, and he's claiming that as the reason he's doing this, but the timing's all wrong." God, she wished that was so. Still... "He doesn't want Colton, Valerie. Think about it. Think about him. He's just doing this to get back at me. It's a control thing, you know that."

She sank down to the kitchen floor, and pulled hard at the cuticle of her middle finger with her teeth. Valerie just had to believe her. She had to.

Alex didn't know about that night she'd found the bastard crying at the cemetery. And she'd die rather than hurt Alex. Besides, Colton was Alex's son.

At least, it was possible that Colton was his son. If she'd been late *before* she got pregnant.

Alex was in the delivery room when Colton was born. He'd been the one to bring her home, care for them both, support them both. He was home every night, helping with baths, watching Susan feed their baby, planning for his future.

Alex was Colton's father. His name was on the birth certificate.

Valerie asked a couple of pointed questions. And then rang off, telling Susan not to worry. The jerk didn't have a leg to stand on and Valerie was going to knock it out from under him, anyway.

Arms wrapped around herself, Susan left the phone on the floor and let all the tears fall.

She'd hoped the pain was behind her.

And was beginning to believe it would never be.

HER AFTERNOON CALENDAR behind her, Valerie picked up the phone to make a couple of calls on behalf of Susan Douglas, but it rang before she could punch in a number.

"Hello?"

"Mom, it's Blake."

"Hi, Blake!" Valerie's heart jumped. "Tryouts over so soon?"

Sitting there at her desk in her navy silk suit with the matching two-inch-heeled pumps, her judicial robe on a hanger not three feet away, she crossed her fingers like a little kid.

"Yeah, we just got home."

Blake didn't sound heartbroken, but...

"So?"

"I made the team."

"Oh, Blake, I'm so proud of you guys! I knew you'd get it." With a grin so big her cheeks hurt, Valerie breathed her first easy breath of the day.

"When do practices start?"

"Right away. Coach thinks we can win a lot but he says we have to practice hard."

Sounded good to her. Brian was going to have to eat if he wanted to play.

She wasn't sure whether to laugh or cry.

She had some leverage. Something to give Brian motivation. Something to begin building the self-esteem his father had done so much to destroy, although neither boy had been fully aware of the damage.

And Blake! He'd finally put forth the effort to get something he wanted. And been rewarded.

She could just kiss the crossing-guard coach.

"What's your coach's name?"

"Kirk."

"Kirk what?"

"I don't know. He told us to call him Kirk."

Kirk it was. She could hardly wait to drop the boys off in the morning and give the man her utmost thanks.

Maybe there was something she could do for him? Give him a step up to a job that would pay more than the minimum wage a crossing guard made. She knew a lot of people and—

"Mom."

"What?"

"Brian didn't make the team."

KIRK CHANDLER WAS the crossing guard's name. She'd read it on the paper Blake had brought for her to sign the night before.

He was a nice guy. It was obvious he had a real affection for kids. She'd go see Mr. Chandler, explain the situation and he'd let Brian on the team. Valerie was so certain of that she sent Blake to school with the signed form in his book bag. And told both boys to show up for practice that afternoon. Everything would be fine.

She'd promised them.

The school's lunchroom was cavernous without the cacophony of sound and movement created by hundreds of young people with half an hour of freedom in the middle of the day. She'd only been there once before, when Blake had forgotten a science report that counted for fifty per cent of his grade, and she'd had to run home between calendars, get the report and meet him during his lunch break to give it to him.

Though there were still several people milling about—a few lingering kids, a janitorial crew pulling large trash cans on wheels from table to table, some cafeteria workers—she spotted Kirk Chandler right away. Dressed in blue jeans and a plaid flannel shirt with the sleeves rolled up, he was over in a far corner of the room, engaged in what appeared to be a serious conversation.

With Abraham Billings.

Not wanting the boy to see her, she backed up and waited until he'd left the room before approaching her sons' basketball coach.

"Mr. Chandler?"

He turned immediately.

"Mrs. Simms."

Completely out of character, Valerie hesitated for the briefest moment to take the hand he held out, but that moment was long enough to make her feel self-consciously foolish. His skin was warm, the size of his palm making her feel small, fragile. His grip was firm.

"*Ms.* Simms," she said. "I'm Ms., not Mrs."

Great, Val, any other imbecile remarks you'd like to throw out there?

"Blake and Brian went back to class half an hour ago. Were you looking for someone?" he asked, his eyes alight with appreciation. Probably because of the figure-enhancing black pantsuit she was wearing.

"Yes. You." She walked beside him to the door of the cafeteria. "I wanted to speak with you before basketball practice this afternoon."

"I'm on playground duty next door at the elementary school in a couple of minutes," he said, starting slowly down the hall. "We can talk there."

His voice was...calming. Masculine, but not too deep. Smooth without being smarmy.

"What does playground duty entail?" She could easily see him out there shooting baskets with the boys. Or refereeing a game of Red Rover.

The clacking of her heels seemed inordinately loud against the tile floor.

"A lot of standing, mostly," he said, sending her a sideways grin as they walked.

The halls were deserted, quiet, as they passed one

classroom door after another, all of them closed. Still, with the low ceilings and colorful banners placed every few feet on the walls, the air felt a bit close.

"You don't organize activities?"

"Not for recess. The kids aren't out long enough. We're just there to make sure no one leaves. And that they don't kill each other."

Sounded like a boring job for someone with so much intelligence shining from his eyes.

And yet she was drawn to the way this man who had apparently dedicated his life to serving children.

She wanted to ask why he'd done that. And, of course, couldn't. Kirk Chandler's life choices were absolutely none of her business.

"I came to talk to you about the basketball tryouts yesterday." They'd reached an outside door. Chandler held it open for her.

"Was Blake excited to make the team?"

"Yes."

"He's a good little player. And he'll get better as the year progresses."

Proud of Blake, pleased that her son was succeeding, Valerie accompanied Kirk Chandler toward the playground several yards away.

Blake's success was a wonderful balm to her heart.

"He's going to be a starter," Chandler was saying, telling her about Blake's aggressive footwork on the court.

Valerie frowned, confused. The man didn't seem to realize that they had a problem here. He hadn't asked about Brian at all, or even expressed any kind of regret for having to leave Blake's twin off the team.

"I'm curious," she said slowly, flicking a lock of hair over her shoulder. "Why didn't Blake's brother make the team?"

"He can't keep up."

"What does that mean?" *Detachment, Val.* "I shoot ball with my boys, Mr. Chandler," she said, softening her tone. "Brian's a much better shot than Blake."

"Possibly." Kirk Chandler stopped outside the gate leading to the playground, leaned his forearms on the top bars and looked over, silently assessing her. And then he spoke.

"Basketball takes energy, Ms. Simms. Lots of it. Brian has none."

She pressed her lips together, as though blending her lipstick, although she'd chewed it off on the way from her car to the cafeteria.

"I can't put him on the team because I can't play him in a game."

"He needs to be on that team, Mr. Chandler," she said, trying to tone down her emotion. "I'll make certain that his energy level is up to par."

Being on the team would take care of that. It would make Brian eat.

Chandler glanced out at the still-empty playground. And shook his head.

"I told Brian he could practice with the team. And as soon as I see his strength and speed improve, I'll consider letting him on. I still have an open spot."

With a calm she didn't feel, Valerie folded her arms across her chest. "I appreciate the offer, but being there with the boys, being constantly reminded that he isn't good enough, won't help Brian."

She shook at the thought. Low self-esteem was at the root of Brian's problems. There was no way she could expose him to something that would make that worse.

"You'd be surprised," Chandler said, his conciliatory tone rankling her. "A lot of times it's something like this that becomes a significant turning point in a boy's life. If Brian wants to be on the team badly enough, he'll get himself there."

"No, he won't, because I can't let him do this." Her words were sharper than she wanted. "Brian's borderline anorexic, Mr. Chandler. Putting him out there every day, in front of his peers—as someone who can't make the grade—could kill him."

"The choice is yours," he said, his gaze steady as it held hers. "But I think you'd be making a mistake. Brian wants to play basketball. If I thought there was any chance he could keep up, I'd have put him on the team for his heart alone. Instead of 'killing him,' as you say, this challenge could very well be what saves him."

"Do you have children, Mr. Chandler?"

It was something she'd wondered more than once.

"No." His gaze had returned to the swings and slide and open field ahead of them.

"I didn't think so."

"I was a boy once, though." With the soft words, an odd tone had entered his voice.

"I'm guessing, however, that you didn't have problems with low self-esteem."

"Every kid experiences some of that."

"The normal bouts, yes. Brian's bout isn't normal."

"The only way he'll ever play on my team is if he comes out to practice and shows me he can keep up. Yesterday he couldn't."

"If Brian doesn't play, Blake won't, either."

"What?" He turned, frowning, his eyes filled with such intensity she was shocked. There was a lot more going on inside this man than the world saw. "You'd actually hold Blake back, *punish him,* because his brother has problems?"

"Of course not…"

His eyes cleared. And that mattered to her.

"Blake made that decision."

"And you're going to let him?"

"You obviously don't understand twins, Mr. Chandler," she said, suddenly weary. So often it felt like life was Valerie and her boys against the world. Trying to find their own place…

"What's to understand? They're two kids with the same birthday."

If she had more time, she'd tell him how wrong that was. She'd tell him how, when the boys were little, one would always know when the other didn't feel well. When Blake had the flu, Brian—at three years old—refused to leave the room and sat quietly beside his brother, eating only the soup that Blake ate, until his brother was better. She'd explain how the boys knew what the other was thinking, completing sentences and thoughts for each other as naturally as if they were their own.

She'd tell him, but she had a feeling he still wouldn't get it. Kirk Chandler was turning out to be an irritating man.

"My boys do everything together," she said now. "They've been in the same classes every year, they play the same sports, they have the same friends. I've got nothing to do with this. It's a natural outgrowth of the bond they share. And," she said with emphasis when he took a breath as though he was planning to interrupt with more of his unfounded opinions, "it's been a gift, giving them the strength and security to weather whatever challenges come along. Including the death of their father."

"And that's why Brian is borderline anorexic, because of all this strength and security."

It wasn't a question.

And Valerie didn't have any more time. She had to get back to Mesa for her afternoon calendar.

"The boys are coming to practice today," she told him, "but don't expect to see them tomorrow."

"The choice is yours," he told her again. "But, for both their sakes, I wish you'd reconsider."

"And I wish you would," she told him, then turned and walked away, leaving him standing there staring out over an empty playground.

An unusual man, a poorly paid servant with a mind of his own and a will of iron.

A man who apparently had the power to ruin her son's life.

And an open spot on his basketball team.

Open spot being the operative words, Valerie reminded herself as she climbed in her Mercedes, put it in gear and accelerated, turning out of the lot.

She'd take care of this somehow. She always did.

CHAPTER FOUR

AT HIS CORNER early as usual the next morning, the day before Halloween, Kirk sipped from a paper cup of coffee and enjoyed the quiet. He had another fifteen minutes before he needed to don the orange vest and take up his sign.

The air was a little chilly, not that he minded. By midmorning, he'd be rolling up the sleeves of his flannel shirt. A lone car pulled up. Stopped. Moved on. Kirk enjoyed these stolen everyday moments. Somehow they never failed to instill a sense of peace in him, along with the assurance that he was on the right course.

Another car approached. This one stopped at the curb a few feet behind Kirk and someone got out. Odd. It was too early for the kids. But he recognized the car. Pulling on his vest, Kirk watched from the corner of his eye.

Abraham Billings didn't wait for his mother's kiss on the cheek. And she drove off before he'd even shrugged his backpack onto his shoulders. Kirk frowned. The woman always waited to watch her son walk into the school.

She always brought him right before the first bell, too. This morning there wasn't another kid in sight.

Head down, the boy, in his customary freshly laundered jeans and T-shirt, ambled to the corner. Kirk held up his sign, although there was no traffic. Abraham didn't seem to notice.

"You got something to do before school?" Kirk asked as Abraham stood there.

"No."

Abraham was looking down the street in the direction his mother had gone, his features drawn into a sullen mask. Still, he made no move to cross the street.

"What's up?"

"Nothin'."

Eyes narrowed, Kirk nodded. There was a job for him to do here; he knew it. He just had to figure out what it was.

And he would.

"Practice is at three today."

Abraham's head swung toward Kirk. "So?" The word was almost thrown at him.

Was that liquor he smelled on the boy's breath? Or something else? Abraham could have gotten into his father's cologne. This was the age for potentially embarrassing experiments.

"I want you there."

The boy's chin tightened. "I didn't try out. I'm not on the team. I can't play."

Three sentences, Kirk mused. He was getting somewhere.

"Come, anyway."

"What for?"

"I left a spot open. Today's practice can be considered your tryout."

Abraham didn't respond. Just stared down the street where he'd last seen his mother.

"You think your mom would mind if you came?"

"No."

"We could go to the office and call her at lunch, just to be sure."

"She won't be there."

"She at work?"

Abraham's body signals were telling Kirk to shut up and leave him alone, but he wasn't going to. Not while the boy was finally talking to him.

"No."

"I see her drop you off here in the mornings. Is it usually on her way to work?"

"No."

Kirk nodded. He had a stay-at-home mom. That was good. Unusual. But good.

"How about your dad? What does he do?"

"I don't know."

Had Alicia known what her daddy did?

"I don't know who my dad is."

With the worst possible timing, a couple of kids came up the street. One on a skateboard, one on in-line skates. Bobby Sanderson and Scott Williams.

Seeing them, Abraham stepped off the curb. He should have called the boy back, warned him to wait until he'd raised the stop sign.

Kirk watched him go instead, hoping the kid showed up at practice that afternoon.

"Hi, guys," he said, signaling that Bobby and

Scott should cross the street. But his mind wasn't on the loud and rambunctious seventh-graders.

If Abraham Billings didn't have a father, that probably hadn't been his dad's cologne Kirk had smelled.

Fifteen minutes later, Valerie Simms's Mercedes stopped across the street, farther down than usual.

"Katie, Cassandra, you have orchestra today, I see." Kirk smiled at the two Japanese-American friends who were standing with him, each toting a violin case.

Looking at each other, they giggled, nodded and, as he signaled, ran across the street, their violin cases banging against their knees.

"Hi, Coach."

He turned, smiled at the twins, took a quick look at Brian.

"Hi, guys. Sore from practice?"

"I sure am." Blake grinned, wrinkling his freckle-covered nose.

"Yeah, he's a lot worse off than I am, Coach," Brian said, elbowing his twin. "Our legs hurt, but his arms hurt, too."

"That's good!" Kirk stepped out into the street. "Your bodies are getting conditioned."

The boys nodded enthusiastically. "See you this afternoon," he called.

And then he wondered if he should have. If the twins' mother had told them they couldn't be associated with the team, he had to abide by that.

Even if he disagreed with her completely.

But perhaps she'd changed her mind. The boys

hadn't given any indication that they weren't allowed to play.

"Hi."

Turning, surprised, Kirk saw the subject of his thoughts. Her presence on his corner explained why she'd stopped the car farther down. She'd actually parked it.

"Good morning," he said. It was the first morning since the beginning of the school year that he didn't smile at her. He had a pretty good hunch this wasn't a smiling moment.

If she was going to capitulate—let the boys play— he didn't want to do anything to jeopardize that.

Like giving any hint of gloating....

Standing there, watching the kids as they walked up, waited and then crossed when he signaled, the boys' mother appeared the epitome of patience. He admired that.

"Brian didn't eat last night."

The kids were gone. And so, apparently, was her composure.

"And you're going to blame that on me."

"No, of course not." He wondered how she could make him feel as though he'd been reprimanded without ever changing the tone of her voice. Must be the judge thing.

He'd been surprised when the boys had told them their mother was a judge.

In juvenile court.

Kirk knew more about that whole scene than he cared to remember.

"Brian's problem existed long before basketball

tryouts came along,'' she continued after another group of kids had passed. ''But I'm absolutely sure that being on the team would help him more than anything else. I'm begging you to reconsider your position on this, Mr. Chandler. Give Brian that open spot.''

Begging. Strong word.

''Please,'' she said when Kirk played the negotiation technique that almost always won—remaining silent. ''It's a junior-high team. It's not like their ranking is going to matter.''

''Tell that to the boys who spend every afternoon in the gym working their butts off.''

Kirk was watching the kids coming up the street, but he caught the slight movement of her high heels beneath the calf-length navy dress as she shifted on the sidewalk.

''I'm sorry,'' she said quickly, then sighed loudly, showing a definite lack of patience as another group of youngsters came to the corner.

As always, Kirk called them by name. Joked with them. Remembered something about them so they'd know he paid attention. And cared.

''I can't let Brian on the team,'' he said as soon as they had the corner to themselves again. ''For the reasons I've already given you.''

''Mr. Chandler—''

''Ms. Simms,'' Kirk interrupted. ''I just saw your boys. They were both smiling, eager. Brian was bragging about being less sore than his brother. And they were both looking forward to practice this afternoon.'' He met her gaze—and ignored the thread of something personal that seemed to pass between them. "They didn't seem to be aware that they were quitting basketball."

"I didn't tell them you'd refused to have Brian on the team."

"He was at practice yesterday. He knew."

"We didn't discuss basketball last night."

"Could it be that the boys want to continue with Blake on the team and Brian practicing but are afraid to tell you so?"

She shook her head, breaking eye contact with him, sending an uncharacteristic bolt of compassion straight through him.

He didn't allow himself to *feel* when he went after what he knew was right. He just went.

"My boys always expect me to do what I say I'm going to do. I'm sure they're certain I'll get Brian on the team."

"You won't."

Another group of kids approached. She looked at her watch. He wondered if court still started at eight-thirty. If so, she'd need to hurry.

"Brian's the only one who can get Brian on that team. If you let him."

The thirteen-year-old girls gathered at the corner, discussing some outrageous-sounding gossip about a boy and girl making it in the girls' bathroom, were obviously completely unaware of the adults sharing their space.

"At another time, I might be willing to try your little experiment, Mr. Chandler, but there's too much resting on this for me to take a chance—"

"They're coming to practice this afternoon," he interrupted automatically, going in for the close without conscious thought.

"I'll tell them tonight."

"Why don't you come to practice?" Kirk delivered the alternative that his instincts were telling him would finish this off. "See what we're doing, what Brian's doing. Watch him on the court with the other boys. And then make your decision."

She glanced at her watch. Flipped a curl over her shoulder. Met his gaze.

"Okay."

He wasn't surprised—had known she'd capitulate. And hated that he'd known. Hated that he could so easily manipulate people. Perhaps Steve McDonald had made a mistake when he'd given Kirk this opportunity to fulfill his promise to his daughter.

"But I'm going to be watching closely, Mr. Chandler."

"I hope so."

Kirk suspected he didn't just mean her son's behavior on the basketball court.

And he suspected she didn't, either.

VALERIE FOLLOWED the sounds of squeaking shoes and bouncing balls thundering up and down hardwood to the gymnasium that afternoon. At four o'clock she was later than she'd wanted to be, but a calendar she'd expected to be light had run longer than she'd anticipated. She'd missed the first hour of practice.

Kirk Chandler looked over as she slid in the side

door and walked softly on her two-inch navy pumps to the row of bleachers pulled out from the wall. She tucked her dress beneath her and sat. Other than nodding acknowledgment, he didn't miss a beat, blowing a whistle and yelling at the boys to pass.

"Dribble! Pass!" he hollered again and again as the boys went repeatedly through a pattern spread out in pairs across the gym floor.

She spotted both twins immediately. Their black curly hair made them easily distinguishable, even though they were dressed just like every other twelve-year-old boy there. In the middle of the room, Blake faced a boy who was half a foot taller, but somehow managed to keep the ball from the other player as he dribbled. It was the footwork, just as Chandler had said.

"Good, Brian," Chandler called out. "Nice pass."

Brian was on the end. Partnered with—Abraham Billings.

Almost instantly, Valerie was transported outside herself, outside the experience, detached. There was a gym. Boys at practice. Her sons working hard.

As far as she'd been aware, her boys didn't know Abraham. Not that she'd asked. She didn't bring her work home with her.

And in her year on the bench, she hadn't run into even one of her kids outside the courtroom.

"Eduardo, like this!" Chandler palmed a basketball and dribbled quickly, showing the boy how to control the ball. He watched as the young man tried it himself. "That's better!" he said, moving down the row.

Eduardo had been at a last-day-of-school swim party the boys had held one Saturday the previous May.

"Good footwork, Blake. Now watch Shane's ball-handling. Shane, you watch Blake's feet."

Valerie observed. Assessed.

And waited.

During the last fifteen minutes of the hour, Kirk Chandler split the boys into two teams and let them scrimmage with each other while he walked up and down the sidelines taking notes and yelling out to them. Only encouragement at that point—earning him Valerie's begrudging admiration. This was the man from the crossing corner. Compassionate. Dedicated to the children he was there to serve.

Abraham Billings was everywhere. He made more shots than any of the other boys combined.

When practice ended, the entire squad gathered around their coach, faces eager, all eyes pinned on the man before them, all ears tuned to whatever he was saying. The gym was silent except for the hum of his voice. He was grinning, nodding and sweating as much as any of them. Fair in all her judgments, Valerie had to admit that from what she'd seen, Kirk Chandler was a good coach. Maybe even a great one.

And after watching the time and effort he'd spent on her son, she was fairly confident Brian would get his place on the team.

She met her boys at the side of the court as they walked off with the coach after everyone else had left through the far door of the gym.

Brian, lagging behind the other two, with his dark

curly hair plastered to the sides of his head, looked from his mother to Kirk Chandler and grinned.

"So I'm on the team, too?" he asked Chandler.

As Blake moved beside his twin, nodding and staring up at their coach with adoration, Valerie held Chandler's gaze.

Don't let me down, she told him as forcibly as she could although she didn't say a word.

He's just a little boy who's struggling with things that are bigger than he is. She knew better than to try to appeal to the man in front of her with that sentiment.

After long seconds, Chandler broke eye contact with her and glanced down at her son, a hand on Brian's shoulder, a ball wedged between his other wrist and his hip. "How many times were you first down the court today, Brian?"

"None." Brian continued to gaze up at the coach, his green eyes earnest.

"How many times did you have to stop because you couldn't keep up?"

"A couple." The boy's expression changed from rapt to tentatively hopeful.

Valerie's stomach tightened. The bastard wasn't going to do it.

"And how shaky were your legs when we finished?"

Brian looked down at the offending appendages. Bony-kneed and far too skinny, his little boy legs stuck out from beneath the silky silver shorts she'd bought them the weekend before for tryouts. And then he turned his attention back to his coach. "Pretty shaky," he said with a shrug.

He knew what was coming. Valerie blinked back a surge of emotion. Why did life have to be so damn difficult? Her sons were good boys. They tried hard and stayed out of trouble. Was it so wrong to want this break for them?

"I'm not on the team, am I?" Brian asked, his voice perfectly even.

"Do you think you're ready?" Chandler asked. He held the ball between both hands, lightly spinning it.

"No, Coach."

"I don't think so, either."

Brian nodded, chin jutting out, maintaining eye contact with Chandler, obviously trying to take it like a man.

"Come on, Bry, let's go get our stuff." Blake elbowed his brother, and the two boys headed across the gym floor to the locker-room door. Valerie didn't miss the quiver in Brian's chin as he turned away.

"How can you be so cruel?" Valerie asked softly. She didn't get it. Tough love was great in a lot of circumstances. Not this one. "Do you honestly not realize that I'm *not* a parent who just wants to see my son play basketball? Or even a mother who wants her son to get his own way? Can't you see that what I am is a parent who's found a way to help her son be healthy when nothing else has worked?"

"Has Brian been in counseling?" The ball between his hands was still.

"Yes, they both have. Their father's unexpected death left some unresolved issues."

His *life* had left some, too, although the boys weren't yet old enough to understand the extent of the damage their father's neglect had caused. Still, they'd been awakened more than once in the middle of the night to the sounds of horrendous drunken yelling.

"What about now, for the anorexia?"

"That's all part of it, but yes. Specifically for the anorexia for the past six months."

He paused, and Valerie thought, once again, that he was finally going to do the right thing. He had to redeem himself. He was the crossing-guard man who'd done more to lift her spirits with his morning smiles these past months than anyone else she could think of.

Purse slung over her shoulder, arms around her waist, she waited.

"Have you talked to his counselor about basketball? Or his doctor, for that matter?"

"I called both. They were encouraging, hopeful that the basketball experience would help."

He dropped the ball he'd been holding, stepped closer as he bent to pick it up, leaving Valerie with a whiff of his musky scent. Sweaty though he was, he didn't smell of it.

Closer now, he nodded at her, but didn't say anything else. Infuriating man!

Silence seemed to be typical for him. And left Valerie with too much to say and a need not to say it.

"You may know basketball, Mr. Chandler." She said it anyway. "But I know my son. If you allow him to play, he won't let you down. But if you don't, you'll be letting *him* down.''

He rested the ball against his side, tucked beneath his elbow. ''Have you ever been a man, *Ms*. Simms?''

''I don't know, Mr. Chandler. I've never done a past-life regression.''

It was his emphasis on the *Ms.* that had taken a lot of the anger out of Valerie's reply. That and the quietly serious light in his eyes. He was making a point. She didn't get it. And she honestly wanted to understand what he was thinking. Why he was being so difficult? He was an intelligent man. He cared about the kids. What was she missing?

''The way I understand things, it's not a need to play basketball, in particular, that's the problem here. It's Brian's self-esteem.''

''That's right.'' She nodded. ''But basketball is the issue, too. It's the only thing that's lit a fire under him in a long time. The boys' father had a hoop installed for them several years ago and Brian's always been a good shot.''

Not that Thomas had ever known that. He'd arranged for the hoop for Christmas one year. But he hadn't been home to see his sons' reactions when the surprise arrived. Nor for any other part of that Christmas holiday. He'd never once seen either of the boys shoot the ball.

''I understand Brian has an attachment to the game,'' Chandler said, meeting her gaze head-on. ''But it will be worse for his self-esteem to give him something he hasn't earned. Something he isn't yet qualified to do.''

"Brian has worked as hard or harder than anyone else out there."

"At shooting, maybe." The coach's eyes narrowed. "But being an athlete requires much more than ball-handling skill. First and foremost, he needs to take care of his instrument—his only real tool—his body."

For a second there, Valerie was reminded of various times on the bench when one defense attorney or another brought to light something the prosecutors missed. She'd look at the file in front of her, the sheaf of papers and reports that were her constant guides, and suddenly see a hole in information that had seemed concrete and actionable.

"It will be much worse for Brian in the long run if things are given to him without his having earned them—given to him before he's ready for them," Chandler repeated.

It was a valid point.

CHAPTER FIVE

"BRIAN'S SEEING a counselor, Mr. Chandler." Afraid to lose such a critical confrontation, Valerie stepped up the heat. "I've been privy to the counselor's findings."

The ball was back between his hands. Spinning slowly.

"Right now, through his own self-sabotage, Brian's physiological needs are not being completely met," Valerie said honestly. "Until those needs *are* met, nothing else matters. Life lessons of the kind to which you're referring, simply pass him by. If we can't get him to eat, we can't get him to a place where those lessons will make any difference. Practicing with the team is not enough incentive to get him to eat. But I really believe that being on the team would."

He spun the ball. Bounced it a couple of times. Opened his mouth to speak.

"You have to understand," Valerie interrupted. "For months we've been looking for something, *anything,* that's important enough to Brian to coax him to eat. We've finally found something he's passionate about, and your decision is standing between us and Brian's cure."

"Basketball doesn't even matter at the moment," Valerie concluded with the rush of adrenaline she used to get when, as a defense attorney, she knew she'd won over the jury.

Catching the ball between his palms, Kirk Chandler held it there.

"The game matters, though," he said softly, but she heard the determination behind his words. "The game of life, if you'll pardon the cliché. And Brian's playing it. Winning isn't everything, Ms. Simms. Getting him to eat will mean less if he's bribed to do it. He has to eat because *he* makes the decision, because of something *he* wants to achieve. With the first, you're giving control of his life, his eating, to others. With the second, the control rests with him."

Eyes narrowed, Valerie wondered if Kirk Chandler had been a lawyer in his previous life. It was sure as hell obvious he'd been more than a crossing guard, lunchroom monitor, playground cop or basketball coach. She'd lost very few cases during her years in court, but occasionally an opposing attorney would outmaneuver her, as Kirk Chandler had just done.

"If he loses one more pound, I'm going to get letters from Brian's doctor and counselor, bring them to Mr. McDonald and have him put my son on that team." Steve McDonald, now the principal at Menlo Ranch, had been the boys' second-grade teacher.

"Then you'd better make sure he comes to practice," Chandler said, apparently not the least bit moved by her threat.

Valerie had more to say but the boys exploded out of the locker room and zoomed across to her.

"Ready, Mom?" Brian asked.

"Yep!" An arm around each of them, she turned with her little family to leave.

"See you tomorrow, guys," Chandler called out.

"Yeah, see ya, Coach," the boys chorused in perfect unison.

They were out in the Mercedes before Valerie realized she'd just lost what might prove to be one of the most important cases of her life. Somehow, without her having consciously agreed, Brian was going to be practicing with the team.

Confused as to how that had happened, Valerie was the one who didn't have much of an appetite that night.

AT FIVE IN THE MORNING on Halloween Friday, Kirk was at his desk, having already sent out enough faxes to keep his line tied up for almost an hour. Paperwork had been signed, sealed and delivered for the Gandoyne/Aster merger on Tuesday of that week, a three-day negotiation from open to close. The rest—well, he wasn't sure what the hell he was doing.

He'd told Troy that Gandoyne would be his only deal. Yes, he could have Chandler Acquisitions up and running again at little more than a moment's notice. Yes, his reputation was still garnering him business opportunities on a daily basis. But he was finished. Had a new life. New goals and priorities.

And he'd gotten up that morning to fax refusals on all of the numerous requests he'd received that week from investors and business CEOs all over the country, begging him to facilitate difficult acquisitions.

It should have taken fifteen minutes. Two succinct lines. *Thanks. But no thanks.*

There was no reason to actually look at the proposals or to be mulling over solutions to million-dollar problems. That was a part of himself he could no longer acknowledge.

Which was why there were thirty-five refusals on the out tray of his fax machine.

By six, his second cup of coffee half-empty on his desk, Kirk was on the phone to the East Coast. Just this one deal. It would take ten minutes of his life. And make an old man millions.

And by six-thirty, dressed and ready to bolt out the door, he was waiting for the return call so he could give his list of orders. Just this one deal, and he'd be done.

"Chandler."

"Coach?"

He'd only given his home number to one boy— and never expected him to use it.

"Abraham, what's up?"

"I'm not going to be at practice today."

Hand in the front pocket of his jeans, Kirk switched gears instantly, slowing his mind enough to be aware the boy's emotional needs.

"I told you if you want that spot on the team you have to be at every practice until the scrimmage game next week."

He wanted the boy on the team. Maybe more than Abraham wanted to be there. But Kirk didn't give anyone anything for free. The consequences of doing that were too damaging.

"I know."

"So you're calling to tell me you don't want to be on the team." What the hell was going on? Abraham wouldn't be calling if that was the case. He just wouldn't have shown up.

"No."

"Then what?"

Silence.

Used to being able to pick up a phone and find out anything he needed to know, Kirk was in new territory. Territory he didn't like. How could he help this kid if he didn't know the rules—the lay of the land?

Abraham still wasn't saying anything. But he wasn't hanging up. Instinctively Kirk remained silent. And waited.

"I have a...job...I gotta do. I arranged it so I can do most of it over the weekend, but they wouldn't let me outta there this afternoon."

A job? At twelve?

What kind of parent had a kid working at twelve? And for so many hours that he'd be working all weekend to have his afternoons free...

"Where you working?"

"An old folks' place."

"Doing what?"

"Nothin' much."

"They pay you to do nothing?"

"I read, okay?" Abraham's tone was only a notch below nasty.

"You read to the old folks who can no longer read for themselves."

"Yeah."

"And they pay you for that?"

"Yeah...sure. I mean, well, no."

Kirk grinned. Abraham was a good kid. He volunteered at an old folks' home. And he couldn't tell a lie.

"Okay, buddy, just this once you can miss. But no more, got that?"

"Yeah, Coach, I got it."

"You make it to next week's scrimmage and you're on the team."

"'Kay."

"See ya soon."

"Yeah, my mom's coming. I gotta go—"

Kirk's grin faded as he hung up the phone. Abraham's tough-guy facade had dropped completely when he'd realized his mother was near, his voice taking on an unsettling edge that Kirk wasn't going to forget—or ignore.

An edge of fear.

BLAKE'S STOMACH HURT again. He was dressed and just waiting in the locker room, waiting for Coach to call them for warm-ups. Their first scrimmage game, and his mom was going to be there. What if he screwed up? Would she hate that?

She was already worried sick about Brian.

For that matter, so was Blake. He glanced over to where his brother was pulling on game socks and shoes. Because it was just an unofficial scrimmage game and no one was suiting up, Coach was going to let Brian play if someone got hurt. Brian hadn't had lunch again that day.

Blake wasn't telling Mom, though. Just like he wasn't telling her how much his stomach hurt. He was the oldest. The man, now. He could handle it all.

As long as Brian quit being so stupid and started eating… He could handle everything as long as nothing happened to Brian.

Mom was worried about that. A lot.

Blake shoved his new uniform shirt into the bottom of his backpack. As far away from Brian as he could put it. There was no way he was going to wear it over his T-shirt like the rest of the guys.

Not when Brian didn't have one to wear.

"You're going to get to play, Bry," he said now as his brother ambled over.

"Yeah, maybe."

Brian seemed cool, but Blake could tell how hard it was on him being here with the team but not part of the team. His brother wanted this bad. Worse than *he* did. And he wanted it pretty bad.

"You shoulda ate today."

"I didn't feel so good. I'll stuff myself with pizza tonight."

Brian wasn't looking so good, either. Every day Blake tried to figure out if his brother was slower than him, slower than he'd been the day before.

"But when you don't eat all day, it doesn't take much to stuff you."

Brian stared up at him and Blake knew what he was going to say even before he said it. "You won't tell Mom, will you?"

"No." Blake elbowed his twin. "'Course not."

"'Cause she for sure won't let me practice with the team if you do."

"I know."

And Blake wouldn't be able to play, either, not that playing mattered as much as his brother getting over this dumb eating thing. Mostly he wasn't going to tell because he knew how much winning a place on the basketball team meant to Brian. It was because of their dad, because he'd bought them their hoop and they'd secretly thought that as soon as they were good enough, he'd come out and play a game with them.

Their dad had been a basketball star in high school. And in college, too, before law school.

Blake just didn't care as much as Brian if they made their dad proud. Not anymore. He didn't figure Dad was an angel watching over them the way his twin did. As far as he could figure, Dad wasn't anywhere near any angels.

Not that he'd tell Brian that.

He knew some things Brian didn't know. Things Mom didn't realize he knew.

Someday, when Brian got better, he'd be able to tell him. He hoped it would be soon. He didn't feel right knowing something Bry didn't.

"Okay, guys, take off the shirts and get ready to get out there and burn the rubber off those shoes." Coach had come in with his new assistant. A math teacher Blake didn't know but who seemed pretty cool.

The guys all took off their basketball jerseys, shoving around and messing with each other. Even though they weren't allowed to play in them yet, they'd gotten their uniforms that day and everyone was pretty psyched.

Except maybe him and Brian.

Abe Billings got one. And Brian didn't.

Blake wasn't going to tell Mom that, either.

VALERIE ENJOYED basketball. It was a whole lot more exciting to watch than Thomas's other favorite sport—golf. Even when the basketball was being played by a bunch of junior-high boys who spent as much time tripping over each other as they did shooting baskets.

She sat there alone in her dove-gray suit, separated from the smattering of other parents because she'd come in late. As she watched, she recognized a couple of good, creative plays amidst the havoc. Coach Chandler had been correct in his assessment that his group of boys could win some games this year.

Blake stole the ball a couple of times. Missed all but one attempted shot, although he could always be relied on to get the ball down court.

Abraham Billings hadn't even shown up for tryouts but played the entire scrimmage.

Brian was never put in the game.

Valerie wasn't going to be one of those moms she detested. The stereotypical stage mom, always pressing for her kids to get the most chances. She'd made Brian get on the scale before school that morning. He hadn't gained, but he hadn't lost, either. She'd said she'd go along with Chandler's plan, provided Brian didn't lose weight. So she would.

She sat there while the excruciating minutes

passed, with alternating cheers and groans from the small crowd, and she didn't even think about what she'd like to say to the coach on Brian's behalf. She detached herself. And cheered. Analyzed. Noted.

Carla Billings, a mother who claimed to be present at every single function in which her son was involved, never showed her lovely face.

Which was too bad. Abraham was a darn good player, showing far more promise than any of the other boys on the court. Whenever she wasn't watching Blake, Valerie's attention was drawn to the agile young man with big brown eyes that ignored her this afternoon but had pleaded with her in another place and time. In her heart he was one of her kids, too, and she was pleased to see him doing so well.

But that didn't make it any easier to sit there and watch her son being rejected.

She didn't seek out the coach after the game. She stayed right in her seat, at the far corner of the court, away from the parents who chatted with Coach Chandler—and each other—while they waited for their sons to emerge from the locker room. As a working mom, she didn't know many of the other mothers who volunteered in the classrooms and had been watching every practice of whatever variety since first grade.

She knew where Chandler was every second, though. Could hear his voice. Could almost feel his presence. And she knew exactly when, finished with the other parents, he headed her way.

Wearing jeans, he'd rolled the sleeves of his red plaid flannel shirt up to his elbows. His hair was short and professional-looking as always. He walked as though he'd just stepped out of a corporate board-room. Or was about to enter one.

"I'm glad you could make it."

Her gaze briefly skimmed his. "I would've been here sooner, but I had a case that ran longer than we expected," she said, hands under her elbows as she looked over at the locker-room door.

"Brian didn't play."

"I noticed."

"He isn't ready."

She could have asked him ready by what standards, but she wasn't going to debate that again. Not as long as Brian was maintaining his weight. She wasn't after special favors for her boys. Her concern was and always had been Brian's health.

And she knew the standards they were abiding by, anyway. The only ones that appeared to matter. His.

"It looks like you've done a great job with the kids," she said. She glanced at him briefly and then back at the locker-room door.

Where were her boys? She wanted to get away from their coach. He was disturbing her equilibrium with messages that didn't add up.

The man was a complete enigma. Charismatic, iron-willed, intelligent, obstinate, compassionate, coldhearted, confident. And a crossing guard making little more than minimum wage. Even with what the school paid him to work as a lunchroom supervisor and playground monitor, his wages had to be pretty low.

"There's no longer an empty spot on the team."

Her gaze flew to his. He'd said Brian wasn't ready.

"Did you notice the kid playing center?"

Abraham. Valerie nodded.

"He took the final slot today."

Valerie wondered how that was going to work with the community service hours she'd ordered as a condition of Abraham's probation. And made a mental note to have Leah file the paper to allow basketball practice to substitute for the boy's time at the nursing home.

And then her heart started to pound with a mixture of anger, indignation, sadness and fear.

"So now Brian's told that even his best effort wasn't good enough."

How the hell was she going to counter that?

"He's still welcome to practice with the team."

"Why would he want to do that?"

"Why don't you ask him," Chandler said, motioning with one shoulder toward the locker room. Her sons had just walked through the door. "He asked if he could."

"So he already knows."

"The rest of the boys got their uniforms today."

"What's the point of torturing him, Mr. Chandler? You're telling me there's no longer a possibility of his making the team."

"If he practices, and someone drops out or gets hurt, he could move up. Assuming he's ready."

Valerie's heart sank. Such a nebulous promise was worse than no promise at all because it would be enough to keep Brian coming back—slowly killing himself for something he had little chance of obtaining.

"You've told him that, I presume?"

"When he asked me."

The boys were almost upon them.

"I can see you aren't convinced and, for Brian's sake, I'd like the chance to convince you before you haul him out of here and don't let him come back," Chandler was saying, speaking faster than she'd ever heard him. "Can we meet someplace later this evening? Just long enough to discuss this."

Before the boys could get within hearing distance, she quickly agreed to see him at a coffee shop not far from the school at nine that evening. But only because it mattered so much. And because he was right about one thing—the way she was feeling, she couldn't bear to allow Brian to come back here, where he'd done his best and still not been good enough. And yet, pulling the boys out now, when basketball was all they talked about, when Blake was diligently applying himself and Brian hadn't lost any weight in over a week… She couldn't do that, either.

CHAPTER SIX

"I WASN'T SURE you'd be here."

Kirk Chandler met Valerie in the parking lot of The Coffee House at nine o'clock that night. It was a place he came often, later in the evening, when the quiet at home got too loud.

"I said I would."

"I expected you to use not wanting to leave the boys alone as an excuse."

She shook her head. "They're almost teenagers, old enough to baby-sit, as they informed me last summer. I don't ever go far when they're alone. And we have an alarm system. Plus I always carry my cell phone."

But he could tell leaving them on their own was still hard on her.

"It was getting a little ridiculous dragging them both to the grocery store every time I went," she continued as they headed toward a table on the patio. "And it's not like I could call a sitter because we ran out of milk."

She'd changed clothes. And looked amazingly good in the faded designer jeans, figure-hugging black turtleneck sweater and black suede boots.

"Do you always wear such high heels?"

"Always."

She'd come, but obviously wasn't happy to be there. He planned to change that.

Convincing people was what he did best.

"Why?"

"So my judicial robe doesn't trail on the ground."

Okay. She wasn't interested in small talk. Kirk asked her preference and went inside to order their drinks. No coffee for her. This late at night it was hot chocolate or nothing.

He bought her a large—with extra whipped cream.

"I realize you have no reason to trust me," he said, setting their cups—her chocolate, his espresso—on the small table she'd chosen. In Phoenix, the first week of November could pass for summer. The air was balmy, perfect. "But I want you to know I have only the kids' best interests at heart. I have nothing personal to gain here, no ladders to climb."

Surprisingly, she nodded. "I think I knew that. Which is why I find myself going against my own better judgment and allowing Brian to continue."

Kirk dropped into the seat across from her. "It's the right thing to do."

"I'm not so sure about that. I just don't have a better alternative."

"I'm watching him closely."

Her blue eyes were fixed on him, and Kirk felt sorry for the delinquents who had to face that uncompromising expression in the courtroom. "I'm counting on it, Mr. Chandler. My son's life could very well be at stake."

For one second, Kirk doubted himself. He was Kirk

Chandler. The best in the business. But not the kid business. What did he think he was doing? Saving himself at the expense of a twelve-year-old boy?

Except that he made his decisions with his heart now, not his head. The predatory instincts had been permanently retired. In their place lay a humility that was guiding him in his new life of service.

"I make him weigh in every day. Did he tell you that?"

"No." And then, "Do the other boys know?"

He sipped slowly, welcoming the heat that traveled through his chest to his stomach, reminding him that although he might feel dead most of the time, he was still very much alive.

"I make them all do it," he told her. "I figured it couldn't hurt."

"You do that for Brian?"

His eyes narrowed. "I told you, Ms. Simms, I'm on his side as much as you are."

"Thank you."

She hadn't touched her hot chocolate. Other than to run a slim finger up and down the side of the cup.

"It must be rough, raising them alone."

She grimaced, glanced down as she dipped a finger in the whipped topping that was slowly melting into the chocolate. "Sometimes."

"How long has their father been gone?"

"Two years ago. But he wasn't around much before that."

Kirk set down his cup. "So you've basically raised them alone from the beginning?"

"Pretty much." She looked over at him. "I've been lucky, though. They're great kids."

"And I guess in your line of work you see the other side of things. Kids who aren't that great."

"They're all great, Mr. Chandler."

Delivered just as his high-school principal might have done.

"Not even the kids call me that," he said. "My name's Kirk."

"Then I'm Valerie, not Ms. Simms."

He leaned forward, about to challenge her. It was something about Kirk Chandler that hadn't changed—his penchant for jumping into situations more cautious people would avoid.

When he was younger, he'd needed the challenge, the relief from endless boredom. And now?

"So, all kids are great, huh?"

"I think so."

"Even the ones you send to jail?"

"They're detained. Juvenile facilities aren't just places to serve out a punishment. Once the kids are stripped of their dignity—once they're humbled—the system's designed to give them a new sense of self, to show them some options to a better life."

Kirk's memory was biased and many years old. Still, the times he'd spent in detention had certainly never left him feeling anything but worthless.

"And to answer your question—" she took a sip of the chocolate "—yes, even those kids are great. They're deserving of that effort. Oh, with a few it's hard to see the good. But for the most part, the kids who end up in my courtroom have had their childhoods stolen from them, one way or another. The original crime was against them. It starts a treacherous cycle.''

Interesting. ''So you're saying the crimes they've committed are not their fault?''

''No, I'm not saying that.'' She smiled sadly, shaking her head, and as the curls fell around her shoulders, Kirk was struck by what a beautiful woman she was. ''We all have free will to choose how to handle our circumstances. There are millions of kids who grow up in bad situations and take another route. Instead of giving in to that influence, giving up, becoming part of it, they hold themselves apart. They climb out and never look back.''

The heroes of the world. That wouldn't include Kirk.

''I'm only saying that my kids in court have as much potential as my kids at home. I look for ways to show them that someone cares, even if that means bringing them back into my courtroom so I can check up on them. And I enter dispositions that I think will help turn their lives around. Counseling, educational and vocational programs, that kind of thing.''

''You really care about them.''

''Of course I do,'' Valerie said. ''You can't sit there looking into the eyes of a scared, lost child and not care.''

Kirk might have been able to. A few years ago. He'd certainly managed to miss the panicked looks in the eyes of the men—very often elderly men—he'd put out of business. Many of them had spent whole lifetimes building something that he'd torn down in the space of a week.

This woman, a Superior Court judge at her age, obviously hadn't wasted a second of her life.

While he'd—

"What about the victims of the crimes these kids commit?" he asked.

"I care about them, too. One of my major considerations in whether or not to detain a child is the threat he or she poses to society. But helping the child helps society. The idea is to help them to grow into responsible, contributing citizens, rather than relegating them to life in adult prisons."

"What did you do before your appointment to the bench?"

"Worked in the public defender's office."

A defense attorney. Why didn't that surprise him?

She'd spent her life defending other people, while he'd spent his destroying them.

And through it all, she'd raised, single-handedly, two fantastic kids. While he'd squandered what chance he'd had to be a father....

Head bowed, he glanced at the woman across from him, feeling insignificant. Ashamed. The almighty and infallible Kirk Chandler, fallen.

KIRK ORDERED a second coffee. Valerie wasn't sorry to see him do that. Sitting there with him was nice. Unusual. But nice.

It had been a long time since she'd gone out in the evening for any reason other than business. Or the twins. They were safely home in bed, probably sound asleep by now, and her usual ten o'clock exhaustion had not made its appearance.

"You saw the kid I pointed out today—Abraham Billings," Kirk said, settling back in his chair with an ankle crossed over his knee, elbows on the arms of his chair, coffee cup held loosely between his hands. "He was the kid playing center."

"The one who got Brian's spot." She couldn't resist the barb, but the words were accompanied by a smile. She couldn't be sorry that Abraham had received this break—or that the boy was eagerly involved in such a healthy activity.

The slow grin he sent her as he nodded elicited an unexpected reaction in Valerie.

"The kid's got real potential."

"I thought so, too." One of her court kids with as much potential as her kids at home. Or more...

"I'd been after him to try out for the team since the third week of school. I could tell he wanted to, but then he didn't show up...."

Kirk's face was drawn, his eyes filled with compassion.

For one of her kids.

"Do you know why?" She heard herself ask a question she probably shouldn't.

Ordinarily, she would never discuss one of her kids outside the system.

But Kirk didn't know that Abraham was one of her kids.

And if there was any way he could help her understand how to help the boy...

"Nope. He never said. But I got the feeling it had something to do with his mother."

"Do you know her?" Valerie was careful to keep her tone neutral, one basketball mother asking after another.

"I've seen her around. The only thing I really know about her is that Abraham gets mad when he thinks a man's looking at her."

Because he was a twelve-year-old boy who didn't want to see his mother in that light? Or because he saw too much of it?

Valerie suspected the latter. But wasn't sure.

And if she was wrong? And took the boy from the woman who loved him? She understood the bond of motherhood.

"Do your boys know him?" Kirk asked.

She shook her head. "Why?"

"Something's not right with that boy, and I can't get him to open enough to figure out what. He's a good kid. I'd like to be able to help him."

"What makes you think something's wrong?" Valerie fought back the twinge of conscience that warned of the dangerous ground she was treading.

Abraham was due back in her court in another few weeks for a review-of-status hearing, and she had to do whatever she could for him.

"During the first part of the year, he missed more school than he attended," Kirk said.

She knew that.

"He missed practice on Friday because he had to do some volunteer work."

Valerie sipped lukewarm chocolate. "Did he say where?"

"An old folks' home."

His community service. There was no reason for Kirk to know that the boy was on probation. It probably wasn't information Abraham would share.

"I can't put my finger on what's wrong, I just know that something is. I've lived most of life by sheer instinct and I know that boy's in some kind of trouble."

"He's lucky he's got you looking out for him."

And perhaps she was lucky, too. If Kirk could somehow stumble on something that C.P.S. was missing...

"Yeah, well," Kirk said, rolling his eyes. "We'll have to see about that."

The conversation wandered then, and a few minutes later Valerie leaned forward, arms on the table, and grinned. "So tell me, Mr. Chandler, what do you do with your life besides help kids across the street, supervise lunchrooms and playgrounds and coach basketball?"

The more she was with the man, the more compelled she was to know what motivated him.

"That *is* my life," he told her emphatically.

Valerie put her crumpled napkin in her cup, disappointed. She'd thought they'd made a connection that evening.

Still, it didn't matter.

"I find it hard to believe that a man who's obviously well educated is content with so little to challenge him."

His eyes narrowed as he, too, stuffed his napkin in his empty cup. "You of all people should know that dealing with children is the biggest challenge of all."

He had her there. Sort of.

They stood. Threw away their trash.

Kirk Chandler wasn't the only one who had well-honed instincts. And Valerie's were telling her that he wasn't being completely straight with her. Something just didn't make sense.

But those instincts were also telling her to leave well enough alone. As long as the man kept his word where her boys were concerned, she had no interest in him, whatsoever.

"Have dinner with me sometime," he said.

He was walking a step behind her in the parking lot. Valerie didn't turn around. Didn't answer.

She stopped at the Mercedes, her key in the lock.

"You didn't give me an answer."

She wondered which of the vehicles left in the lot was his. It couldn't be the Corvette. Not on a crossing guard's salary. Which meant it was either the beater in the corner that looked like a combination of a couple of different cars. Or the Ford Taurus.

She couldn't see him driving either one.

"No."

"No, what?"

He was leaning on the outside of her open door.

"No, I won't have dinner with you."

He radiated confidence. The man had not learned how to look like that while standing on a street corner. As much as she wanted to, she couldn't tear her gaze from his.

"Do you mean that?"

"No."

She didn't know where the word came from. She just knew she had to get out of there. Immediately.

Before she did something else that contradicted her position. She had no intention of having dinner with him, yet she'd just undermined her own refusal.

Kirk Chandler had an alarming habit of getting that reaction from her.

Forcing herself to look away, she slid into her car and drove off.

It wasn't until she was halfway home that she realized she still didn't know which of those cars he'd been driving.

THE GRANITE TOMBSTONE shone bright in the afternoon sun. Kirk pulled at the grass around its edges, but there was really no need. Sunny Acres' landscaping was immaculate, as always. Reaching over to prune a slightly browned petal from the sprig of baby-pink roses he had delivered there every Friday morning, he fought back the helplessness that plagued him every single day.

This was a lesson he'd learned the hard way. One that had irrevocably changed his life. There was no going back. No closing the door on a knowledge he didn't want. Or wished he'd had ten years sooner.

He didn't really know why he'd come today. Why, every single Saturday afternoon for the past two years, he hadn't missed a date with his little girl. He was rubbing salt in a wound that would never heal. Keeping alive a regret that was already choking him.

And still he came. In spite of the self-loathing he always experienced here, Kirk had also come to know a level of peace as he tended to a child who no longer needed his attention. Pulling a paper towel from the back pocket of his jeans, he wiped off the top of the stone. In Arizona, dust could settle in a matter of minutes.

Then he stood. Blinked back an emotion he'd never thought himself capable of feeling, resigned now to its constant companionship.

"Sleep well, little angel," he whispered, walking slowly away.

They were the only words he ever said to her.

ABE BILLINGS HUNG OUT at Sunny Acres sometimes. It was the only nearby place where no one would bother him.

Not many people liked to hang out at cemeteries.

As for Abe, he thought it was pretty cool. Here he was never alone. And no one ever did raunchy things. The way he saw it, the cemetery was as safe a place as he could find.

Pulling out the cigarettes he'd snitched from the pocket of a pair of pants that had been hanging on the outside knob of his mother's bedroom door, Abe dug for the lighter, then slung his backpack over his shoulder. A year ago he'd put anything he really cared about in that pack. And he'd been carrying it everywhere he went ever since.

Lighting up, Abe wiped away the tears that sprang to his eyes from the first shock of smoke in his throat, held his breath so he wouldn't cough and started walking again. He'd smoke every single one of the bastard's cigarettes.

He'd show them. He'd show *all* of them.

How dumb did they think he was?

"Abraham?"

Shit. Abe froze. And felt the heat of that cigarette as he turned it backward in his hand.

"Abraham! Wait up!"

What the hell was Coach Chandler doing here? Abe had heard he lived up near the foothills with all the rich people.

He slowed, but didn't turn, frantically searching for something to do. He thought about putting the lit cigarette in his mouth the way he'd seen on television.

But he was too much of a wimp.

"Abraham, it's good to see you." Coach wasn't even out of breath as he caught up to him.

"Yeah," Abe said, dread seeping through him.

This was it. He was caught like a rat in a trap and there wasn't a damn thing he could do to save himself.

Story of his life.

CHAPTER SEVEN

"I THOUGHT YOU HAD to work on Saturdays." Coach Chandler acted like it was any old day.

"I got done early." He actually hadn't gone at all. As long as he was playing basketball he didn't have to go back to the old folks' place. He'd been shocked as hell when he heard Judge Simms had ordered that. He'd figured for sure he'd lose his spot on the team as soon as she saw that it meant her kid didn't get one.

That lady scared him. When she looked at him, he swore she could see every thought he'd ever had.

He felt kind of sorry for Blake and Brian having to actually live with her.

"So what are you up to now?"

"Going home." In another minute, the cigarette was going to be burning his palm.

Just like his butt was gonna get burned. Smoking was in violation of his probation.

"You live around here?"

"Around the corner."

"In the trailer park?"

"Yep."

"Just you and your mom?"

The heat was getting close. "Yeah."

"You like it there?"

He shrugged, forgetting about the cigarette for just that second. And almost hollered as the movement brought the smoldering tobacco in contact with the flesh of his hand. He dropped the cigarette. And just kept walking.

He wanted to put it out. There was no way he wanted to set anything on fire. But he just dropped it and kept walking.

He couldn't help it.

"It's okay, I guess," he answered a little jerkily.

But the coach didn't seem to notice.

Was it possible that he hadn't noticed the cigarette, either? For some reason Abe seemed to get lucky breaks around this guy.

"You got a pool there?"

"Yeah."

"Is it heated?"

"Nope."

They reached the corner. Turned. And started to sweat when it occurred to him that Coach Chandler might be planning to walk him home.

He'd step out in front of a car first.

"You like to swim?"

"I guess."

"I thought I might have a swim party for the team. What do you think?"

Was this guy for real?

Abraham knew the answer to that. And hated himself for hoping.

Abe was nothing but a stupid wimp.

"Sure, that'd be good," he said. "You got a heated pool?"

"Yeah."

"Cool."

The trailer park was only a block away. But there was a convenience store just before the entrance. He'd make up some story about getting stuff for his mom.

And hope to hell the guy left him.

Because there was no way he could buy a damn thing. He didn't have any money.

"Well, my car's down this street, so I'll be seeing you," Coach said, turning away.

"Yeah, see ya."

With a lighter step than he'd had in a while, Abraham headed home. His mom always kept Saturday evenings just for him and her, and it was after four o'clock. Their time.

But before he went in, he ran back to peek around the corner so he could watch Coach drive off. He didn't know why. Maybe he just had to make sure he was really leaving and not coming back to spy on him or something.

Coach got in a car, all right. A Milano Maroon 1965 vintage Corvette.

Sweet.

THE THIRD Friday in November, at night no less, and Valerie was sweating as though it was midsummer. Whacking the tennis ball as hard as she could to deliver an impressive spike, Val stumbled on the court of the fitness complex not far from her home. She righted herself in time to land her racket on the return that came speeding over the net. Unfortunately, her responding volley was uncontrolled and the ball landed outside the line. Actually, it landed outside the court.

She should have agreed to have dinner with him. Then maybe he wouldn't have asked her to play tennis.

"That shot wasn't too impressive," Kirk called over his shoulder, jogging over to the next court to retrieve the ball she'd hit.

"Sore winners aren't too impressive, either, Chandler," she called back. She was tempted to walk off the court and refuse to give him this last serve to finish off his game, set and match victory.

Except that would make her a sore loser.

And she was having fun.

Kirk was back, wicked grin and all. Beneath the bright lights of the tennis court, he reared back to administer another one of the lethal serves that had been killing her all evening. His leg muscles stood out in stark relief beneath the white tennis shorts, his shoulders and forearms those of a natural athlete. His slim midsection, as he lifted the racket and tossed up the ball, was more distraction than she could easily deflect.

The sharp sound of his racket connecting with the ball had barely reached her ears before the ball itself was there. She thought about standing there and letting it whiz on past.

But Valerie was Valerie. She never just stood around, gave up or otherwise turned away from a respectable and honestly delivered challenge. Even if the outcome was already certain.

With an effort of which she could be proud, she leaped for the ball, made a satisfying comeback. And didn't even see his return hit.

Only because it was dark, of course.

"You're buying."

His grin victorious, Kirk met her at the net.

"Buying what?"

This was the third time in two weeks that they'd met for tennis. The third time he'd beaten her soundly.

"Dinner." And the third time he'd tried to get her to go out with him afterward.

"It's eight-thirty. I had Mexican take-out with the boys three hours ago."

With the net between them, they walked over to the bench on the side of the court. Valerie was sweating in her short-sleeved knit top and black exercise slacks—but not as much as he was.

"We're just in time for dessert, then."

The boys were at a friend's for a birthday party. They'd taken sleeping bags.

"I have responsibilities, Chandler. I have to get home." He always stayed at the courts after she left, to hit volleys against the side wall. Each time, as she'd driven away, he'd been there, smacking the wall so hard he left marks.

As Kirk dropped the balls into their canister and snapped on the lid, his grin faded. "I'd like to talk to you," he said. "Remember I told you I was concerned about the new center on the team?"

Abraham Billings.

"Yeah?"

"I saw him last weekend."

"And?"

"Come have coffee and we can talk about it."

Leah had left the latest report on the Billings case on her desk yesterday afternoon—a report from the doctor who'd provided the mandatory counseling she'd ordered. Abraham had given no indication of problems at home.

His probation officer, Diane Moore, said Abraham was one of the best-behaved kids she'd ever had.

And his caseworker, Linda James, suspected there was something bad going on in the boy's trailer-park home. Carla Billings had explanations for the men's pants hanging on her closed bedroom door one afternoon, and an excuse for her own supposed absence from the home at the time. In spite of the fact that the caseworker had heard her in the bedroom. She also had explanations for the presence of different men on two other unplanned visits from the state. And for her ability to support her son without any proof of being gainfully employed.

The caseworker was a woman Valerie knew and respected. One who'd told her in confidence that she believed Carla Billings was turning tricks—a crime in the state of Arizona. And worse, doing it in her home while her son was there.

Kirk stopped walking at the curb of the almost-full parking lot.

"A cup of coffee." He reminded her of the question she'd never answered. "What can it hurt?"

"At The Coffee House again?" It was just a couple of miles.

His head tilted in surprise. "Yeah."

She stepped off the curb. He didn't. "Now?"

"Yeah." He paused. "I'll follow you." He still hadn't left the sidewalk.

Valerie was in her Mercedes, releasing her hair from its ponytail before Kirk's odd behavior hit her. She still didn't know what he was driving. But if, as she suspected, it was that beater she'd seen in the parking lot a few weeks ago, he probably felt embarrassed.

She didn't see him again until he pulled into the parking lot of The Coffee House twenty minutes later. He'd obviously done something in between leaving the fitness complex and joining her. She would've had enough time to go in, order coffee and drink half of it.

She'd decided to wait for him, instead.

"Close your mouth, Judge," he said as he slid out of a mint-condition vintage Corvette, locked it and walked toward her.

"Unusual transportation for a crossing guard."

Stupid thing to say.

But damn, there was a lot about this man that didn't add up.

"I haven't always been a crossing guard."

No kidding. "What did you used to be?"

He held the door open for her. "An unhappy member of the corporate world. Now I'm a happy crossing guard."

An explanation of sorts, if somewhat flippantly delivered. But no answer at all. How could someone with his drive and intelligence be satisfied not using his talents?

"You could always get a different job in the corporate world, one that might make you happier."

"You're probably right," he said, standing beside her at the counter. "But since I have no desire to do so, I'll let the opportunity pass."

"You're going to be a crossing guard for the rest of your life?"

"You have a problem with that?" His tone was light. Valerie wasn't sure the conversation was.

"No." Maybe. It just seemed like such a waste.

"It's honorable work."

"I completely agree."

They were next in line.

"The kids deserve the best."

"Of course they do." But it didn't take a young businessman successful enough to drive a mint-condition vintage Corvette to provide that at a low-traffic side street.

He stepped up to the counter. Ordered a hot chocolate for her—remembering that she liked extra whipped cream—and a coffee for himself.

And Valerie knew, without another word being said, that this particular conversation was over.

The man was frustrating the hell out of her.

"So what's up with Abraham?" she asked as soon as they were seated in the cushioned armchairs in a private alcove.

Abraham was, after all, the reason she was there.

At least in part.

"He was smoking a cigarette."

She set her cup down, carefully keeping her face neutral. Smoking was a violation of Abraham's probation. She could detain him for it. Get him out of that home for a bit, give the state time to come up with something on Carla, one way or the other. Was she the loving mother Abraham was protecting? Or was she, as his caseworker unofficially claimed, unfit to raise her son?

Valerie didn't particularly care what Carla Billings chose to do with her life—except insofar as it affected Abraham.

"He tried to hide it," Kirk was saying. "To the point that it burned his hand. He was favoring it in practice this week."

"Did you see his hand?" Valerie's mind was spinning. She couldn't possibly use this information.

And she might *have* to use it to protect a young man in her care.

"Yeah. The burn's right in the middle of his palm. Looked painful."

"Was he taking care of it?" And where was Carla Billings when her twelve-year-old son was out smoking?

"It looked okay." Kirk shrugged. "Making a big deal of it wasn't going to do anything but make him defensive. I got a close enough look to see that it wasn't infected and let it go."

"I wonder where he got the cigarettes."

"I don't know."

"What did you say to him?"

He sipped his coffee. "Nothing."

"What?" Valerie sat forward, her arms wrapped around her middle. "You condoned his smoking?"

"I pretended not to notice. I have a pretty strong suspicion that Abraham needs a friend right now, not another authority figure."

"What makes you think you could ever be that friend?" She picked up her cup of chocolate. Stirred in the whipped cream. Took a sip.

"Because I've got the time and the willingness to be the best friend that kid ever had."

"Can you do that?"

"Do what? Be a friend?"

"Play favorites with the kids."

Paper cup in hand, he sat back, crossing an ankle over his knee, his tennis shoe glistening newly white beneath the lights of the café. "I don't play favorites. Ever. I'm there for all of them. Completely. Abe just seems to need more at the moment than most of the rest."

"*Most* of the rest?" He'd looked away when he'd said that.

"Has Blake said anything to you about stomach discomfort?"

The chocolate in Valerie's cup jostled, splashing over onto her hand. Burning. Valerie hardly noticed. She wiped it away only when Kirk handed her a napkin.

"No, Blake hasn't complained to me. Why, has he said something to you?"

Along with Brian, he'd had another physical a couple of weeks ago, although it had just been a once-over for his basketball eligibility. Still, he'd been in perfect health.

Unlike his brother, who was still ten pounds under his ideal weight.

"No," Kirk said. "But I've seen him rubbing it a few times, and the other day I think he was sick before practice."

"You *think* he was?" She sat up straight, scared to death. "You don't know?"

"I thought I heard him getting sick. He swears he wasn't."

"Did you ask Brian about it?"

"He was already out on the court."

"Maybe it was just something he ate." God, she hoped so. She could handle anything—anything—so long as her boys were healthy. Brian's recent troubles had put the rest of her life very firmly in perspective.

"Maybe."

With narrowed eyes, Kirk watched her.

"What?"

"Tell me about your husband."

"He was killed in a car accident two years ago."

An expression of sorrow crossed Kirk's face during a long moment of silence.

"What did he do?" he asked softly.

Grateful to him for not trying to find words where there were none, she answered, "He was an attorney."

"You met at work?" He was holding his cup, but not sipping from it.

"We met in law school."

"What was his specialty?"

"Family law." The quintessential irony.

"Yet he wasn't around much for his own family?"

The man had a good memory.

Sitting back, Valerie held her cup between both hands. She took a sip more for the comfort of having something to do than because she wanted anything to swallow. The Coffee House was relatively busy even after nine o'clock at night, but sitting in their alcove, Valerie felt separated from the rest of the world.

"We graduated from law school with dreams of changing the world."

"Doesn't everyone?"

She chuckled, but without humor. "One would like to think so."

He grinned. "Too idealistic, huh?"

"Law school is about the most cutthroat place I've ever been," she told him, remembering the experience of that first year. "They only give so many seats. The schedule is so arduous, you have no life outside your studies. You deal with it or you're out." He watched her, the interest in his eyes compelling. "You're in all the same classes with all the same people getting all the same assignments," she continued. "Students would check books out of the library and purposely not return them so that a fellow student couldn't complete an assignment."

"Sounds charming."

His droll tone elicited a real grin.

"Yeah, well, it doesn't take long to figure out who's decent folk. And to align yourself with them."

"I take it he was one of them?"

She'd been certain of that.

And never been more wrong about anything in her life.

"He was planning a career in public law."

"I take it he didn't follow through on that."

"For a couple of years, yes."

She wasn't sure quite when her ideals and his had grown so far apart. Perhaps because the change had been so gradual...

"I'd taken a job as a defense attorney in a private firm." And the more self-supporting she'd become, the more critical he'd been.

"Defending criminals?"

"Defending people accused of committing crimes. I always believed my clients were entitled to every protection the system could provide. That was my job, and I took it seriously. I worked hard to ensure that my clients got the best results under the circumstances."

"Sounds like an overwhelming task."

"Sometimes. It meant I went to trial a lot more often than most defense attorneys. Fortunately, I won the majority of my cases."

And the more cases she won, the more prestige and respect she'd gained—and the more her husband drank.

"Eventually I left private practice," she continued, "and went to the public defender's office." She paused. "Everyone's entitled to the best defense. Not just the wealthy and privileged."

"I take it your husband didn't share your philosophy."

The man was a little too good at reading between the lines.

"Money was more important to him than it was to

me.'' Giving up on the chocolate she didn't really want, Valerie set down her cup. Forearms resting across her knees, she stared at her tennis shoes. ''I don't know what happened to him.''

And she didn't know why she was telling this man anything about it. Her life was her own.

Still, there was such a sense of nurturing about him. Glancing up at Kirk, she couldn't look away. That quirk in his mouth, the warmth in his eyes—it was as though he was genuinely interested in knowing about her pain. As though he cared. As though he understood something she didn't think *she'd* ever understand.

The sensation was unusual. Compelling.

''Once he went to work, the job consumed him.''

''Money has a way of speaking to people.''

''I don't think it was just the money.'' Running her hand through her hair, Valerie shook it out over her shoulders. ''At least, that wasn't his biggest priority.''

''Prestige, then?''

Again she shook her head. ''I think it was the winning. The power. He became obsessed. Right didn't matter. Justice didn't matter. Not as much as winning the case. It was scary how he'd manipulate the law to benefit his client. At some point beating his opponent seemed to be his prime motivation. He'd strip women and children of everything they had, giving it all to the men who'd left them, and see nothing wrong with that.''

And somehow, in the midst of everything else, alcohol had become his first obsession.

''The more cases he won, the more he'd take on.

It got to the point that we hardly ever saw him. He missed every one of the boys' birthdays. He was either working or traveling with clients or partners in his firm, even on the major holidays. Christmas was about the only time some of the single partners would take off, and he used to insist that he had to party with them. According to him, those social occasions were when most of the real business was done.''

Kirk was still watching her attentively. But he said nothing. She wanted to know what he was thinking.

''I'd talk to him, try to reason with him, even beg, but it was like talking to a wall. He just didn't get it. He kept saying that his values hadn't changed. That those values were driving him to do the best job he could.

''He'd miss school plays, Cub Scout functions, parent-teacher conferences, Sunday dinners. I'd tell him the boys needed their father. He'd say they had a father who worked night and day to provide for them. A father who was making the world a place in which his sons could succeed.''

''It's all about control.'' Kirk said, glancing at her through lowered lids. ''If he controls the world, or his portion of it, he has something solid to pass down to his children. Which is just an illusion, of course. The only true freedom comes from an ability to surrender and not lose self.''

Valerie stared. Nodded. He understood—and he was attributing nobler motives to Thomas than her deceased husband deserved.

Kirk's sense of perspective, of the balance between public and private, between the material and the spiritual, made him as different from her husband as a man could be.

"I used to wonder how he could look at the boys and me and not see what he was doing…"

And then she'd just stopped wondering.

"Sounds to me as though he probably didn't look."

He was right.

Of course.

CHAPTER EIGHT

"You comin' Billings?"

"Nah, you guys go ahead."

Walking around the corner in the mostly deserted locker room after practice the Monday before Thanksgiving, Kirk stopped suddenly, listening as his players gathered their things and jostled their way out. He wasn't interested in eavesdropping. But he'd learned to pay attention to his instincts. And his instincts were telling him to stay right there and listen.

The door had closed. They might all be gone. Still, leaning against the wall, a basketball tucked under each arm, he waited.

"What's the matter with him?" Abraham's voice echoed between empty lockers. There was no other sound. No rustling of clothes or collecting of personal belongings.

But someone was still there.

"Nothing."

Brian Smith, in protective mode.

Abraham and the Smith twins. Blake's stomach must be giving him problems again. If Kirk didn't miss his guess, the boy was sitting on the bench between the lockers, doubled over.

"I ate something bad." Blake confirmed at least one of Kirk's suspicions.

Silence fell and Kirk pushed against the wall, righting himself.

"What?" That was Brian again. Kirk stopped.

"Don't know," Blake muttered.

"Why didn't you go with the other guys?" Brian challenged Abraham. To distract him from Blake?

"Didn't feel like it."

"So what're you hanging around here for?" Brian asked, with none of the usual insertions from his twin.

"No reason. You got a problem with that?"

"Maybe."

About ready to make his presence known, Kirk grinned at the entire exchange. Male bonding at its best.

"So what's the matter with *you?*" Abraham was obviously talking to Brian now. His tone had changed, softened as much as a twelve-year-old tough guy's voice could, stopping Kirk yet again.

"Nothing's wrong with him." Blake's voice was still a little strained.

"Why's he so much skinnier than you?"

"He just doesn't eat much."

"Yeah," Brian chimed in. "I just don't eat much." He sounded more like a little kid than the man holding his own he'd been just seconds before.

"You guys got a ride home?"

"Eventually," Blake said. It sounded as though he or someone had stood up.

"Our mom comes after work. Sometimes she's late," Brian added. "Why, you need a ride?"

"Nah. I can call my mom. Or walk."

"So why you hanging around?" Brian asked yet again.

"Just don't feel like going yet, that's all."

"Stuff at home, huh?" It didn't surprise Kirk that Brian had picked up on that. He was the more sensitive of the Smith twins.

"Maybe. What's it to ya?"

"Nothing," Blake said. "It's nothing to us. Come on, Bry."

"It's cool," Brian said, apparently ignoring his brother for once. "Everyone's got stuff at home sometimes."

"Come on, Bry," Blake said again. "Mom's probably waiting."

"She won't be here for another fifteen minutes."

Leaning back against the wall, Kirk listened to the boys.

"You got a dad?" Blake asked.

"Doesn't everybody?"

"He a jerk?"

"I wouldn't know."

"He dead?"

"Nah."

"Took off, huh?"

"Yeah. Before I was born."

"Yeah," Brian said. "Ours is dead."

Silence followed. Kirk could picture the boys standing there. Perhaps nodding awkwardly, while frantically searching for what to say or do next.

"You want a cigarette?" Abraham asked.

"You smoke, man?" That was Blake. "That'll kill ya."

"Yeah, maybe."

"Or your mom will if she catches you," Brian said.

"Right." Abraham's voice turned nasty. "Like she'd ever notice. Besides, I get 'em from her."

"She knows you smoke?" Blake's voice held something akin to admiration, setting off Kirk's internal warning system.

"Sure." There was a lot of bravado in the answer. And then, "Hey, you guys ever seen a *Playboy* magazine?"

"Who hasn't?" Blake asked with enough bluster to reveal it as a lie.

Kirk, sensing that Abraham wasn't nearly as innocent as the Smith twins, decided it was time to make his entrance. He wasn't going to have Valerie's boys led astray right under his nose. Moving quietly to the door that lead from the gym, he swung it open, banging it against the outer wall.

"Hey, guys," he said cheerfully, coming around the corner.

The boys had all changed back into street clothes, jeans and sweaters. Kirk was still wearing the sweats, T-shirt and tennis shoes he'd had on for practice.

"Coach." All three boys stood a little taller.

"How's your stomach, Blake?"

The dark-haired boy started, then looked away guiltily. "Fine."

"You tell your mom about it yet?"

"There's nothing to tell."

Brian's face, as he listened to the exchange, was pinched.

"You think something's wrong with him?" he asked Kirk.

"Probably nothing serious yet, but if it's not taken care of, it could be."

"See, *Blake!* I told you to tell Mom."

The boys shared a look heavy with an unspoken and weighty message. Adopting a bored posture, Abraham watched them. But he didn't manage to camouflage the interested glint in his eye.

"She's got enough to worry about," Blake said, turning worried green eyes on Kirk.

"You won't tell, will you?"

Abraham looked away.

Kirk had mastered the subtle art of answering with neither truth nor lie long before he'd reached the age of these boys. Evasion. Prevarication. Distraction. In his former life, an indirect response was second nature.

"I'm hoping you will," he told the boy. "You're a good player, Blake. But skill is only part of it. You have a contract with this team, and with yourself, to be the best athlete you can be. That contract includes maintaining your equipment. Your shoes. Your uniform. And your body."

Blake stared down at the floor. "Yes, sir."

"How about you?" He looked at Brian next. "Are you eating three meals a day?"

"No, Coach." The words were mumbled, and Kirk wrestled with a mixture of compassion and frustration.

"You're working harder than any other boy here," he told Brian. "If you'd put even a tenth of that determination into your diet, you'd be on the team."

"There's no spot open."

The boy had him there.

"And if one does open, you aren't going to be ready for it."

Brian didn't respond.

"Tell you what," Kirk offered, his gaze moving between the twins. "Blake, you come see me during lunch tomorrow, and you and I can have an honest talk about the severity of your stomach upsets, and we'll go from there."

The boy's eyes lit up. "Okay, Coach, thanks."

"Brian." He nodded at Blake's brother. "I want you to keep a log of everything you eat. You have to turn it in to me before you're allowed to practice each day."

"Yes, Coach."

"And I want to see balanced meals there," Kirk added. "I want you to tell me how large of a serving of everything you actually ate, not just what your mother put in front of you."

"Can I do it in pencil or does it have to be in ink?"

Kirk shook his head. Working with kids was so different from anything he'd ever known.

"I don't care what you write with," he told Brian. "Nor do I care if it's on a napkin, in a notebook or on your arm. Just get it to me."

Brian grinned. "Yes, Coach."

"Now scram, you two. I imagine your mother's outside waiting for you."

At ten after five, he knew she was. He'd called her earlier to try to talk her into a game of tennis that evening and, during her very ladylike rejection, she'd mentioned her light calendar that afternoon. She'd be at the school by five to take the boys out for pizza, she'd said. Then they were going shopping.

Not that he could tell them. Valerie's boys had no idea their coach even knew their mother's first name.

Let alone that he had a slight case of hero worship for the beautiful judge.

"Abraham, hold on a sec, will ya?" Kirk called as the boy started to head out with the twins.

The young man turned back. "Yeah?"

"Have a seat." Kirk indicated the long wooden bench, straddling one end.

Abraham sat on the very corner, hunched over with his backpack on his shoulders. Turning his head, he looked at Kirk.

"You're an incredible basketball player, Abe."

Staring, Abraham said nothing.

"The game could very well be your ticket to whatever freedom you crave—whatever you want to achieve in your life."

Still silent, the boy sat there, perched for flight.

"Think of it," Kirk said. "Free to go, to make your own destiny, to study, to become whoever you want to be."

Kirk didn't bother to subdue his intensity. This young man, who touched him in such an elemental way, was on the brink of making the most important deal of his life. And if he made it with the devil he could be sentencing himself to seventy years that were far worse than anything he was experiencing now.

"As your coach, I need to know what's holding you back."

Abraham stared at the floor. The boy was harder to read than many of the hardened and world-wise businessmen he'd brought down in his time.

"I know you care about the game."

Kirk understood the boy's silence. And was concerned.

"I also want you to know that I care about you."

A slight jerk of a shoulder was the only reaction he got, but it was all Kirk needed. He'd scored. The win was within his grasp.

But the real winner, ultimately, would be Abraham Billings.

"CHANDLER." At home that evening, Kirk answered his phone on the first ring.

He'd stopped avoiding calls.

"The statute protects them," his lawyer's voice said. "Nothing's going to happen unless we can show that the father named on that birth certificate is not the child's biological father."

Troy Winston wasted no words, as usual.

"So do it."

"It'll mean publicizing the reason you were at the cemetery that day, including details of your emotional state. As well as reports on Susan's."

"That boy is mine. Do it."

"This isn't business, Kirk. We're talking about personal lives here."

"Yes, mine. And my son's."

"No judge will want to touch this. Chances are it'll get thrown out."

Gazing out the rounded wall of windows circling the atrium in the middle of his home, watching the shadows reflected by the lights and plants over the pool, Kirk detached himself from the situation and welcomed the numbed relief.

"You get the depositions, file whatever you have to file. I'll work on the judge end."

"You have connections."

"Maybe."

Troy chuckled. "Only you, man."

"What?" In the old days, Kirk would be grinning. Now he just frowned out into the night.

"Only Kirk Chandler could find connections in high places while he's working as a crossing guard."

Kirk didn't know about that.

"This is probably going to take some time...."

The warning, Troy's version of goodbye, was the most upsetting part of the conversation as far as Kirk was concerned.

TUESDAY WAS THE DAY she heard delinquency cases, and this particular Tuesday was busier than usual, since everyone wanted to push as much business through before the holiday as possible. She'd spent the morning on a molestation case—a fourteen-year-old boy with his eight-year-old brother—and had heard testimony that was buffeting everything sensitive inside her.

With the lights out in her office, Valerie lay back in her chair, taking a couple of minutes to herself before going to pick up the boys. They'd had a game that afternoon—an away game—and wouldn't be back at the school until almost six.

"Excuse me, Judge Simms?" Leah knocked at the door.

"Come in." Sitting up, Valerie switched on her desk lamp—and only then realized that she was still wearing her robe. Slipping it off, she hung it in the closet behind her desk as her assistant approached with a couple of folders.

In just her slacks and matching tunic, she felt lighter.

"I have a request for immediate action here," Leah said. "April Bradley's P.O. wants you to issue a bench warrant."

Listening as Leah outlined the sixteen-year-old's probation violations, Valerie looked over the papers, signed and initialed them, and handed them back.

She reduced probation on another one of her kids from intensive to standard just in time for the holidays. The things that made her job worthwhile.

And there was a pretrial motion to sign.

"Here's the Billings file you asked for," Leah said, placing the manila envelope in front of Valerie. She opened it. Hesitated.

She hadn't yet reported the smoking violation. Had decided instead to order twice-weekly drug testing. She wrote out the order.

Knowing full well that nicotine wasn't going to show up there.

If they pulled Abraham from his home, moved him someplace in another part of the city—or state—they could monitor any potential nicotine problem. Right now, she just wanted to make sure they didn't have any more serious substance-abuse issues to deal with.

Leah didn't ask any questions when Valerie handed back the signed form.

KIRK FELT A LITTLE BAD. But not enough to deny himself the victory. It was ten o'clock Wednesday night, and he'd convinced Valerie Simms to go for a walk with him. Just around her neighborhood. Which also happened to be *his* neighborhood, although he was fairly certain she didn't know that. The boys were in bed, and, calling on her cell phone, he'd played on her sympathies. Tomorrow was Thanksgiving and he'd be spending it alone. Surely she could spare him a few minutes tonight.

"Your manipulation didn't work, Chandler," she said as she joined him at the end of her driveway. He couldn't see the front door of her large, secluded ranch-style home. It was hidden behind a walled-in alcove surrounded by rosebushes. "I agreed because I wanted the exercise and didn't feel safe going out alone."

"No lunchtime skate today?"

"Yeah, I skated."

She looked cute in black spandex pants that outlined her legs and derriere. He liked her in the tennis shoes she often ended up wearing around him instead of her usual high heels. The flat shoes made her seem less imposing. More accessible.

There were no sidewalks in the elite mountain community. Walking on the edge of the wide, quiet road, Kirk kept enough of a distance to avoid touching her. But it was hard. Something he hadn't expected. Until that moment, he'd thought himself permanently immune to any kind of passion.

Let that be a warning to you, he told himself. If he could have extricated himself from the situation—this…relationship—without raising questions, he would've done so. Immediately.

"What are you doing on Thanksgiving?" she asked after several minutes of silence.

Visiting the cemetery, he could have told her. But didn't. "Same thing I always do," he answered instead. "Eating out."

"Eating out? Whoever heard of eating out on Thanksgiving?"

"You'd be surprised." Of course, in the past, eating out might have meant in a five-star resort restaurant at a table filled with powerful people, but now it meant a meal at whatever local diner he found open.

"You don't have any family in town?"

"Nope." He wouldn't allow self-pity, understanding that a man reaps what he sows. He'd rarely shared the holiday with his parents or his ex-wife and his daughter, when they'd been part of his life.

They were walking too slowly to get any real physical benefit, but the pace allowed him to see when she peered at him in the comforting semidarkness, which was broken only by a moon that hung bright and low—and an occasional muted street lamp.

"You alone in the world, Chandler?"

So many questions—and just when he'd realized there was a real temptation to become more intimate.

Odd, to want something so badly and not go after it. At thirty-four, he was forging his way through yet another new experience.

"No," he told her, refusing her sympathy. "I'm an only child, but my parents are healthy and thriving—in a home on a golf course in Florida."

"Oh!"

He took minor pleasure in having surprised the good judge.

"So what about you, what do you and the boys have planned?" he asked. A good offense was often the best defense.

"Dinner at home," she said. "We were invited to some friends', but—"

"Brian probably wouldn't eat."

"Right." She took a couple more steps. "And I wouldn't be able to give him a hard time about it, either. Not in front of other people."

"How many people know about his problem?"

"Besides his doctor and counselor?"

"Yeah." Hands firmly in the pockets of his jeans, Kirk took a wide step when her arm came close to brushing his elbow.

"One." It was her turn to surprise him.

"I'm the only one who knows?"

"Yeah." She nodded. "Leah, my judicial assistant, knows he's seeing a counselor about some self-esteem issues—she has to block out my calendar for Brian's appointments—but that's all."

She'd trusted him—and only him—with a problem she held very close to her heart. He had a role to play here. Kirk's hasty but very strong decision, made only moments before, changed again. He couldn't turn his back on a woman and child who needed his help.

CHAPTER NINE

THANKSGIVING PASSED uneventfully. Valerie's younger brother called from Texas, where he'd been living since college, and they shared their requisite holiday chat, catching up on all the news since their Fourth of July phone call. At thirty-three, Adam was in school again, going for his fourth degree. And he was dating a woman six years older than himself. He was planning to make her wife number two.

Valerie hoped the woman knew she'd be signing on for a life of supporting her brother's academic habit. Adam was a great guy. Funny. Kindhearted. Handsome. He'd just never grown from student to responsible, bill-paying adult.

And she'd talked to her parents. They'd moved from Arizona back to Indiana several years before, when her grandmother died, leaving her parents the house her mother had grown up in. They might not be rich in any financial sense, but they considered themselves wealthy in a spiritual way. They'd joined a new church upon returning to Indiana and it had become their life to the exclusion of all else. Sometimes Valerie wasn't sure they even heard her when she spoke to them about her own life—about anything outside of their church family.

Which made getting any kind of emotional support from them nearly impossible.

And yet, the things they'd tried to teach her—things like not taking personally what other people said or did, about the power of choice and, particularly, the assurance that she was never alone—did sometimes calm her heart.

While so many people spent their lives searching frantically for an elusive peace, she just had to call her parents to feel its presence.

Lying back in bed with moonlight shining through her bedroom windows, Valerie listened to the strains of her favorite New Age jazz CD and thought of everything for which she was thankful.

She had a job she loved, one that allowed her to contribute to society in a very real, satisfying and measurable way. At home she was not only comfortable and secure, but surrounded by beauty both inside and out. The custom-built house she and Thomas had commissioned when she'd made partner was landscaped with rock gardens featuring native plants.

And most important, she felt grateful for her sons. What mother wouldn't be thrilled with Blake and Brian? Thinking of their identical rounded cheeks with a smattering of freckles, the dark curly hair that was so like their father's, and those incredibly clear shining green eyes, she smiled.

"Mom?"

"Yeah?" Valerie sat up, focusing easily on Blake in the dim light. He was in the gym shorts and T-shirt he always wore to bed. She'd thought the boys were both asleep.

"Can I talk to you a second?"

"Of course." She patted the bed when Blake remained in the doorway. Though the boys would die rather than have anyone know, they still climbed into bed with her on Sunday mornings—one on each side—as they discussed whatever might be on their minds. Or made plans. Or just picked on each other.

They climbed into bed with her anytime they needed to talk. Valerie pulled back the covers, feeling the cold through the thin cotton of her pajamas.

Blake sat on the edge of the bed. "There's only one month left of basketball. And that's if we make the play-offs."

"I know."

Her son was frowning. And so, consequently, was Valerie. Blake wasn't usually the one who worried about the future. That was Brian's area. He was the more sensitive and emotional of her boys.

Blake, on the other hand, was the more logical, easygoing twin.

"What if Bry doesn't get on the team, Mom?" Blake's green eyes were wide as he turned to look at her. "He's working so hard."

"I didn't think there were any spots left."

"I know, but Coach could always make an exception, couldn't he? Just for a game or two?"

"I don't think so, sweetie." Her eyebrows drawn, Valerie tried hard to read her son.

Blake scrambled close to her on the bed. "I do. I think he can, Mom." With a hand on the mattress, he leaned forward until his earnest young face was only inches from hers. "You have to talk to Coach, Mom. You're important. He'll listen to you."

She nodded. "And what am I supposed to tell him?"

"That Brian has to play—at least in one game. Just so he can say he's on the team."

Arms wrapped around her middle, Valerie took several deep breaths. Calmed herself. Listening. "Why?"

Blake's gaze dropped. "Because he's earned it."

"You know better than that, Blake," Valerie said softly. "Nothing in life is automatic. Even with hard work."

The boy looked up again. "But Brian has... problems, Mom. If you tell Coach about him, he can make an exception."

An expected shard of fear shot through Valerie's heart. That had sounded far too much like the boys' father. Instead of honoring the laws he'd studied, he'd used them, manipulating the justice system to his own benefit.

Because he'd felt he was owed.

By whom, or why, she'd never understood.

"It doesn't work that way, Blake. You do the best you can do, and then you have to be at peace with the results. You have to trust that, somehow, things happen the way they're meant to."

Blake smirked, his eyes filled with frustration. And a curious glint of pain. "Not another one of your lectures, Mom. Please. Not now."

"I'm sorry. But it's not just one of my lectures. It's the truth. An important truth." Sitting there, staring at her troubled son in the darkness, Valerie had never wished more for someone to share the responsibility of raising her boys.

But, as usual, it was only her.

And whatever part of her father's wisdom she'd retained over the years.

"So you're just going to let Brian die?"

Had Blake's face not been so pinched with distress, Valerie might have smiled at his dramatic words. "He's not going to die," she told him. "Believe me, Blake, I'm watching very closely. As is your coach. Brian hasn't lost a pound since you made the team."

"He always drinks a ton of water before weigh-in."

Any hint of peace emanating from the day, the music, the quiet of the night immediately fled. Valerie didn't move, her expression understanding, compassionate, reassuring—and frozen in place. It was the best she could do.

"He's...not eating?"

Blake shrugged, twisting the hem of his shorts around his finger. "Sometimes."

Gazing at the top of her son's head, Valerie couldn't remember a time she'd felt so completely helpless. She understood now why Blake had come in alone.

And had a feeling he hadn't said everything he'd come in to say. He was only glancing up at her for seconds at a time. And was about to tear his shorts, they were so tightly twisted.

Leaning forward, Valerie ran her fingers through that curly dark hair. "Blake, look at me."

It took a long moment, but she waited until he did. "Is Brian skipping lunch again?"

"Sometimes."

He tried to look away. She grabbed his chin. "What else?"

"Coach said I had to tell you—"

"About Brian? He's right, you should. Although I don't know why Brian's drinking all that water to weigh in if your coach knows he's not eating…"

Shaking his head as much as he could manage with her hand on his chin, he said, "No, not about Brian. He doesn't know about that."

Dropping her hand, Valerie asked, "Then what?"

What *did* Kirk Chandler know that he hadn't mentioned to her the night before?

"I've been having some stomachaches."

Oh. Kirk *had* mentioned that. But when she'd seen no evidence of it herself…

If she could've lain down and cried, she would have. "Where does it hurt, hon?"

"Here." He ran his hand over the middle of his stomach.

She placed her hand over his, slowly rubbing the belly that had somehow firmed from baby fat to that of a young man. "When does it hurt?"

He shrugged. "Different times."

"Always after you eat?"

"No."

"How long does it last?"

"Depends."

"On what?"

He was staring down, twisting the hem of his shorts again.

"I don't know."

She needed Brian. He'd fill in the blanks.

"How often does it hurt?"

"Sometimes a lot. But it didn't hurt at all today. Until—"

"Until when?"

When he looked up, there were tears in his eyes. "Until I got into bed and started thinking about stuff."

"What stuff?"

"I don't know," he said, his eyes, in contrast to moments before, never leaving hers. "Like Brian. And the team. And Christmas coming."

"What does Christmas coming have to do with anything?"

"I don't know."

Holidays were hard when you didn't live in a traditional family. She understood that. She'd just thought, perhaps mistakenly, that she'd compensated enough so her boys didn't miss out.

She asked Blake a couple more questions that he grudgingly answered. She determined that his body was functioning as it should and told him she'd call his doctor on Monday.

She already knew what she was going to hear, though. She'd be told to get him off soda, on to milk, to keep antacids readily available, watch the fried food and get him into counseling.

All things she'd been told herself four years ago when she'd been on the verge of developing an ulcer.

Blake stayed with her for another half hour, sometimes talking, lying on the side of her bed. And when he was finally sleepy enough, he got up and stumbled across the hall to the room he shared with his brother.

Valerie went with him, tucked him in. Both boys insisted they were too old for the nightly ritual, but they always let her do it, anyway. Kissing him on the cheek, she whispered a promise that she'd take care of everything, and watched his eyes drift shut.

When she'd repeated the motions with his twin—including the quiet promise she had no idea how to keep—Valerie returned to her room.

Judging by her twelve-year-old kids, she wasn't doing such a hot job of single parenting.

AT NINE-THIRTY on Monday night, the first of December, Kirk's phone rang.

"Want some coffee?"

He liked the fact that she didn't feel a need to introduce herself. And then refused to like it.

"I was just heading over to The Coffee House. Meet me there?"

"Yeah."

Something was wrong. She wouldn't be calling him otherwise.

Kirk just hoped it was something he could help her with. If she was planning to try again to get Brian on the basketball team, she was going to be disappointed.

Because he wasn't letting her son on his team until Brian gained at least one pound. He'd made a deal with the boy.

Kirk arrived before she did, ordered for both of

them and chose a table outside on the patio. Only in places like Arizona could you enjoy a balmy evening warm enough to be out without even a sweater on a December night.

"What's up?" he asked as soon as she sat down.

"I couldn't just want coffee with a friend?"

Dressed in a black blouse tucked into jeans, with black high-heeled suede boots, she was every man's dream of a "friend." And more.

"Are we friends?" he asked, sliding down in his seat at a sideways angle to the little glass-topped table, his jean-clad legs crossed in front of him.

She blinked, tilted her head to look at him. "I guess I don't know."

Because he didn't know either, he let her off the hook. "Blake told me he talked to you about his stomachaches."

She stirred the whipped cream in her hot chocolate. "Yeah. I called his doctor today."

"And?"

"He prescribed antacids, an ulcer diet and another round of counseling. He's sure, as I am, that Blake is worrying himself sick about Brian."

"And about you."

She'd obviously freshened her makeup before she'd come, because he couldn't see the freckles that were always so prominent after she'd been sweating it out on the tennis court.

"About me? I'm doing fine."

"Boys worry about their mothers. Especially when there isn't a dad around," he told her. Unless they were self-centered like Kirk. Then they just didn't see when their mothers' hearts were breaking.

Head slightly bowed, he looked over at her. "Blake also said that you'd promised Brian a spot on the team, at least for one game. He seems to think you have more power over things than I do."

With a deep breath and closed eyes, she appeared to be considering her response. Her tension made the cords in her neck stand out.

"I promised him I'd take care of the things he spoke to me about," she finally said, so gently her words were like a brush against his skin. "He just assumed that meant Brian could be on the team. And I'm his mother, Kirk. Mothers are gods and have the power of gods, didn't you know that?"

"Mine didn't." His mother, a rich socialite, had been a servant. His servant.

"Mine did."

That didn't surprise him.

"But what I'm about to do isn't very godlike," she said, pushing her cup away, leaving folded hands on the table. "I'm narcing on my son."

"I haven't heard that word in a while." He would have smiled, except that she looked so serious.

Too serious.

"What's wrong?"

"Brian's filling up with water before weighing in."

His eyes narrowed. "Instead of eating."

"Right."

The little shit.

Disappointment fought with anger. Compassion

won out. "He wants a place on the team more than anything," he said, thinking aloud.

"I know."

He glanced across at her. "So why doesn't he just eat?"

"The sixty-four-million-dollar question," she said sadly. "It has to do with control, and self-worth. He's asserting control over his life by controlling his appetite. And punishing himself for not being good enough to earn his father's love and attention."

Oh. God. The caffeine he'd consumed that evening burned at the edges of Kirk's stomach. Every time Valerie had spoken about her dead husband, Kirk had recognized pieces of himself. But she'd never talked about him from the perspective of her children.

Had Alicia ever once thought that she was unworthy of her father's love? Was that how she'd explained his continual absences?

"What about Blake?" Kirk half blurted. "He doesn't seem to have self-esteem problems."

"His just manifests in different ways," Valerie said, sinking Kirk into further darkness. "Brian's my sensitive child. He internalizes. Blake is more logical, and projects his feelings on to the things he does. Ever since he started school, I've struggled with getting him to apply himself, to give his best effort. His counselors attribute a lot of this to a feeling that there's no point, because his best isn't good enough."

"He gives his all on the court."

"I know." Her gaze met his and held enough to establish an intimacy he couldn't afford. "It's the first time in his life he's felt this way. Which is why I couldn't pull him off the team.''

He'd had no idea. The whole time she'd been fighting for Brian, she'd been fighting for Blake, too. Fighting a very real and frightening battle. He'd screwed up. Underestimated the risks.

"So what do you suggest?" he asked. He could put Brian on the team the next afternoon. A junior-high team wasn't as strict as later teams would be about the number of players. He could squeeze in one more.

And he'd institute a grade-check program. Although he was doing it for Blake, it wouldn't hurt any of his kids to have a little extra motivation to do their best academically as well as on the court.

She looked him in the eye, her blond hair framing her face and shoulders, giving her an illusion of fragility. "Do you think Brian's ready for the team?"

"I made a deal with him." He told her the truth. "I told him he has to gain a pound to play."

Her mouth opened in surprise. "The boys didn't tell me that."

Kirk couldn't help it. He felt sorry for her. "It was a guy thing," he said inanely.

"Okay." She tapped the table. "I'm going to fill him up with every fattening thing I can think of for the next couple of days. Butterfinger bars, Oreo ice cream, chocolate sheet cake, French fries, all the things I don't normally let them eat until they've had something healthy. I can probably bribe him to eat enough to gain one pound. Then he's abided by your rules and earned his place on the team."

Her solution was a good one. Blake would win.

And Brian, too; he would've met a standard he'd agreed to—albeit with help and not in the way Kirk had intended. But there would be time after Brian made the team to work more with the boy.

"If he's on the team, it'll be with the proviso that I monitor his lunch every day," Kirk told her. "Obviously, keeping a list of what he's eating wasn't enough."

Valerie's smile was shaky. "Thank you."

He shrugged off her gratitude. Told her it was nothing.

But it wasn't.

AN HOUR LATER, he was walking her to her car, basking in the admiration shining in her eyes as she laughed up at him. He didn't bask long. If Valerie Simms learned anything about the man Kirk Chandler had been all his life, her admiration would quickly fade. She was a judge. A woman who heard the facts and passed judgment every day of her working life. He wouldn't have a hope in hell.

Not that he cared. His life plan no longer included self-gratification. He'd already had more than his share of that. And he'd taken far too much from too many people.

"So," she said, climbing into her car, "we never decided for sure. Are we friends?"

Could the woman read his mind?

"Sure," he told her. Because he would be a good friend to her, watch over her sons.

She nodded. And then her eyes grew shadowed. "But just friends, and the boys can't know."

"I agree."

"And not just because you're their coach."

"Because you don't want them thinking their mother's friends with a mere crossing guard?" he asked, intending the question to sound light and teasing.

He was surprised it didn't come out that way.

Valerie glanced through the front glass, shielding her expression. "They've already lost one father, Kirk. And obviously they have a lot of unresolved issues with that. They're my first priority and I can't risk letting them think they might have another father, because I don't know how it would affect them if it didn't work out. So I just can't get involved right now."

"Hey." He reached in the open door, laid a palm on her shoulder, ignoring her softness. "It's okay," he told her. "I understand."

She looked up at him, her eyes clouded with an uncertainty he wasn't used to seeing.

"Honestly," he added. "I don't want to make any of the other boys feel any less special, and if it got around that I was friends with the Smith boys' beautiful mother..."

She smiled, as he'd hoped she would.

Good. That was settled.

They'd be friends. On a joint mission to save the children of the world.

Friends.

And nothing more.

CHAPTER TEN

THE WEEK AFTER Thanksgiving, the Menlo Ranch Rangers won all three of the games they played, landing them a chance to make the play-offs. With Abraham Billings's skill, Blake Smith's footwork and Brian Smith's heart, the team appeared unstoppable.

Abraham, Blake and Brian had become quite a team off court, as well. Valerie didn't know this just because Kirk had told her so on the two occasions they'd met that week, but because if her boys weren't talking about basketball, they were talking about their new friend, Abraham.

"They invited him over to spend the night," Valerie told Kirk late Friday night. He'd called to talk her into a late-night walk, but she'd already been in bed—reading. They'd been on the phone for the past hour, instead.

"He's there?" Kirk sounded surprised.

"No." Valerie frowned. "He said he was busy tonight."

Just as he'd been busy the other three times the boys had invited him during the past week. Just as he'd be busy the next hundred times they asked—if they asked. Valerie was fairly certain Abraham Billings would rather die than be a visitor in the home of his judge.

Not that he'd tell her boys or, if her guess was correct, anyone else about that.

And, ethically, Valerie couldn't say a word, either.

She was sitting on the floor of her room, leaning against the far wall under the windows. As far from the bed as she could get.

And she'd put on a pair of sweats with her sleep shirt, too.

"I don't think he was busy," Kirk was saying.

"Why?" Senses honed, Valerie sat forward, her arms on her upraised knees. She shouldn't have asked. And she shouldn't be paying such careful attention to anything and everything her sons told her about Abraham Billings. It wasn't right.

And yet, with a boy's life possibly at stake, how could she not? Would it be right for her *not* to do everything she could to protect a boy under her care?

"I don't think he's ever busy," Kirk said. "He sits at home with headphones on and plays video games."

"How do you know that?"

"Listening to him talking with the team, mostly. He has a tendency to quote alternative-rock lyrics, and when some of the guys asked him why he's so good at it, he said he listens to them every night. Twelve years old and he spends his nights listening to alternative rock." Kirk sighed. Valerie knew he was worried about Abraham. She wished she could discuss the case with him. Fill in some of the blanks. Ask for his opinion. "And when he's discussing strategy or explaining a move on the court, he'll often preface it with 'It's like the video game I was playing last night…'"

"That doesn't mean he spends his nights—"

"I ask him," Kirk told her. "Every day I ask what he did the night before."

She hadn't realized he was that involved. But she should've known. It didn't surprise her.

"So maybe he's just giving a pat answer to avoid your question," she said now, running her fingers through the curls hanging over her shoulder. Hoping the boy wasn't shut off in his room at one end of the trailer every night while his mother conducted business at the other end.

"He's been working all week to beat the Fire Wizard on 'Earth Invasion.' I get a report at every practice."

Oh.

"And I've tried to call him a couple of times this week, just like I've called the other boys, to remind them to tell their parents what time the bus will get back to school after the games. He never picks up. Because he's constantly wearing headphones."

"What about his mother?" Valerie asked, curling her bare toes into the carpet. "She's never home to answer the phone?"

"He says she's home, but working. I guess she's some kind of bookkeeper or something."

Yeah, that was what they'd heard, too. Except that she could never produce a firm for whom she worked, or a pay stub, or any evidence of a license or college degree…

God, this was hard. Being two people at once. Both of whom wanted to do what was right for this child.

"That's not the worst of it," Kirk said. "Tonight he hung around school for a long time after practice." His voice was hesitant, as though he was choosing his words carefully. Or maybe he just wasn't sure he should be speaking to a parent about someone else's child.

Valerie wasn't sure he should be, either. And couldn't stop him if her life depended on it.

"Was he waiting for a ride?" she asked, pretending she knew nothing more about the boy than what Kirk was telling her.

"That's what he said, but I left shortly after he did—and saw him walking home."

"Does he know you saw him?"

"No."

"So why do you think he was hanging around?"

"I don't know," Kirk said, and Valerie could hear a note of worry. "But what I *think* I saw was fear. Which makes no sense at all."

Heart pounding in her chest, Valerie held the phone with a sweaty palm. "Afraid of something at home?"

"I hope not," Kirk said, his voice grim. "I was hoping it was more like someone waiting to mess with him on the way home. You know, older guys. That's why I followed him home—from enough of a distance that he didn't know I was there, of course."

Valerie smiled. Kirk Chandler was a good guy.

"I take it there was no problem."

"None."

"You sound disappointed."

"If the problem wasn't on the way home, where was it?"

"Unless waiting made the route safe." Valerie hoped so.

She could make a phone call. Sign an order, even though she wasn't the judge on call that weekend. Have the boy removed from his home.

She had the smoking thing to back her up.

Sort of.

Official channels had not brought her that piece of information.

"What are you doing this weekend?" she asked, needing to think about something else. She just couldn't get a clear read on the Billings case. Couldn't quite find the detachment that came so naturally in the courtroom.

Perhaps because she wasn't in the courtroom.

And that was the only place she should be dealing with the Billings case.

"Not much," Kirk said. "Studying films for our games next week. Working on plays."

"You aren't Coach Chandler all the time," she told him. Didn't the man do anything outside his school functions? They simply weren't consuming enough to fill a lifetime. Especially not the lifetime of a man as dynamic as he obviously was.

"These boys actually have a chance to make the play-offs," he said. His voice didn't sound quite as...excited, as engaged, as she had a feeling it should be. *Could be.* He always seemed to be holding something back. "It'll be a first for Menlo Ranch. And I'm going to do everything I can to help them get there."

"Surely watching films isn't going to take all weekend."

"You hinting for a date, Judge Simms?" The lazy tone took on a hint of sensuality. Valerie lowered her legs to the carpet. Crossed them.

"Of course not. I promised the boys a trip to the science museum. And there's a movie they want to see.

They spent the next few minutes discussing movies—most of which he hadn't seen.

"You did it again," she said, breaking into his commentary on sequel films and the capital they generated—a commentary that could have been given by a financial analyst.

"Did what?"

"Sidetracked me from gaining any insight whatsoever into the real life of Kirk Chandler."

"You know what you need to know."

"I thought we were friends."

"We are."

"Friends get to know each other."

"What do you want to know?" He didn't sound irritated exactly, but he wasn't nearly as relaxed as he'd been seconds before.

"Your hobbies," she told him, surprised to find just how much she did want to know. That and everything else about him.

It had been a while since she'd had a close friend. She could be forgiven for finding the experience addictive.

"I don't have any."

Other than tennis. Which he'd already told her he

hadn't played in years until she came along. And now he only played it with her.

"None?" What kind of person had no hobbies?

Except maybe her ex-husband. Work, getting ahead at any cost to anyone, had been Thomas's all-consuming pastime.

"No."

"Why not?"

"Seemed like a waste of energy."

Turning off the light in her room, she returned to the floor, watching the moonbeam that pierced her wall of windows and landed on the navy carpet. An Enya CD was playing softly in the background, partly as a camouflage for her voice if the boys awoke, mostly to soothe the tension that had caused several restless nights in a row.

"What do you do for fun?" she asked in spite of his obvious desire to talk about something else.

"Spend my days with kids."

Great answer. And no answer at all.

"You don't watch movies, you don't have a hobby. What happens on weekends when you don't have basketball films to watch?" She had no idea why she was pushing this. Except that the darkness and the privacy of the telephone—where she was just a voice talking to another voice—gave her a sense of protection. Enough to take the chance.

"I wait for Monday."

He didn't sound the least bit sad about that. But his response brought tears to her eyes.

THE REPORT WAS WAITING for her when she got off the bench Monday afternoon. Abraham hadn't shown up for school, and the principal's office, upon receiving no answer at home, had called Diane Moore. The probation officer had called Abraham's caseworker from Child Protective Services. When they'd arrived at the home, Abraham was there, as was his mother. The boy had been in bed, the covers up to his neck, apparently suffering from flu.

But when Abraham moved, the C.P.S. officer had seen bruises.

Carla Billings had been questioned about her order to call the school anytime Abraham was absent. She said she'd meant to. Asked why she hadn't answered the phone, the response had been that she hadn't heard it ring.

Her son was on probation, in danger of being removed from her home, and she hadn't been able to do any better than she'd "meant to."

"I want them both in my courtroom first thing tomorrow morning," Valerie told Leah.

Abraham's probation officer would make the call, ordering Carla to bring her son to court. There would be no reason given—a status hearing, under the circumstances, was not unheard of—because Valerie wasn't going to risk giving Carla a chance to take the boy and run.

In the morning, the woman would no longer have the chance.

As of tomorrow, Valerie—the Arizona court—was going to be Abraham's guardian. The thought left her feeling slightly sick.

And Kirk Chandler would never understand.

KIRK TRIED SEVERAL TIMES to call Valerie on Monday night. He couldn't leave a message at home in case her boys picked up. And although he'd left a message on her cell phone, he knew she rarely had it on when she was with her sons.

"Damn." He slammed his fist against the pantry door in his sinfully large kitchen. Frustrated. Concerned. And uncharacteristically helpless. Kirk Chandler had a contact list long enough to fill a book. And no one to call.

Worse, he had no knowledge upon which to draw.

Grabbing his cell phone from the built-in counter desk next to the pantry, he punched the automatic dial.

"This better be good, buddy. It's after midnight here."

He'd forgotten Troy was on the East Coast for the next couple of days.

"I need some advice."

"Now, there's a surprise."

Kirk let his attorney's derision slide. "I got a kid on my team I think was roughed up over the weekend."

When Abraham hadn't shown up for practice that afternoon, he'd gone looking for the boy. And found him right where he'd expected to. Along the back wall outside the cemetery. Apparently it was a favorite place of his.

"So call the cops."

"And say what? That a kid has some bruises?"

"Yeah, why not?" Troy asked. It was then that Kirk heard the slur in his voice. Troy must be entertaining a woman. It was the only time his friend drank.

"He said he fell out of a tree."

"So don't call the cops."

"There aren't a hell of a lot of trees here for climbing."

"So call the cops."

"What are they going to do?"

"Listen, Chandler, I'm in acquisitions. I do mergers. Remember? The kind that make billions of dollars? I don't know a damn thing about juvenile law."

"You had to learn something about it in law school," Kirk reminded his friend. They'd been in college together. Kirk knew that Troy had had a pretty thorough overview of his profession.

Troy sighed, sobering. "They'll probably call Child Protective Services, who'll most likely visit the kid in the morning," he said.

Kirk heard a whisper in the background. Followed by what sounded like a female whine. Or maybe a cat that wanted to eat?

Troy didn't have any cats. And he wasn't even at home.

Thanking the only man still left on his payroll, Kirk rung off.

If nothing was going to be done until morning anyway, he'd wait and call Valerie at work. He had no idea what she'd be able to do, but he couldn't just turn Abraham over to the police. He'd been on the receiving end of their compassion a time or two himself. And found it nonexistent.

At least Valerie cared about her kids. Maybe she'd know a sympathetic cop to call.

In the meantime, he was going to break open that scotch he'd been saving, sit out by the pool, slowly emptying the bottle, and pray that Abraham would be safe until morning.

"ABIE?"

He turned his head slowly, searching out his mother's shadow in the darkness.

"Yeah?"

He almost flinched when she sat down on the edge of his bed, but not quite. He couldn't make things any worse for her.

"I'm sorry, baby."

"I know."

Under cover of the plain white sheet, protected, Abe felt stronger. His room wasn't much—box spring and mattress with a plain blue bedspread, no designs on his sheets or walls or anything, but the bedding was soft from the stuff his mom used when she washed it. And his wall held a mammoth CD rack that was almost completely filled.

"I had no idea he was—"

He would've felt stupid sleeping on cartoon characters, anyway.

"It's okay, Mom. I know."

His room was small, but then he didn't have much junk. Just the old dresser he'd helped his mom bring in from someone's trash a couple of years ago, and his desk with an old computer she'd gotten from someplace he didn't want to know about. And the television set and video games she'd bought him for Christmas the year before when she'd had a bunch of money.

"But he hurt you, honey."

Resting her weight on one arm, she leaned toward him, brushing his hair back. He felt like a baby when she did that. But as long as no one else knew, he figured it was okay.

"It's okay, Mom. It's just a few bruises. They stopped hurting already." Or they would if he could just stop thinking about them. A whiff of his mother's soft perfume took his mind from the way life had become.

"But what about basketball? You're not allowed to play if you miss practice and you're so close to making the play-offs."

He shrugged. And couldn't breathe for a second from the burning stab in his shoulder blade. The stupid tears came back and he had to turn his head sharply away from her.

"Coach'll let me play. I'm the best guy on the team." The lie was safe. She couldn't make it to games. He'd just hang out until they were over.

Her soft lips on his cheek made things good. Or as good as they got in his life.

Until a drop of water smeared on his cheek. She was crying again. The kind he hated most, when there was no sound. Not even sniffling.

"You're my best guy, you know that, don't you, Abie?" she whispered.

"Yeah." Someday he was going to be her only guy. Someday real soon. He already had some ideas about how to get enough money to lock the bastards out of the trailer for good. He'd spent the whole day thinking about it.

That and trying to forget about those fat hands on him last night. Coming at him again and again when he wouldn't...

"Diane Moore called today."

Shit. "Why? You called McDonald and told them I was sick."

She kissed him again, her fingers soft and slender against his head. "I forgot."

Rigid, staring at the wall, Abe silently recited a slew of words that Blake and Brian Smith would never in a million years say.

Didn't she get it? He couldn't help her if they hauled his ass away.

Not that *that* was going to happen. He'd make damn sure of it. One way or another. He'd run if he had to.

"Ms. Moore said we have to be in court in the morning for a status hearing."

He didn't care how much it hurt to turn his head, he stared into the darkness until he could see her eyes. His mom didn't look him in the eye and lie to him. Ever.

"They're going to send me to jail," he said. He felt as if he might throw up. Or have diarrhea.

"Oh, Abie." His mother smiled right at him. Abe's throbbing shoulder and the place on his back didn't burn quite as badly. "They aren't going to throw you in jail for missing school."

"I broke probation—"

"You missed school, Abie," she said, her voice sounding all momlike. God, he wished she was like this all the time. "We're due for a status hearing. I probably just lost the slip of paper with the date."

He didn't remember there being a date, but it wasn't like he paid that much attention. Mostly, he just tried to forget the whole court thing. He still couldn't figure out why those official types had to get involved. It wasn't as though he was stupid. Missing school didn't hurt him. He got straight As and knew a lot more than most of the kids.

"Okay," he finally said, wishing he could put on his headset and go to sleep. 'Course, if it was like last night, every time he moved in his sleep he'd just wake up again.

Life sucked.

"We have to be there at eight-thirty, so I'll just take you to school afterward."

Great. Damn great. Judge Simms first thing in the morning.

"Can we get breakfast before we go?"

"You bet."

"At McDonald's?"

"Of course."

That was something, then. "Thanks, Mom."

She kissed him one more time, right next to his mouth. A longer kiss. And he knew everything would be okay. Somehow.

He wanted to kiss her back, to wrap his arms around her neck and hold on, but he'd quit doing that ages ago. He wasn't a little kid anymore.

And if he moved his shoulders that much, she'd for sure figure out he was hurting....

She looked him in the eye once more before she left. She had to be the most beautiful mom in the world. He was lucky.

Everything was going to be great soon.

With him and Mom, it always was.

Eventually.

He tried to sleep after she left, but he was afraid. After last night he wasn't closing his eyes until he saw the outside light go out. The one that meant his mom was done working. While he waited, he thought about basketball. The team. Their chances of making it all the way. Coach.

And that was when he started to cry.

CHAPTER ELEVEN

THE FOLDS of her black robe swirling around her ankles, Valerie stepped through the private back door into her courtroom and up to the bench on Tuesday morning. One quick glance showed her that Abraham and Carla Billings, a C.P.S. worker, Diane Moore, Abraham's probation officer, and his court-appointed attorney were all in place, standing as she entered.

She waited, but the boy refused to look up at her.

"You may be seated." She opened the boy's file. And thought about Blake and Brian on their way to school that morning, talking quietly about their friend. Wondering if he'd be at practice. If he'd be able to play in the upcoming tournament game.

And, characteristically, they were as concerned about whether or not Abraham was all right as they were about their current favorite sport.

It wasn't like him to miss practice without an excuse, they said. And they'd started to weave a fantastic story around the boy. With their scanty knowledge, spurred on by the fact that he'd never come to their home or invited them to his—and mixing in a bit of twelve-year-old-boy darkness—they'd invented a scenario horrific enough to shut them both up.

The truth was worse.

Valerie forced back another twinge of guilt as she thought about her duplicity in using Kirk Chandler as an unsuspecting source of information.

"Judge, we're going to Abraham Billings. This is #JV324555."

Valerie only half heard the bailiff. She glanced up a couple of times. The boy, dressed in clean jeans and button-down shirt, was staring at the table in front of him, rubbing the edge with his right thumb. With his tanned skin and perfect features he seemed more suited to a movie set than her courtroom. Carla, circumspectly dressed in expensive-looking navy slacks and an off-white ribbed sweater, was watching her son.

She loves him.

Valerie didn't want to know that. Not right then.

She read aloud from the document in front of her and then asked, "Have all parties received and reviewed the report?"

The reply was affirmative.

With a knot in her stomach, Valerie proceeded with the delinquency hearing—knowing full well that it was a front for the real reason Abraham was there. She'd already signed the dependency petition that had come from the attorney general's office that morning; Abraham would be removed from his home. C.P.S. was going to take him directly from the court.

Quietly, almost imperceptibly, Carla took her son's left hand. Clasped, their hands fell beneath the table, out of Valerie's sight. She stared at where they'd been, heart pounding.

Abraham's left sleeve had risen slightly when his mother had taken his hand.

"We're here because you missed school yesterday," she said, reaching deep inside for the composure to continue this long enough to get what information she could. "What happened?"

"I was sick." His voice was strong. Clear. If he lied that well, things were worse than she'd thought.

"Abraham?"

"What?"

"Could you look at me, please?"

He glanced up, but wouldn't meet her gaze.

"You were sick yesterday?" she asked.

"Yes." No wavering there.

"Why didn't the school know about that?"

"I thought they did."

Valerie looked at Carla Billings.

"I forgot to call," the woman said, her voice uneven. "I'm sorry."

Valerie had the right to remove Abraham from his home. But she also knew it was critical to give him more of a reason than broken probation. She couldn't bring up the smoking. Couldn't tell him what they both knew—that his mother was prostituting in her bedroom while her son was at home.

"What was wrong with you?" she asked him.

"I had the flu."

She turned back to his mother. "Is that true?"

"Yes."

"Did he have a fever?"

"No. Not that I could tell."

She nodded. Looked at the folder. Then back at Abraham's mother. "You didn't check?"

"No, ma'am."

"Did you see a doctor, Abraham?"

The boy was sitting up so straight, he wasn't even touching the back of his chair.

"No, ma'am." He looked at her when he answered. At her, not her eyes.

"Are you better today?" she asked, compelled by something that was not yet clear to her.

Carla Billings reached over to her son, rubbing his back.

Abraham flinched. So it was more than just the hint of a bruise she'd seen when the boy and his mother had clasped hands.

"Show me your arm, Abraham," she said.

He held out his right arm.

"Not that one."

The boy flung his left arm out and then drew it back.

"Again," Valerie said. "And roll up your sleeve."

Slowly, gazing at his mother the entire time, Abraham did as she'd ordered.

An ugly, multicolored bruise covered the boy from his wrist to his elbow.

"Now, would you please show the court your shoulder?"

"Judge, I hardly think—" Abraham's attorney began.

"Now, Abraham. Please," Valerie interrupted.

Abraham's big brown eyes implored his mother,

who finally nodded. She helped her son get his shirt off enough to expose one shoulder blade.

He stood, turned, displaying the welted and broken flesh, and then quickly sat, pulling his shirt back on without apparent regard for the pain he must be causing himself.

"I see there are bruises on your body, Abraham. What happened?"

"I fell out of a tree."

"He was playing out by the cemetery," his mother said, her eyes wide and innocent as she faced Valerie.

"The one by Cypress Lane?" It was the only cemetery anywhere near the trailer park where Abraham lived.

"Yes."

"I'm not aware of any trees in that vicinity. At least not ones suitable for climbing."

"That's because I fell off the cemetery wall," Abraham said, his right thumb thumping on the table as his chin jutted out at her.

"Is that the truth, Abraham?" Valerie gave him another chance to talk to her. To help her help him.

"Yes, ma'am."

"You're sure about that?"

"Yes, ma'am."

She took a deep breath. It didn't release the ache inside her. "Abraham, I'm ordering a C.P.S. investigation," she said, writing on the page in front of her. "In addition, I'm ordering that temporary custody be given to C.P.S. until the investigation is completed."

Abraham nodded, his expression stoic. Valerie couldn't look at his mother. But she heard her gasp.

And could practically feel the energy seep from the younger woman.

"Is there anything else you'd like to say?" she asked the boy.

"No, ma'am."

Taken aback by the boy's complacent reaction to the news she'd feared would unhinge him, Valerie turned to his mother.

"Ms. Billings, you are entitled to a hearing in this court five days from now to contest this decision if you feel so inclined."

She wished she hadn't looked at Abraham's mother. The utter despair in the woman's posture, her expression, her eyes, was mirrored deep inside Valerie. She'd known it would feel like this.

And she'd let that feeling get in the way of doing her job. If she'd followed her first instinct and removed Abraham from his home the last time he'd been here, the boy wouldn't be so bruised that he couldn't even sit back in his chair. She could have spared him that, at least.

Tears streamed silently down Carla's face. And Valerie wondered if she'd done the physical damage to her son.

She turned to the C.P.S. officer. "Martin, before you place Abraham, I want him to have a complete medical examination."

"Place me?" Abraham rose perceptibly in his seat, his voice ricocheting off the walls of the small court. His eyes, wide and frightened, were trained on his mother. "Place me where?"

"You are, at least temporarily, in the state's custody, Abraham. Mr. Lewis will be finding a place for you to stay.''

''Mom?'' The boy continued to stare at his mother, as though she were the only person in the room.

Carla opened her mouth to speak, but a huge sob tore through the room. Wordlessly, she nodded.

''For missing school one day?'' he asked her, his voice high.

Shaking her head, his mother reached for both of his hands, squeezing them. ''For the bruises, Abie.'' She spoke so softly Valerie could barely hear the words. ''They don't believe you fell.''

''I did!'' Abraham cried. ''I did fall! Tell them I fell.''

When Carla pulled the boy onto her lap, Valerie nodded at the officer, who'd risen behind mother and son.

''Come on, Abraham, it's time to go,'' Martin Lewis said from behind them. He reached for the boy and then withdrew, and Valerie knew he was thinking of the bruised flesh they'd seen. And the fact that they had no idea how many more bruises were hidden under his clothes.

Valerie had no idea who'd done this to Abraham, but she knew she'd do everything in her power to make absolutely certain it never happened again.

Abraham clung to his mother so tightly, Valerie realized he must be hurting himself. She nodded at Lewis again.

''Abraham, it's time to go,'' the man said more firmly.

And when the boy still didn't react, Lewis took Abraham's hand.

"No!" The single, shrill word shot out, followed by another. And then another. The tough young man she'd seen at school with her sons was crying, begging, screaming, clinging to his mother. Refusing to let go even when Martin Lewis held him by both arms.

At that point Valerie had to leave the room.

HE WAS NOT HAVING a good afternoon. For the second day in a row his star player had cut practice. There was no way Billings was going to be ready for the play-off game on Wednesday. But Kirk didn't give a damn about that.

He'd been trying to get Valerie all day to tell her his fears about Abraham. To ask her advice. She hadn't picked up.

And he hadn't left a message. He'd been hoping Abraham would at least show up for practice. Basketball meant so much to him.

So where the hell *was* the boy? Kirk didn't even wonder if Abraham was okay. He knew he wasn't. Abraham Billings had not been okay the entire time Kirk had known him.

He'd been planning to change that.

Pushing in the number to Valerie's cell phone before he left the school parking lot on Tuesday evening, he held the phone to his ear with one shoulder, started the Corvette and pulled slowly into the street.

She picked up on the sixth ring. And after only minimal cajoling on his part, agreed to walk with him that night after her boys were in bed. That meant he had four hours to kill.

As he headed home, he listened to the messages that had come through on his cell phone that day. One from his mom and dad in Florida, their monthly call telling him that the weather was great and the golfing even better.

It was all the conversation any of them could manage with each other and keep up the appearance of a happy family. Unspoken recrimination lay so close to the surface that any talk more personal than that posed too big a threat.

The elder Chandlers had plenty of money to live out the rest of their lives in easy luxury. And, because of Kirk's heartlessness in pursuing his father's business in a hostile takeover—for financial reasons and financial reasons only—his father had no life that he cared about anymore.

He wouldn't say so, though. Kirk's whole life, his parents had justified his actions, spinning gossamer fictions around them. Unfortunately, this last web was just too thin to hide the ugly truth.

He'd had a call from Troy, too. The Arizona statute his lawyer had warned him about was going to protect Susan. Unless Kirk could come up with much more substantial evidence to show that the father named on Colton's birth certificate was not his biological father.

Kirk needed a new lawyer.

And someone who had authority in the Arizona court system.

After ten minutes of pacing, Kirk was back in his car, heading out of the elite neighborhood that no longer felt like home. A few minutes later, he parked in the space he'd grown, over the past couple of years, to think of as his. He had some serious issues to ponder. And the only place he could find solace was with his daughter.

Alicia might not need him there. But he needed her.

And maybe, if he got lucky, Abraham Billings would wander by.

KIRK SEEMED DOWN when she met him at the end of her driveway at ten o'clock that night. More likely, she was projecting her own mood on to him. She'd just had one hell of an evening, to top off one hell of a day. She'd fixed sloppy joes for dinner—the twins' favorite—and even that hadn't been enough to ease the frowns from their faces.

Chandler's problem was almost certainly the same as her boys'. They were worried about Abraham. Valerie sighed. There was no way she was going to escape the inner turmoil this night. She, who always played straight, hadn't done so in this particular situation. She'd assumed the end justified the means. Like Thomas?

And maybe that was fitting. She could have prevented at least some of this.

"The boys tell me that Abraham Billings missed practice again today," she said, determined to get the discussion over with.

Starting off down the street, Kirk nodded, though the motion was barely discernible in the darkness.

He told her about his concern for Abraham, expressing a level of caring she hadn't realized he felt for the boy. She'd known he watched out for Abraham, not that he'd become so involved, so determined to help the boy and end his suffering.

"I'm sure he'll be back tomorrow," she blurted when she could think of nothing else to say. She was too tired.

And she'd just spent the past few hours serving platitudes to her sons. What she'd needed to do was tell someone that she was making herself crazy worrying about the boy. At various moments she found herself imagining what Abraham might be doing right then. And hoping he was okay. That he was accepting things for now. Settling in.

"Steve McDonald said Abraham had the flu yesterday." Kirk couldn't seem to get off the subject, no matter how little she contributed to it.

She felt like such a fraud, walking beside him, listening to him as though she knew as little as he did. When, in fact, she knew exactly where Abraham was.

He was in a specially chosen foster home on the west side of Phoenix. Far enough away that there was no risk he'd run into his mother or anyone he knew. Seeing familiar people made the transition so much harder.

"Then he was probably still sick today and he'll be back tomorrow," she said again, wondering why on earth she continued to suggest something she knew for certain wouldn't be happening. Why couldn't she just plead ignorance and let him talk?

Why did this boy, this case, matter so much?

He shook his head. "He wasn't sick in bed yesterday."

Valerie slowed, too exhausted to keep up the pace they'd set on earlier excursions. "How do you know that?" She was careful to sound merely curious—continuing the duplicity.

"I saw him yesterday afternoon, hanging out not far from the park where he lives."

She had to know if the boy had acted strange—stranger than warranted for ditching practice and being caught by your coach. Strange enough to suspect he'd already been bruised by then.

Or had somebody hurt him the previous night?

"You think he just lied about being sick to cut school?"

"No." Kirk shook his head. "Something was wrong. I just don't know what."

She slowed her pace more as her adrenaline sped up. "Why do you say that?"

"He was pretty bruised."

She hadn't wanted to hear that. Although hearing that he'd been okay the previous afternoon wouldn't have changed what she'd seen that day.

"Did you ask him about it?"

"He said he fell out of a tree."

At least his story was consistent.

"Did you believe him?"

"Not for a second. And he knew I knew he was lying."

"What do you think happened? A fight after school?"

His mother? She almost hoped it was Carla who'd hurt the boy. As horrendous as that was, it was still better than the other possibility—that one of his mother's "clients" had gotten to the boy.

"He wasn't at school."

"A street fight, then?"

"Maybe." Hands in the pockets of his sweats, Kirk slowed as they reached the small private park that was part of the gated community in which she lived. "You want to sit?"

"Sure." She was actually kind of relieved. Walking had been too much effort.

"You wouldn't happen to know some nice friendly cop we could call to check up on him, would you?"

She didn't need a cop to do that. All she had to do was make a phone call. "Yeah. I can think of a couple. I'll get on it first thing in the morning."

They discussed the boy for another few minutes, until Valerie wished she'd never agreed to the outing. She'd just needed a few minutes of feeling good.

And Kirk Chandler had a way of making her feel good.

Especially when he touched her without touching her, running his finger through a strand of her hair, close enough that she could feel him, but not so close that he intruded on her carefully plotted life. Not so close that skin touched skin. Not so close that she was tempted to lose the misery of the day in the sweetness of a man at night.

He was restless beside her. Tapping the heel of his tennis shoe on the concrete beneath their bench. Nodding his head slowly. Something was bothering him.

But he wasn't telling her about it.

Valerie didn't want to care one way or the other.

She didn't want to think at all anymore. At least not until she'd had a chance to sleep off the worst of her pain and worry and guilt.

Kirk's hand moved slowly through her hair. Taking up one strand. And then another. Occasionally shooting a ray of sensation down her body as he brushed her scalp. A full fifteen minutes passed in almost complete silence before he dropped his arm along the back of the bench right where her shoulders were leaning.

She settled into the bench.

She asked him how playground duty was going. About Brian's eating habits at lunch that week. And, wincing slightly, she asked about his team's chances of winning the play-offs if Abraham was still too sick to play in the game the following night.

She was glad when his hand slid from the bench to her shoulders, massaging lightly. The action was harmless. They were in an open, if dark and deserted, park. And touch was good sometimes.

Her exhausted body came alive, giving her renewed energy when she needed it most. His touch revived her strength and once again she felt as if she could carry on. Forge ahead. Make a difference in the world. And for her sons.

His hand moved to her neck and her head dropped back. He kneaded the taut muscles of her neck, bringing immediate relief. But even as her eyes closed, she knew she couldn't stay there much longer. She had to get home. Check the locks. Turn off the lights. Look in on the boys. Wash her face, brush her teeth and find a clean nightshirt…

The lips touching hers were so light, so perfectly part of that moment, she simply accepted their rightness in being there. And when their pressure increased, when they began to move, her own moved beneath them, as naturally as her skin had responded to the healing touch of Kirk's fingers. She was alive with sensation, euphoric almost, and yet sedated by the night. The quiet.

He kissed her a second time. And a third. The fourth time Valerie opened her mouth to his, deepening the kiss. Tasting him.

And then, slowly, she became aware of who she was.

And pulled away.

CHAPTER TWELVE

THEY SHOULD JUST GO HOME. They'd crossed a line and there was nothing left to do but leave.

And still Valerie sat there. Kirk wasn't moving, either, although he hadn't said a word.

"This isn't fair to you," she finally murmured.

"What isn't?"

She was glad for the cover of darkness. It had been almost two decades since she'd been in the beginning stages of a relationship with a man. And never had she knowingly begun a relationship when that was all there could ever be.

"You. Me. Us."

"Our friendship is unfair to me?" he asked.

Seated several inches away, he emanated life and vitality. His casual navy sweats and white long-sleeved T-shirt actually looked elegant on him.

"I'm sure you feel the same way." He was a man. He'd just shown her how much of one.

The shake of his head was dimly perceptible in the night. "I think I'm where I want to be."

She had a feeling he meant that more than literally. And she had to get things straight, once and for all. She couldn't afford to compromise here. Not at this time in her life—in her sons' lives. Brian and Blake had already suffered enough at the hands of their parents. Perhaps they didn't wear their bruises as obviously as Abraham Billings, but sometimes that was worse. Their scars were internal, psychological. The kind that could continue to inflict damage and skew everything else in their lives for years to come.

It was much harder to heal wounds that couldn't be seen.

It was much harder to give a boy back his self-esteem than it was to remove him from an unhealthy environment.

"There cannot be a repeat of what just happened," she said, perhaps more sharply than she'd intended. And maybe she said it as sharply as she'd known she had to. There was just no room to give.

No room for her, her needs or wants or desires, whatever they might be. Not here.

"I agree."

Although she couldn't really make out his expression, she turned to look at him, anyway. His hands were resting lightly in front of him. "You do?"

"Yeah." He nodded. He was looking at her, too.

"Why?"

"Well..."

"I mean—" she half laughed "—I know why for me, but you're young and gorgeous, unattached. What you did, kissing me, was perfectly natural. There was nothing wrong with it at all."

"I'm glad to hear there was nothing wrong with it," he said with a chuckle. "But I have to argue with you on one point."

"What?" She frowned but was breathing easier.

"I wasn't the only one doing the kissing."

"Oh." She kept peering at him because she knew he couldn't really see her. "Well, maybe not, but..."

"But it won't happen again." She might not be able to decipher his expression, but she knew it had grown completely serious. "Because that was your second error," he said.

"What?" She kissed badly? She could believe that. She hadn't had a lot of practice. Not in too many years to count.

And hadn't been all that experienced before her marriage. Law school was no easy task. And Valerie had been determined to graduate at the top of her class. Yeah, she could believe she wasn't a great kisser. Thomas had certainly told her that often enough.

Still, it was rather embarrassing for Kirk to know that.

"I'm not unattached."

Considering that she'd just made it very clear to him—and to herself—that there could be nothing between them, she should not be disappointed to hear him say that he was committed elsewhere.

"You...have a wife, after all?"

"No."

"A girlfriend?" Then why wasn't he off being friends with *her?*

Making *her* stomach turn over with his kisses?

She hadn't figured him for a man who disregarded monogamy. He was so completely the opposite of Thomas.

"I don't have a girlfriend." His voice was tentative, as though he wasn't sure what to say next. But she waited because she knew there was more. "Like you, I have a son."

"Where?" She couldn't help it; her voice rose at least two octaves. "How old is he?" *Who is his mother?*

"I just found out."

Valerie began to detach herself from the situation, the same way she did at work. "You got someone pregnant and now you have to marry her?" She said it matter-of-factly.

"No."

"You aren't going to marry her."

He cocked his head. She thought he might even be grinning a little. "You want to let me tell this story? Might save time—and help you get the facts straight."

"Sorry."

"No problem, Judge. I understand how it is with you court people. Always probing for the truth."

She was missing something. There'd been a sarcastic edge to that statement.

"So tell me about your son."

"It's not a story I'm proud of." He shrugged, hands still loosely in front of him. Was the man ever *not* comfortable in his own skin?

"Okay."

"I had one night of sex almost a year ago."

Valerie sucked in a breath, apparently not as detached as she'd thought. His son was a newborn baby.

"So you *are* thinking about marrying her."

It didn't matter. She could be friends with a married man.

"This really would be easier if you'd just let me tell it," he said, his voice lighter than before. He was enjoying the opportunity to tease her.

She'd remember that.

She hoped.

"I won't say another word."

"Mmm-hmm."

She glared at him—not that it did any good. Glares needed to be seen to be effective. "I won't."

"You just did."

Damn.

"I recently found out that a child resulted from that night." He paused. Swallowed.

What mattered was doing the right thing when you were faced with the situation.

"His mother didn't want me to know."

"Why not? You'd think she'd want support if nothing else."

"She's married."

"You slept with a married woman."

"She wasn't married at the time." He stood, turned to face her, his expression more shadowed now than ever. Straining to see in the dark, she could tell that he'd shoved his hands in his pockets. "She was engaged to be married, but I didn't know that." One foot on the bench, he continued, "I'm not proud of myself. It was just…one of those things."

She understood. She'd had one. Once. Right before she met Thomas.

"But the point is, the boy's mine. I'm his father.

And I am not going to be able to live with myself until I can be a proper father to him. If that means child support and nothing else for now, then fine. But my son is not going to grow up thinking his father didn't want him.''

She believed him.

"So tell her that.''

"I did. She didn't thank me for the problem I was causing. It seems she told her husband the child is his.''

Life could be surprising and full of unexpected co-incidence. At a time when Valerie's faith in men was at an all-time low, this decent, honorable man had dropped into her life. Ironically, she was helping a friend, albeit a distant one, with a situation that was the reverse of his. But while Susan fought for the right to have her son's father raise him, her manipulative and controlling ex-husband claimed that *he* was the father. This man, who'd apparently first made an effort to get to know his seven-year-old daughter when she lay dying in a hospital, had already shown that he had no idea what fatherhood was about. For him, trying to prove that he was the child's father was a means of control, of asserting ownership over the ex-wife who'd walked out on him.

Susan was so distressed by the man that in those long, agonizing conversations they'd had during the month or two she and Valerie had consoled each other, she'd never even called him by name. It was usually "the bastard.'' Or sometimes "the jerk.'' But then, Valerie very seldom called Thomas anything other than "my husband," or most often, "the boys' father."

And here was Kirk, a decent man with no other goal than to be accountable for his actions. He was a man so conscientious of his obligations, so driven by the need to do the right thing, he couldn't tolerate being denied that possibility.

Susan's situation had been depressing Valerie, reminding her far too much of her life with Thomas. Not just because her husband was responsible for the death of the other woman's daughter, but because Thomas had been the same type of negligent father as Susan's first husband. He'd gone to his grave never having known the two remarkable children he'd had.

If ever a man was the antithesis of her ex-husband, it was Kirk Chandler. And still, Valerie was not, *absolutely not,* going to fall for him. However, she wasn't averse to having some of her faith in humanity—particularly the male variety—restored.

Finally silent, Kirk sat back down beside her.

She turned toward him, cursing the darkness that wouldn't let her read his expression. Or let him read hers...

"I'm guessing the husband is named as the father."

"Yes."

"Arizona law is pretty clear about the significance of that, but if you're willing to go to the wall on this, I'll do what I can to help."

"I've already called an attorney, prepared to do whatever is necessary. I'd appreciate any and all help you can give me."

Intimacy engulfed them. Much more intense than before. And he wasn't even touching her.

IN HIS CUSTOMARY JEANS and flannel shirt, Kirk was leaning against the wall outside Steve McDonald's office at six-thirty the next morning.

"You're in early," the sandy-haired ex–baseball player said.

Kirk held up a paper bag. "I brought you a doughnut."

McDonald was the official-looking one in his gray suit, white shirt and tie—unlike previous years when Kirk had been the one dressed for success. He frowned. "Krispy Kreme," he said. "That means you want something."

"You saying I have to bribe you to get your help?" Kirk challenged, following his one real friend into the office.

"I'm saying you think you do."

With far more important things on his mind, Kirk let that comment pass.

"Abraham Billings hasn't been at practice for the past two days."

"He's been absent."

"Monday it was the flu. What about yesterday?"

"I don't know."

"You know where he is?"

"No." Steve seemed inordinately interested in a file on the top of his desk. A file that was a good four feet from eyes that had recently been diagnosed as needing glasses.

Kirk had good instincts about people. He could

read them in seconds flat. And those were the ones he didn't know. With Steve it didn't take that long.

"But you know *something*."

McDonald looked up, resignation in his eyes. "Give me the damn doughnuts."

Kirk silently handed them over.

"You want one?"

He stood in front of Steve's desk, the tips of his fingers in his front pockets. "I don't think so."

"Abraham won't be coming back."

"What?" Kirk didn't bother to regulate his voice. That early in the morning, the school was deserted. "Where is he? Wouldn't you think someone ought to let his basketball coach know that, seeing we've just made the play-offs and he's our star player."

This had nothing to do with basketball. Steve's lingering scrutiny told Kirk the principal knew that.

"You'd have received a notice in your box this morning, along with the rest of Abraham's teachers."

"A notice that says what?"

"That he's withdrawn from Menlo Ranch."

"And?"

"That's all."

"It's not enough."

"Look, Kirk, I can't say any more. There are privacy issues here."

"Oh, and there weren't *privacy* issues when you partied all night before your English final in senior year and stole the test key to commit it to memory an hour before the test?"

It was information that, if released, could hurt the

reputation of a junior-high-school principal. Not irreparably after all this time, but hurt just the same.

McDonald studied him, his blue eyes piercing. ''You'd actually let that out.''

''I have to know where to find Billings.''

''You haven't changed a bit.''

''I'm going to help that boy.''

''So the end justifies the means?''

''I need to know where he is.''

After another moment of study, McDonald nodded. ''I understand. And we both know that I'm going to give you the information.'' He looked over at Kirk, his gaze not wavering for a second. ''But we both need to acknowledge something else, first,'' he said. ''Whether I tell you about Abraham Billings or not, you and I both know you had no intention of saying a word about my past.''

Kirk appreciated Steve's loyalty. But he spent much more time in honest introspection these days. ''I've been known to do whatever it takes to get what I want.''

''You've never sold out a friend.''

''I sold out my own father.''

''Only after he and your mother spent a lifetime selling *you* out.''

Kirk reared back. ''What the hell are you talking about?'' Steve must be getting his story mixed up with someone else's. Not that it really mattered, but Kirk was insulted, anyway.

''They couldn't be bothered with the hard work of raising a kid, so they paid your way out of every mess you got into.''

"They paid my way out of jail."

"They robbed you of every chance to make mistakes, be accountable for them on a kid scale, and learn the necessary lessons. Instead, you had to learn them a much harder way, and pay on a much grander scale."

Kirk stood there for a full minute, attempting to arrange the pieces Steve was trying to give him into the puzzle that he knew was his life. Any way he looked at them, they didn't fit.

"Remember when we were five years old and all the guys were trying out for T-ball?" Steve asked.

"Vaguely."

"We all had a great time at the try-outs. Yeah, we were scared we weren't going to make the team, but we worked up the courage to try anyhow. And experienced the thrill of genuine victory when we were all chosen."

"So?"

"Your father sponsored the team, bought brand-new uniforms for everyone with the Desert Oasis logo on the back, and in return, you automatically got a place on the team. You didn't get the chance we did to face the possibility of failure. And then to succeed. And I don't think any of the guys ever forgot that the whole year."

He never felt a part of that team. But then, in his old life, Kirk had never been a team player. He was the *only* player. And a winner.

"And what about that time in high school when you were running for student body president and your father bought boxes of pizza on voting day?"

Kirk looked at his watch. "Much as I'd like to continue this trip down memory lane, I've got to get outside," he said. "What's the scoop on Billings?"

HE MADE IT OUT to his post but had to force himself to gentle his voice so he didn't bark at the kids. The only thing keeping him focused at all was watching for Valerie's car. He had to talk to her. She'd know what to do.

Hell, small as the juvenile court community was, she probably knew the judge who'd made such an incredible error.

Not that the *who* mattered to him. What he wanted from Valerie was a way to undo the damage that had been done yesterday to a very special boy—before it was too late to get him back.

Valerie had a meeting downtown and started to drive off before Kirk even managed his morning wave. He flagged her down instead. And got a quick affirmation that she'd meet him for coffee that evening. Then she was speeding away from him. Leaving him with a frown on his face and a load of frustration building inside.

How the hell was he going to wait until nine o'clock that night to set in motion the plan to save his star basketball player? And what was happening to Billings in the meantime?

Whatever it was, Kirk had a feeling that ignoring a minor infraction—the kid smoking a cigarette outside a cemetery—would have been a better option than sending him away.

BY THE TIME Valerie's car pulled up outside the coffee shop that evening, Kirk had passed beyond angry to livid. Frustration and worry—with no action—did not set well with him.

For the first part of the day, he'd alternated between living in the past, reliving his own brief stint under the state's care, and hoping Abraham was someplace other than the detention cell he'd been in. The state might not call it jail, but anyone who'd been sent to detention knew exactly what it was.

Judges could do anything, but surely they wouldn't send a kid to detention for missing school.

He'd pressed Steve McDonald. The other man had no idea where they'd taken the kid.

And then later, once he'd found out where the boy actually was, he'd railed against his own helplessness.

"Hey," Valerie called as she slid out of her Mercedes.

"You have your heart set on coffee?" Kirk asked.

"Not really."

"Let's go for a drive. My car."

She frowned, but walked beside him, climbing into the passenger side of the Vette as he held the door open for her.

"What's up?"

He shook his head. This wasn't a conversation he could have while driving. Not with the emotion churning through him—worsened by near panic at the fact that he could still experience such negative feelings. He'd thought, since his transformation, he'd left all that behind him.

He'd meant to.

"I just wanted to get away from the glare of the parking-lot lights," he told her.

"Okay. You mad?"

"No."

"Did I do something?"

"God, no." He gave her a quick smile. At least he hoped not. Juvenile court was a relatively small place. It wasn't completely unlikely that Valerie was the judge assigned to Abraham's case.

It wasn't likely, either. Surely she would've said something. All the conversations they'd had about Abraham... No, he'd just had too many hours to blow the whole thing out of proportion.

"But you *are* angry about something?"

He nodded. "Let me find a place to park this thing and I'll tell you all about it."

"Did my sons do something wrong?"

"Of course not. Brian ate an entire hot dog for lunch today." It was the highlight of Kirk's day.

"The whole thing?" He could see her grin as a car approached from the opposite direction.

"Every bite."

His key player was out, but they'd won their game.

He turned off at the first lay-by he came to along the Beeline Highway—a scenic view during the day. He shut off the ignition and turned to face her in the darkness. Would he ever have a conversation with this woman during which he could see her face?

"So what's up?" Her voice was soft, compassionate, soothing him with the reassurance that she'd do whatever she could.

A car passed, and then nothing. The highway, really just a two-lane desert road connecting Fountain Hills to the Mesa-Phoenix area, had very little traffic this time of night.

"Abraham Billings has been taken by the state."

Once the car was out of sight, they were engulfed in blackness.

"Oh."

Not quite the reaction he'd been expecting.

"He's been withdrawn from Menlo Ranch."

She was facing him, one knee resting against the stick shift. "That's standard procedure when a child is taken into state custody. It's best to transfer him from a place that isn't serving him well to an environment where he can get a fresh start."

"You sound as though you approve of this decision."

"I'm sure that if indeed the courts removed him from his home, the decision was made with all due consideration."

Well, at least now he knew she wasn't the judge he was furious with.

"It's the worst thing that could've happened to that kid!" He'd meant to keep the intensity out of his voice, but some habits apparently didn't die.

Even when whole lives did.

CHAPTER THIRTEEN

CALMING HIMSELF with a skill created by years of discipline, Kirk noticed Valerie's expression in the lights from an oncoming car. He'd expected compassion. Concern. What he got was—stoicism. "He wouldn't have been removed without substantial evidence," she said. He'd sure as hell called this one wrong.

When billion-dollar hostile takeovers were at stake he could get it right every time. But to save one relatively small boy...

"I'm sure there was evidence," he said, scrambling for plan B. Caught unprepared. Something else that wouldn't have happened during a negotiation. Kirk had never gone to an important meeting without at least six backup plans of varying degrees. "It was obvious the kid had problems," he continued. "I'm not arguing that. It's the approach to handling those problems to which I object. They took him away from the one thing that had a chance of saving him."

"What's that?"

"Basketball."

Her sigh said it all. Or at least as much as he needed to hear. "The state has incredible facilities,

Kirk, with highly trained professionals who will see that Abraham gets everything he needs."

"He's not going to respond to a bunch of professionals," Kirk said, getting frustrated all over again as he tried to make her understand. "Abraham is far too closed off for that. He's been there, done that, heard and seen it all—and doesn't believe any of it."

"I've seen them work miracles on kids a lot tougher than Abraham Billings."

"He isn't like most kids. He's got more savvy, more insight than a lot of adults I know. I have a feeling he's lived most of his life on instinct, and at this point, he's positive that the only person he can trust is himself."

"Even more reason for him to be in a place where people are watching out for him, showing him that there *are* people he can trust to look out for his best interests."

Kirk released a long, heavy sigh, shaking his head in disappointment. How was he going to get her cooperation if he couldn't even get her to see the truth? It was like talking to her about Brian and basketball all over again.

"Abraham had hope in nothing when I first met him," Kirk said. "The change that came over that kid when he got on the basketball court was phenomenal to watch. He slowly started to believe that there was something to work for. Something that was good in life—something that could be *his*. Basketball was his ticket to college, to the hope of a better life."

"He's in junior high, Kirk. There'll be plenty of time for that."

"Not if he gives up the hope. Don't you see? Abraham acts like a kid who's always had everything that mattered taken away from him. This move only reinforces that belief. Not only did he lose his mother—whom he obviously adored—but he lost basketball, too. The chances that he'll go back to it at some later point in his life are pretty slim. If for no other reason than because he'll have quit believing in anything.

"And that aside, this kid who's had a shit life finally finds something he loves, something for himself, something he's good at, someplace to shine and get some positive attention. He's no sooner beginning to gain some confidence from that than it's snatched away from him."

"Judges don't make decisions like this lightly, Kirk," Valerie said, her tone probably not as condescending as it sounded to him. "If Abraham is in custody, it's because that's exactly where he needs to be."

Kirk knew all about judges and their decisions. Often made after reading a folder full of papers and seeing a kid for—what—five minutes? Maybe a little more, depending on how much there was to discuss.

"You sound as if you agree with this," he said, quietly now. The Vette was too small for this conversation.

"I know all the judges in the juvenile court system. I trust them all. Completely."

The day had gone from hellish to unbelievably hellish. "You judges are all alike," he snapped, rejecting the truth even as he had to face it. He'd thought she was different. "You're always playing God, thinking you know everything because you're privy to a damn report. Thinking you automatically know what's right in any given situation. Do you even know how arrogant you are?''

She turned, faced the windshield, her arms crossed in front of her. He'd pissed her off. Well, he was pretty damn pissed, himself. He'd expected more from her. And from himself.

"I wish I had some of God's insights," she said. He wasn't fooled by the softness with which she uttered the words. "It would make my job a whole lot easier."

He could feel the defensive energy coming from her. And still couldn't stop. The Kirk Chandler of old. "How does a piece of paper and a couple of questions asked of a scared kid give you the right to determine the shape of his entire life?''

She looked over at him, seeming to study him in the darkness. She didn't answer right away. When she did, she sounded more weary than anything else. "People come into my court counting on me to make a decision," she said. "What if I'm not sure? They don't want to hear that. They want an answer. Even if it isn't the right one." She laid her head back against the seat, eyes facing out into the night. "Every day when I enter the courtroom, I remind myself that all I can do is my best. I make the calls as I see them. And pray that the kids under my care will be okay.''

He couldn't argue with that. No matter how much he hated what had happened to Abraham, he'd be the last person to expect people to do better than their best.

"I'm assuming this means you won't be in favor of trying to help me get him back."

"If he was removed by the court, his mother has the right to a hearing in five days," she said.

"Do you know the judge in charge?"

"I'm not free to answer that question."

He'd already guessed that. Soft thuds filled the silence as Kirk tapped the leather steering wheel with the side of his thumb.

"If he's not coming back, I'm going to see him."

She started. He could only see her silhouette, but her face was turned toward him. "You know where he is?"

She sounded more alarmed than amazed at his abilities.

"I'd given him my number. He called this afternoon."

"You talked to him?"

"No." Kirk shook his head. He slumped down, his head along the back of the seat as he stared out into the darkness. He didn't need to see the terrain to know that it was a huge expanse of seemingly barren desert. "He left a message."

But no phone number. And Kirk had been kicking himself half the day for missing that chance to connect with the boy.

"What did he say?"

"He called to tell me he was sorry he wouldn't be at the game. And before he hung up, he gave me the address of his foster home."

Abraham had not sounded pleased with the place.

At least it wasn't jail.

But listening to a kid who'd clearly given up, it might as well have been.

Valerie faced the front, both feet on the floor, her hands on her knees. "You can't go see him, Kirk."

It was no plea.

"Is that a court order?"

"Of course not. The judge on the case would have to order it, and there's no reason to do so. It's just common sense."

"It makes no sense to me at all, common or not."

"Abraham needs a chance to get used to where he is, to need the people he's with, to see that they can help him and to learn to trust them."

Her words carried the compassion of a mother—if a misguided one.

"I think he trusts me." He put on his seat belt.

Doing the same, Valerie ignored his hint that the conversation was over. "The people he's with are trained to help him."

"You know who he's with? Where he is?"

"I know how the courts work. They wouldn't take a child from his mother without making sure he was getting the proper counseling and care."

"I've got news for you," Kirk said, pulling out on to the highway, breaking the speed limit to get back to town, to her car. To free himself from her presence. "Courts make mistakes."

He wasn't sure whether he was relieved or disappointed when she didn't argue with him. When she gave up any attempt at conversation at all.

CAREFUL NOT TO WAKE the boys, Valerie wandered around the house late that night, picking up knickknacks, running her fingers over them, sometimes smiling, sometimes not. Remembering. The picture of the twins on their fourth birthday, both of them with faces full of birthday cake and innocent green eyes, was on a side table in her home office. Lifting it, she studied those sweet faces and felt a surge of painful memories.

She'd hired a clown for their party that year. They'd insisted on waiting for their father to get home before the show started. And ended up with a ten-minute show because the clown had obligations elsewhere and finally had to start.

A ten-minute show without their father. Thomas hadn't come home that night.

Valerie was fairly certain that was the first time he'd been unfaithful to her. She'd told him no the night before when he'd reached for her under the covers shortly after yelling at her for spending two hundred dollars on the clown for the boys' party the next day.

He'd left her alone—but only after squeezing her breast so hard it'd borne bruises in the shape of his fingertips.

Moving slowly, a ghostlike creature in her own house, she found herself in the kitchen, wishing she hadn't cleaned up the mess from dinner before going out to meet Kirk for coffee. Wishing the boys had disobeyed and gotten out of bed for a snack, leaving crumbs and spilled milk behind on the counter.

Wishing she had something that needed to be done, some menial task that would give her purpose. Something mundane enough, normal enough, to pull her out of the blackness. Something to redirect the thoughts and feelings consuming her.

She ended up in the front hall, sitting on the cold tile, guarding a front door that didn't need to be guarded. Or was she there because it was as close to escape as she could manage? She'd come in to put a note in her purse to remind her to call Brian's doctor in the morning. He was due for his next checkup.

She'd dropped the note on the floor.

And started to cry.

"Do you even know how arrogant you are?" Kirk had railed at her. He'd been angry; she understood that. And he'd hit a mark he'd had no idea was there. A private place—a wound—Valerie had been nursing for ten years. Ever since Thomas had first ripped it open. And then again every single time he'd bruised it after that. No matter what the issue between them might be, it had always come down to the same thing. That she was too arrogant—too judgmental. And after she'd been appointed to the bench, that she passed judgment on people *outside* her courtroom.

"You're always analyzing people, Val." She could hear her dead husband's voice as clearly as if he'd been standing there in front of her, just as he'd stood so many times before—feet spread, hands on the hips of his tailored slacks, the sides of his suit coat pressed back. *You think you're better than everyone else. Always passing judgment..."*

He'd most often been referring to himself. Once, after having come home with another woman's makeup smeared on his shirt. After he'd missed trash day, having forgotten to get the cans out of the locked gate that housed them. Always after he'd missed something with the boys—including their birth. He'd been on the golf course that afternoon.

She'd tried so hard not to judge. To be fair.

"Fair from your *point of view."* Thomas had spit the words at her more times than she could count. Usually followed by accusations of her small-mindedness. Her inability to see others' points of view.

"I'm sure Kirk would agree with that," Valerie told the note she still held, watching as tears dripped slowly off her chin to smear the paper. Twice now they'd had serious disagreements about the lives of the children in their collective care. And twice she'd refused to budge from her position.

But how could she budge when she knew she was right? Should she be untrue to herself, to the intuition that had been guiding her throughout her life, simply to please a man she happened to like?

If she'd done a little more of that for her husband, would he still be alive? More important, would Alicia?

"It was my point of view the governor appointed to the bench," she told the soggy note, not really even seeing it through the blur of tears. Crumpling the paper in her fist, she leaned her head against the wall, wondering how life had come to this.

"If my judgment is good enough for the people of Arizona, one would think it should be good enough for my private life, as well," she whispered.

The words only brought more tears.

She'd had such great goals, studied hard, worked hard, giving a hundred and fifty percent, always doing what she said she would. She had a great job. Great kids. A great house.

And, suddenly, no faith in herself.

WITH THE PINK BABY ROSES covering the entire front of the headstone, Kirk could almost pretend he was in a little girl's room. Almost.

"So what do you think, my wise child, does a man ever really change?" He'd spent the first ten minutes of his Saturday-afternoon date with his daughter telling her about Abraham, and his resultant anger.

Sitting on the ground, leaning up against the side of the stone, he tried to help her understand.

"I don't know if you remember or not, but when you were little, Daddy always expected things to go his way. And he'd get mad if they didn't. Which usually made people do what he wanted."

Yeah, that summed it up pretty well.

Running a hand through his hair, he remembered he had to make an appointment to get it cut. He hated when it grew over his ears. Not that he had an image to care about anymore.

"So what do you think, baby girl?" he asked, his voice quiet and low in the deserted cemetery. "Am I always going to do whatever it takes to make things go my way?"

He uprooted what might be the beginnings of a weed in the beautifully manicured grass between his upraised knees.

The December air was cool but not cold, blowing

lightly against his forearms where he'd rolled up the sleeves of his flannel shirt. Bright sunshine beat down on the glorious array of color surrounding him, the vast collection of live and cut blooms that graced the cemetery. Head back against Alicia's resting place, he stared up at the pure blue sky, wondering if she could see him.

Wishing he could see her.

"I made Valerie mad," he told her softly. "Three days ago." Though no replies ever came, he always waited. "I haven't heard from her since." He answered the question he supposed she might ask. "I waved to her at school, but I don't think she looked over at me."

A newer-model black sedan pulled in on the opposite lane, stopping about halfway down. A young woman emerged with roses, laid them on a grave. And stood there frozen.

Who was she mourning? Her husband? A parent? Alicia would know.

Not a child, Kirk prayed.

"The boys have been to practice, though, and they're as friendly as always. They're great guys, Licia," he told her. Only three years older than Alicia would be had she lived. "Funny and sweet, tough and innocent. And ill. Each in his own way."

His daughter wasn't old enough yet to wonder if they were cute, so Kirk didn't bother telling her they were. Nor had he told her about Abraham's striking good looks.

"We've got our last play-off game on Tuesday," he said instead. "If we win, we go to the finals."

He'd already explained the sport to her, the day he'd gotten the job as coach. He figured she'd been bored to tears but had listened politely.

And then he just sat there, as he always did at some point during his sojourns in that strange place where life met death, smelling the roses he had delivered for her every Friday. Facing the fact that he could talk all he wanted and Alicia would never answer. She'd still be lost to him. Gone away without hearing how much he loved her.

And, as always, his thoughts were drawn back to that last week of her life, keeping vigil outside her room, all alone and too late.

"I gotta go see him, sweetie." The words were no less ragged for their softness. "Valerie told me to stay away, but I can't do it. Abraham's hurting. And I can't be too late for a child again. I promised."

He'd promised *her.* He'd promised his little girl the night before she died that he'd spend the rest of his life taking care of children.

"I have to know who hit him. And why."

He wondered if Alicia knew.

He wanted to tell her about her brother. But couldn't bring himself to do it. Not yet. And if Susan had told her—well, the news would still be new when Kirk got around to it. He planned to ask Alicia's advice every step of the way when he finally got to be a father to his son.

His butt was starting to hurt from the hard ground, so Kirk slowly stood. He never knew what to say at this point. Goodbye was too final. See ya, a lie.

"I'm going to visit Abraham."

He backed away, unable to turn until he'd passed the two stones directly behind hers. Focusing on the baby-pink roses.

Christmas was coming. Maybe he'd buy a poinsettia next week. Or better yet, bring a miniature tree, decorated with colorful baubles.

He turned, walking swiftly through the grass, not slowing until he reached his car.

CHAPTER FOURTEEN

HE COULD HEIST a car. He just wasn't sure it was his best bet. Driving it didn't worry him. But what about when people looked in and saw a kid behind the wheel?

Walking was out. Not because he didn't know where he was, which he didn't, but because it had taken them over an hour to get there by highway.

Still, if it was his only option, it wasn't like he had to make it home.

Just away.

Abraham stepped off the porch. And liked how that felt. Another step would probably be even better.

He tried it out. Looked behind him to make sure his jailers were still inside having their Saturday-night dinner. He'd said he wasn't hungry. Which wasn't entirely true. He just didn't want to eat more of their food than he had to. It wasn't his. And he didn't need their charity.

He also hated sitting at their family table, listening to the chatter of the little girl who'd been born to the Mortons. Mrs. Morton was a bored housewife who'd been some kind of counselor at some point.

They'd told him she'd be good for him.

She wasn't helping a bit.

A few more steps and he was out of their yard. No bells going off, no hidden alarms. And then, steps weren't enough. With only the jeans and shirt he was wearing and the tennis shoes on his feet, Abraham broke into a run that would put Blake Smith to shame. Gaining his freedom. Taking care of himself, just as he'd been doing since the day he was born.

And one way or another, he was going to make it home and get back to taking care of his mother, too.

Now that the bruises were almost healed.

On the outside, anyway.

SATURDAY NIGHT Blake lay on the couch staring at the large-screen television across from him. And sometimes, when the excitement didn't make his stomach feel worse, he looked over at the shining Christmas tree they'd put up that morning and tried to figure out what might be in the giftwrapped packages that would soon be showing up underneath. Brian was on the other sofa, laughing at a rerun of *The Simpsons*. They were supposed to be at Fiddlesticks, playing miniature golf and video games.

But Blake's stomach had hurt too much for him to go.

And Brian hadn't eaten all his dinner, so Mom had said he couldn't go, either. Not that Bry would've gone without him.

Still, Saturday night lying on the couch sucked.

He glanced over at his mom, who sat in a chair with her leg flung across the arm. She was pretending to watch the show with them, but he could tell she wasn't seeing it. Her expression never changed, even during the commercials.

He rolled over, trying to find a more comfortable position, something that would relieve the burning pain between his ribs. Mom didn't know he was hurting. She thought they'd stayed home because of Brian.

He couldn't tell her. She'd just worry.

And then Brian wouldn't eat.

Taking care of the two of them was tough.

But he'd manage.

Once his stomach quit hurting.

Yeah, Saturday night on the couch sucked. Big-time.

KIRK LEFT SCHOOL during his morning break. He had a couple of hours if he wanted them. And Monday morning, two days after his visit to Alicia, he wanted them.

He'd taken his break a couple of other times recently, to go home and make a few business calls for people, but today what he had to do was important. Something that mattered.

The court building looked exactly as he remembered. Every brick exactly the same. Even the crack in the sidewalk as he approached the front door was something he remembered.

He'd called ahead so they knew he was coming. After he made it through the metal detector, the receptionist called Valerie's J.A. to come get him.

Leah she said her name was.

Kirk told her it was nice to meet her, though he

wasn't really thinking about her at all. He was too busy trying not to remember.

He concentrated on the Christmas decorations, the tree in the lobby, the pictures on the walls.

He'd been in the building many times. But never in the judges' chambers.

Silently following the girl with braids sticking out in all directions, Kirk couldn't quite stop himself from taking a couple of extra-big steps. Just because he could. No shackles on his feet this time around.

And then he caught a glimpse of Valerie. He'd expected her to be in her office waiting for him. Not coming out that door he'd only seen from the other side. The private back door of Courtroom One that led to the bench. Or, in this case, away from it.

"Hi." She smiled at him, looked down and then back up.

She wasn't sure if they were friends anymore or not.

He wasn't sure, either.

"Hi."

He fell into silent step beside her. Waiting for privacy before he said what he'd come to say. And probably stalling.

Kirk didn't eat crow often, or well.

"How was your weekend?"

She looked intimidating in that robe.

Not that Kirk was intimidated. At all. He'd outgrown that a long time ago. Still, she no longer seemed like the woman he'd snapped at in his Corvette several nights before.

And not at all like the woman he'd kissed....

"Good. We put up our tree."

Christmas, a time he celebrated—when it was over.

He should have put on something besides jeans. And tennis shoes.

She led the way to her inner office, thanking Leah and closing the door behind them. Efficiently removing and hanging her robe in the closet, she took the high-backed leather chair behind her desk, motioning him to one of the chairs in front.

"What's up?"

Kirk declined the chair. This was a standing moment. A hands-in-the-pockets-of-his-jeans moment.

He'd never felt less like a valuable human being than he did right then. Especially compared to her. Here she was changing lives, saving kids.

And he'd spent the first fifteen years of his adult life ruining other people. And deserting his kid.

"I came to apologize."

He wasn't planning to tell her about Saturday evening, the hour it had taken him to talk Abraham into going back to foster care after he'd found him hitchhiking on the freeway exit. If he hadn't gone to see the boy…

Alicia had probably had something to do with that.

Valerie wasn't saying anything, just looking at the pen she was flipping between her thumb and forefinger, a frown on what he could see of her downcast face.

"I had no business calling you God."

"You didn't, exactly."

His friend was back. At least tentatively.

Kirk sat down, reaching across to lift her chin so

he could see her eyes. "I know you agonize over every decision you make here," he told her with complete honesty. He'd known that the other night. "So does probably every other judge in this building." As an adult, he understood that juvenile court was a breed different from the rest. Here they tried to reshape lives instead of just punish. Here they believed there was still time.

"You save lives, Valerie," he said, his words no less intense for their softness. "Every day, while most people are out eating fast food on the way from one appointment to the next, driven by the mighty dollar, you're on a path that makes a real difference."

He was evidence of that.

"Thank you," she said, studying him as though she wasn't sure what was going on. "I think. Sounds like you just laid a whole lot of pressure on my shoulders."

"You're going to tell me that's not what you do?"

"I..."

"Tell me you don't stay in contact with every single one of your kids, one way or another, follow up on them, make sure they're doing okay or haul them back in here to find out why not."

"It's my job to watch out for them." Her dark blue eyes were luminescent, touching a chord in him he didn't understand. "They're under my care."

"Exactly." He stood, needing to move, to get out—almost as much as he wanted to spend a few more minutes with her. "Instead of writing them off as troubled kids, you see value in them and give them every chance at a successful life."

Valerie stood, too, frowning. "You've certainly had an epiphany in the past few days."

He'd said too much. Or maybe not enough.

"Can you take a walk?"

Her morning calendar had been short. She said she'd have some time to see him.

"Sure."

Her calf-length black skirt swirled as she came around the desk, walking as easily in those high heels as she did in tennis shoes.

There weren't many places to walk near the juvenile court facility. An RV dealership. Other industrial property. And a wide sidewalk.

In deference to those heels, Kirk chose the sidewalk.

"You seem to know your way around," she said.

He slid the tips of his fingers into the front pockets of his jeans. He seemed to be doing that a lot, lately. Maybe it was time to wear something other than jeans. Until a year ago, he hadn't even owned a pair. "I've been here before."

"Testifying?"

He supposed that could be a valid explanation, considering he worked around kids all day. Maybe there'd been a ruckus on the playground that had gotten out of hand... No, he decided. Too complicated to lie. And what would be the point.

"I was here...before."

"For what?" She'd put on sunglasses. Which made her look, in her long skirt and stylishly tight gold sweater, like a Hollywood star. "When?"

"Sixteen or seventeen years ago."

"What, you were here for a tour? I know they used to bring all the kids in for a 'scared straight' type of experience."

Once they were away from the front parking lot, there were very few people around. Just an occasional car driving by on the street. A voice calling somewhere off in the distance. The rumble of the nearby freeway. The birds. And the blue sky and sunshine.

"I had kind of a tour," Kirk said. "And I'd like to say it scared me straight."

She glanced over at him. "You're trying to tell me you were here as a perpetrator?"

"Actually—" he shrugged "—I think I'm trying not to tell you that."

"But you were."

"I was."

"For what? You get caught jaywalking?" She was grinning. Apparently she didn't believe him. Kirk allowed himself a second to be gratified.

"The first time was for breaking and entering."

Her step faltered. "The first time."

"The second was breaking and entering with robbery thrown in."

He made light of it. But the memory made him sick.

"Oh my gosh."

"The third time…"

"The *third?* Kirk! You go to *jail* for these things."

Some people did. And eventually, briefly, so had he. He'd begun to wonder, mostly since his talk with Steve McDonald, whether his life might have turned out differently if his father had forced Kirk to pay his own debt to society that first time.

"The third time it was car theft."

"You stole a car."

His father's Corvette. The car Kirk had driven there that day. He'd been driving it most of his adult life.

As a reminder.

"Charges were dropped on that one."

He'd been brought in, booked. Strip-searched, required to shower where anyone could—and did— walk by. Dressed in the same blue cotton pants and T-shirt as every other juvenile locked up in detention.

And then his father had found out who'd stolen his car.

And Kirk had been taken out for a steak dinner to recuperate from his dreadful experience. While his mother had sat in a corner of the booth with silent tears trailing down her cheeks.

"The fourth time was aggravated assault."

Valerie laughed out loud. "Now I know you're kidding."

Yeah. That was how it felt to him, sometimes, when he remembered.

But he knew.

Who he was. What he'd done.

"I pleaded not guilty for reasons of self-defense." He felt compelled to finish what he'd started. It was time she knew the nature of the man.

"You're not kidding."

They stopped under a tree, just standing there, staring at each other through their tinted lenses. "I'm not kidding," he admitted, his voice completely serious.

"What happened?"

"A punk football player grabbed my date in the parking lot after a dance one night. He'd had too much to drink. He kissed her, squeezed her breast. I hauled him off her. He hit me. I hit him back."

Again and again and again. It had been his first introduction to an anger that could drive him to the bitter end. And it was the last time that anger had been given a physical outlet.

"Then it was self-defense. I can't believe they even pressed charges."

"He was the mayor's son."

And had been unconscious after the first punch. With his bare hands Kirk had nearly killed an unconscious kid. He would have if his date hadn't started screaming at the top of her lungs.

Only the fact that Kirk's father had been the mayor's biggest financial supporter and that the mayor's son had been unable to recall what had happened had saved Kirk that time.

He'd eventually married his date.

"Was there a fifth time?" Valerie asked, starting to walk again.

"No."

"Were you ever detained?"

"Only until my dad came to get me." But it had been enough. That last time, when he'd been booked for beating up the mayor's son, Kirk's folks had been up in the mountains. Unreachable for four days.

Four days for him to be grabbed in the shower by some pervert, spit on by another of his fellow inmates, treated—it seemed to him at the time—as though he were no better than cow dung, forced to submit to the ignominies of a full physical, to undress and leave his regulation blue pants and prison shoes in a brown paper bag before he could walk down the secured hall to his cell each night. To use the rest room in full view of anyone who wanted to watch. And to *remember*.

Kirk had been plenty angry by the time his parents came to get him.

Driven by something he hadn't understood then, he'd made their lives hell for weeks after that.

His father had given him the Corvette.

He understood now, though. Courtesy of Alicia's death. He'd been driven by fear, by the knowledge that he couldn't control everything in the world around him. Even though he'd been taught that was his right since the day he was born.

It had taken him years to figure out what made him resent his parents, what created the underlying anger he felt when he was with them. They'd given him a world where he could have anything he wanted, taught him that he was the lord of his existence. They'd set him no limits. Seventeen was a hard age to learn that he wasn't always in charge, that he couldn't control everything.

Too hard. While Kirk learned that he never wanted to be on the wrong side of the law again, he hadn't learned the part about control. Instead, he'd spent the next seventeen years of his life proving that, on the contrary, he controlled all.

Or so he'd thought.

"You're awfully quiet." Her words sounded more like a question than a statement.

The court buildings no longer in sight, Kirk put a friendly arm around Valerie's shoulders, half expecting her to call him on it—or shrug it off.

"Just remembering." He grinned—sort of. "So how much damage did I just do?"

"To what?"

"That pedestal I've been put on."

She sputtered and laughed. "You were never up on a pedestal, Mr. Chandler," she said. "Far from it." Sobering, she added, "And you didn't do any damage at all."

"Come on, Judge, I'm just another one of your juvies."

"Hardly." She bumped his side. For safety's sake, he chose to believe it had been by accident. "Not a single one of my kids has a body that—"

She broke off.

"That what?"

"Nothing."

Because he was treading dangerous ground himself, Kirk left it at that.

"Actually," Valerie said, bumping his side again as they walked, "I'm impressed, and very grateful to you." Her tone had dropped to a more serious level.

The Kirk Chandler of old would have taken that straight to his ego. "Why?" he asked now, honestly perplexed.

"Impressed because, despite those rough experiences, you built something to be proud of. Look at your life, dedicated to the betterment of children. But you haven't done like most of us, working our jobs and going home. You've taken it steps further. Your life *is* those kids. You let them know they matter, give them a sense of value when they see how much you value them.''

If she got that, then why didn't she understand how important it was for him to see Abraham Billings? Kirk dropped his arm.

''And grateful?'' he asked. They turned a corner, bringing them back in sight of the Arizona Superior Court, Juvenile Division.

''Because you just validated the one thing that gets me through my days here.''

''Which is?''

''The belief that troubled kids can and do grow up to be good, law-abiding, caring and successful citizens. Every decision I make is geared toward that end.''

He wouldn't abuse that belief by telling her exactly what kind of citizen he'd grown up to be. Ruthless. Out to win. To be the one holding all the cards—at almost any cost. He'd drawn the line at breaking laws that could land him in jail. But the laws of human decency and kindness he'd trampled on whenever necessary.

And without compunction.

Those were things she'd never know about him.

Traffic was picking up as the morning calendars drew to a close and court personnel were leaving for lunch. Someone in a dark blue Mercedes honked at Valerie. She smiled and waved.

''Have you heard any more on the paternity suit?''

she asked him as they neared the front parking lot where he'd left his car.

"Nope." Troy had told him it would take time. The first step had been a formal letter to Susan requesting that she submit her son to a paternity test. The second had been a pleading filed in family court.

"Have you thought about just asking her for the test yourself?" Valerie asked.

"No." When he'd found out about the child, Susan had refused to speak to him.

Stopping at the side of the building, where there was a private entrance for employees with clearance, Valerie turned to smile at him, squinting beneath the bright sun.

"Speaking as a woman, not as a member of the legal profession, I'd suggest that, given the intimate nature of the situation, it might be best to handle this on a personal basis rather than through lawyers. Reassure her that you aren't trying to take anything away from her. That you just want to share in the responsibility."

Kirk doubted that Susan, even in the good days, had ever thought as logically as Valerie. But he was desperate. He'd give her another try. He wouldn't accuse. Or challenge. He'd simply ask.

It could work.

In a different lifetime.

CHAPTER FIFTEEN

ROCKING HER SON, Susan Douglas studied his perfect features and fought the ready tears that threatened whenever she really looked at Colton. She just couldn't escape the memory of another time. Another warm body against her breast. Another face with exactly the same features.

And still, she loved this child fiercely. For himself. Not in place of the sister he'd never know.

Which was why she didn't feel the least bit guilty about the phone call she'd made an hour before. She'd caught Valerie Simms just as the judge was leaving her office for her Wednesday-afternoon session. The conversation had to be quick.

She'd received a call from Kirk. A confusing call. She hated the man she'd divorced three years before.

But she'd adored the man she'd married ten years before that. To distraction.

And although she knew it was inconceivable, he'd almost convinced her that he'd really changed. That fathering Colton mattered.

There was a time she would've given *anything* to have Kirk be a father to her child. To his child. And those old aches still had power over her.

The power to destroy reason.

She couldn't let him do that.

So she'd called Valerie. And didn't feel the least bit guilty about telling her friend that things were getting desperate and she really needed the paternity issue settled once and for all. A court order, anything Valerie could do to get her ex-husband off her back.

And when Valerie had asked what was going on, she'd told her she was afraid for her life. That Kirk had threatened her. That he had a horrible temper and she was afraid of what he'd do.

Smoothing the top of her son's head, Susan relaxed a little more. Her tactic had worked.

But then, she'd known it would.

Susan Douglas had learned from a master.

COACH HAD PROMISED come hell or high water, that he'd be there Wednesday afternoon. Four o'clock sharp. Abraham came straight home from the school he hated worse than being slugged by a disgruntled trick—though definitely not worse than having the bastard grab at his pants—and hung out at the corner where he could watch for the Vette. If he went in the house, his foster mother would start analyzing crap she knew nothing about and never would, playing Donna Reed or June Cleaver. She didn't have a clue what the real world was like.

Mothers still loved their kids, but they had responsibilities nowadays, had to work for a living instead of hanging out wearing aprons and baking cookies. And they sure as hell didn't have time to analyze a kid and think they knew all the answers.

Thank God for that.

He started to sweat at twenty to four. Something might've held Coach up and he might not be coming. Maybe he forgot. Or found some other kid he could help. He might've decided that Abe's new place was too far to drive.

Sinking down onto the curb, he didn't care that he was making the backside of his jeans dusty, since he and Mom didn't have to wash them, anyway. They hadn't even let him bring his own clothes and he hated the stiff new things they were making him wear. He picked up a handful of pebbles.

His backpack still strapped to his shoulders, he jiggled the rocks in his palm. It wouldn't matter if Coach didn't come. He'd be free to head out then. He was only staying because he'd promised the coach. And if Chandler didn't keep his promise, then Abe's was null and void. No second chances.

Not for a world that didn't give him any.

Ten minutes to four. Abraham stood up. He might as well head out. Chances were Coach wasn't going to show. And he'd feel stupid standing there like a little kid, waiting for him anyway. Backing up to the stop sign, he considered his options.

There was no reason to return to the house. Every morning when he left there, he had everything he needed in his backpack. Glancing up and down both streets at the quiet intersection, he pondered which way to go. He wasn't quite sure where the freeway was, but knew he'd find it.

Abraham always found his way.

At five to four, just as he was heading north, away

from the corner, Coach Chandler pulled up to the curb.

"Hop in."

Quenching the relief in his belly, he did.

"DOES MRS. MORTON KNOW you're with me?" Kirk eyed the sullen-faced boy as he slouched down in the leather seat of his forty-five-thousand-dollar car.

"Yeah." The sweater they'd bought for the boy wasn't anything Kirk could imagine Abraham choosing for himself. Seeing Abraham in it irritated him. They'd taken the kid from everything he knew. Couldn't they at least leave his clothes alone?

"You told her I was taking you to dinner like we discussed?" he pressed, mostly because Abraham was staring out the passenger window.

As though he could read Kirk's thoughts, Abraham turned his hard eyes directly on Kirk. "I said I would, didn't I?"

With his years of honed instincts, Kirk wasn't satisfied with that look, but he trusted the boy anyway. Someone had to. So Abraham was plotting something. But the boy wasn't lying to him about this.

He'd just have to be smarter than Abraham, talk him out of whatever plan he had for the evening. And make sure the boy was still in the car when he pulled up to the Mortons' later that evening. Abraham Billings had no idea who he was dealing with.

Though he suggested every restaurant he could think of, Kirk ended up eating fast-food hamburgers and French fries with the boy. In his car. It was the only thing he'd agree to.

Abraham obviously didn't realize that eating in a vintage Corvette was a sin.

Just as Kirk didn't realize what kind of bomb he was going to detonate when he asked how Abraham was doing.

After the string of cusswords, the boy spent fifteen minutes talking about all the things going undone in his mother's life.

"Don't you think she's old enough to take care of herself?" Kirk asked, chomping on a double burger and fries as though he ate in his car parked in the back of a hotel lot every night of the week.

Abraham's tanned, perfect features turned toward him, and Kirk had trouble swallowing the bite of food he'd just chewed. Those big brown eyes had never looked so completely sincere.

"Not my mom, Coach," he said. "She's one of those women who are too sweet for their own good. She always believes the best is going to happen. She'll forget to pay the electric bill because she figures no one's really going to turn off the power when it's a single mom and her kid living in a trailer. Especially since she 'most always pays it.'"

"You paid it, didn't you?" Kirk read between the lines.

"Sometimes."

"And the other bills, too?"

"Mostly. She kept her money in a little chest under my bed and I'd take it and buy money orders to pay for stuff."

Abraham didn't seem to be very hungry. He held his hamburger in one hand and picked at his fries.

"She can't live alone, Coach. She's afraid when she's alone. She'll go crazy and invite some jerk to stay with her because she won't think she has any other choice."

Kirk wondered if anyone had ever wrung that woman's neck.

As if by mutual agreement, they shied away from uncomfortable conversation and tended to their food for several minutes.

"If they don't let me go back there, Coach, I'm running," he said suddenly, his voice as filled with determination as any judge's had ever been.

"Whoa, buddy, remember what we talked about? Think of your future."

"What future?" The brown eyes were sullen again, staring out into the early darkness that had fallen. December in Phoenix meant it was dark by five. A fact that had gone unnoticed by Kirk for most of his adult life. As had the blue skies and sunshine that characterized Arizona days.

He opened his mouth to give Abraham an answer.

"Forget it," Abraham said before Kirk got out the first word. "I'm supposed to take care of my mom. I've known that for a long time. If I can't even do that, what good am I?"

Kirk had a ready answer for that one. "You're—"

"There's no point in my being here," Abraham interrupted, his voice bitter. "There's nothing for me to do, and everyone else just wants to tell me what I'm thinking and feeling, and telling me they understand when they don't know a damn thing."

Kirk nodded. He had a feeling the boy was more right than wrong about that.

"There were problems at home, Abraham," he said, looking inside for the intuitive sense that had guided him through years of successful negotiations. "You were pretty badly beat up."

"I fell—"

"Don't give me that line of bull," Kirk warned before Abraham could compromise himself with another lie. "I'm guessing one of your mother's friends did it to you."

His stomach came close to rejecting the dinner he'd just eaten when Abraham's silence acknowledged the truth of Kirk's words.

"Did he do anything else?" Kirk wanted to avoid the path he was taking, but knew he couldn't. "Before he hit you?"

"No!" There was too much vehemence in the boy's voice. More than mere offense at the question.

"Did he try?"

The boy turned, and while Kirk couldn't be sure, he suspected there was a hint of moisture in the boy's eyes. "So what if he did?"

"So nothing as long as he didn't succeed," Kirk said, his blood boiling with a need to find the bastard and squeeze the breath from his body.

"He didn't." Abraham was staring at the floor and Kirk could tell the boy wasn't being completely honest. But because he was fairly certain from Abraham's tone that the man hadn't done more than try, he didn't know, at that moment, how much it mattered that Abraham talk about it.

"And you don't think that was reason enough to take you out of there? Next time you might not get so lucky."

"I wasn't at home when it happened," Abraham said, looking over at Kirk. "The guy wasn't one of my mom's, uh, anyone she—he'd never been to our house. He *wanted* to come over and she'd told him no because he gave her the creeps. He was just some drunk that asked her out and she turned him down."

"So how'd he find you?"

"I don't know." Abraham shrugged. "I was hanging out down the street and he pulled up and started talking to me. Asked me if I knew where Carla Billings lived. I lied to him. Gave him directions to where one of my old teachers lives. An hour later he came looking for me."

The muscles in Kirk's neck were so tight they hurt. "And where was your mother when all this was going on?"

"Home," Abraham said. "Working. But she's the one who saved me, Coach. I was in that parking lot, thinking I was a goner and she came rushing up out of nowhere like she's a superhero or something. She kicked the guy and screamed so much he took off before someone could come arrest his ass."

An ideal life for a twelve-year-old.

"I know what you're thinking," Abraham said, his voice calm now, as though he were the adult and Kirk the child, the one needing assurance. "But that kind of stuff happens to all kinds of kids, Coach. It could happen to me here just as easily as it did there, probably easier 'cause I don't know the ins and outs like

I do at home. And my mom takes care of me, Coach. I know things don't look so great, but we're all the family we've got. And family is everything. Haven't you learned that yet?''

Out of the mouths of twelve-year-old kids....

''Yeah, I learned that,'' he said, his throat dry. ''But, honestly, Abe, wouldn't you prefer a normal home life?''

''Normal compared to what?'' the boy asked. ''I know kids at school whose dads beat 'em up on a regular basis. I just got beat up once. Besides, this is the life I was given.''

''It doesn't have to stay that way,'' Kirk said, arguing a side he wasn't sure he agreed with. Valerie had made a mistake about Brian, and Kirk believed she'd made a mistake in supporting her peer on this one.

''Listen,'' Abraham said, an adult in a kid's body. ''At least before, I had something, you know? Now I got no family at all. Maybe for some kids this would be better, but not for me.''

''You haven't even tried.''

''What's to try?'' he asked, bitterness returning to his voice. ''My mom's the one I belong to, she's where I have a place and a job to do. If I can't do that, I'm nothing.''

The boy was wrong about that, but Kirk was unable to help Abraham to see things any other way. Maybe because he wasn't clear on the whole thing, either. Instead, he saw something in a disadvantaged young man that, as a thirty-four-year-old multimillionaire, he hadn't understood himself. *A sense of what mattered most.*

Against the prompting of an inner self he didn't often get along with, Kirk pulled up in front of the Mortons' at eight o'clock sharp, just as he'd said he would, and dropped off a young man who'd lost everything that mattered to him. A boy who was giving up.

A STRANGE KIND of adrenaline pumping through her veins, Valerie barely got around the corner from dropping off the boys the following Friday afternoon before picking up her cell phone.

"How would you like to go to dinner?"

"Valerie?"

She couldn't blame him for his surprise.

"Yeah, I know, we don't do dinner, but I just left the boys with friends who're taking them camping overnight. I have a free evening and I don't want to waste it."

Strange how spending some time with him was the only thing that *didn't* seem like a waste of time at the moment. Freedom did strange things to an otherwise focused and responsible single mother. "Besides," she continued before he could answer, "I want to thank you."

"For what?"

"I'll tell you at dinner."

"Is that a bribe to get me to go?"

She pulled up to the stop sign at the next intersection. And, with no traffic behind her, stayed there. She'd been thinking about him all week, about his teenage years. And the man he'd become.

She admired him. A lot.

"Do I need one?" she asked.

"No."

She hadn't thought so.

IT MUST HAVE BEEN the wine.

There was no other explanation for the fact that she was sitting out by her pool with Kirk Chandler later that night. They'd had dinner—her treat, although she'd had to excuse herself, find their waiter and pay the check before Kirk figured out what she was doing. She'd thanked him for the miracle of Brian's doctor's appointment that week. Her son had gained ten pounds. And she'd admitted that his way of handling Brian's problem had worked.

Then, somehow, they'd ended up with a bottle of wine and two glasses, relaxing on the upholstered lounge chairs on her landscaped patio.

"Did you ask the doctor about Blake's stomach-aches?" Kirk asked after they'd been sitting there, quietly enjoying the night, for several minutes.

She nodded, smiled again. It had really been a good week. "He said to give him a daily laxative for the next week or two. Who'd have thought the solution would be so simple?"

"Has it helped?"

God, it felt great to be here with him, sharing concern for her kids. "It's too soon to tell."

Christmas carols played softly in the background, piped outside through the sound system Thomas had had installed when they'd built the house.

"I can't believe there are only two more days of school before Christmas break," Valerie said, thinking of all the shopping she had left to do. She still wrapped and hid Santa gifts for her sons, although she suspected the tradition was really more for her. Thomas had disillusioned the boys about Santa when they were seven. He hadn't been willing to expend the effort to keep up the pretense.

At least she'd already sent off all the packages to her various family members.

"Did the boys tell you they're supposed to drop off their clean uniforms at the gym tomorrow?" They'd lost the last game before the finals the previous afternoon.

"Yeah. They're all ready to go."

She sipped her wine, astonished by how different life could feel in such a short period of time. A week ago she hadn't been sure how she was going to hang on. Tonight she thought she could take on the world. And win.

"Who did your fountain?" Kirk asked, gesturing to the rock waterfall and flowers by one end of the pool area.

"My husband."

"Talented man."

He'd had a lot of talents. Just not a lot of values. Something she hadn't known until it was too late.

The antithesis of Kirk Chandler. She'd never met a man with his priorities so completely focused on the things that mattered in life.

Leaning her head against the cushion, she let the wine, the unusual freedom, take her away.

"So why aren't you doing more with *your* talents?" she wondered aloud, finding herself in a state of drifting relaxation…and giving in to it.

One part of her recognized that if it hadn't been

for that state, she would never have asked the question.

"Which talents might those be?" Kirk's voice sounded just as relaxed.

"Whichever ones allow you to afford a mint-condition 1965 Corvette." Her boys had told her the year. And many more things about the car that she couldn't remember.

"That would be merely the gift of receiving," he said lazily. "The car belonged to my father."

"How long have you been driving it?"

"Seventeen years."

"And you're what, thirty-five or six?"

"Thirty-four." He glanced over at her. "How about you?"

Three years older than he was. Valerie took another sip of wine, watching the lights from the pool reflect the natural-rock waterfall.

"Thirty-seven."

The youngest female judge ever to sit on the bench in Arizona's Superior Court. And three years older than he was. When she was a senior in high school, he'd have been a freshman. But hey, her brother, Adam, would've been in sixth grade when his current girlfriend was a senior.

She lowered her glass, stared at him in the soft patio lighting. "Your father gave a vintage Corvette to a seventeen-year-old?"

He shrugged. Sipped his wine. Frowned at the pool. "He liked me."

"I like my boys, too, but I sure won't be giving them even a beat-up nonvintage sports car at that age.'' It was too much too soon. In the hands of a young and restless spirit.

''I was an only child.''

''That's still no reason. Did you at least have to work for it?''

''No.''

''Was it always that way? Expensive toys just handed to you?''

He emptied his glass, refilled it, and topped hers off, too. She didn't intend to drink it. Based on how loose her tongue had become, she'd already had too much.

''Always,'' he said several seconds later. ''Toys and clothes. And places on teams.''

Valerie would have gasped out loud if his sardonic tone of voice hadn't stopped her.

''You never had to work for *anything*,'' she said, her voice softening as she glanced over at him. Wishing he'd look at her instead of out into the night.

''I worked hard at getting into trouble.''

''You rose above it.'' And she knew the value of that. Knew how seldom it happened.

He sipped again. ''So it would appear.'' His eyes narrowed as he spoke.

Finally, she understood his lack of motivation. He'd never had to work for anything, which meant he'd never been taught a proper work ethic. She could help him with that. Work ethic was something she'd been born with.

And if she hadn't, her parents had instilled it in her as a child.

Valerie took a couple of sips of the wine she wasn't going to have.

She had to sit down with him, list his talents, find out what he loved. And hated. They'd find a place for him—something to do that used all aspects of his talents instead of just some.

His parents should have done that with him before he ever left high school. Was this why he'd been so unhappy in the corporate world? Because he'd had no goals? Nothing to work toward?

"What did your father do?"

"Owned and ran the Desert Oasis regional supermarket chain."

"Oh!" She shifted in her chair, smiling. "I used to go to one of those stores—about ten minutes from here. I loved that place! And it was always so crowded. I couldn't believe it when it closed five years ago. What happened?"

More wine. More staring. "He slowly handed his stock over to someone he trusted—who turned around and sold him out to a national chain."

"And they closed him down?"

"He was well compensated."

"Yes, but some things matter more than money." She shook her head. "To have worked so hard and then lose everything like that…"

"He survived." With a glance at his hardened expression, Valerie let it go. Yet she couldn't help wondering about the bitterness in those last words.

CHAPTER SIXTEEN

KIRK WASN'T GOING to sleep with her. He knew that. He didn't even want to. On an analytical level. But physically… Emotionally…

"I don't even know where you live." They were standing at her front door, allegedly so he could leave. He just hadn't opened the door yet. Neither had she. And they'd been standing there for more than twenty minutes.

"Not far."

She frowned. "Kirk, don't you think, after all this time—after I bought you dinner and acknowledged that you were right in the way you handled my son— you could lose at least *some* of the evasiveness?"

She had no idea what she asking.

"Is our friendship only one-sided, then?" she asked, taking a step back.

"No." It was because he valued her friendship that he didn't tell her who he'd been before he became Kirk, the crossing guard. Didn't tell her he'd been exactly the same as her ex-husband. The things that man had done to her had raised enough walls inside Valerie to keep Kirk locked out forever if she ever saw the two of them in the same light.

"I live a couple of blocks over." He named the street.

She stared at him. "It backs up to the mountain."

"Right."

She stepped forward again, so close he could smell her perfume. And the wine on her breath.

"Those are the most expensive homes here in the foothills."

He nodded, his gut tight. She was getting too close to something he'd shut away. His past? Or a future he couldn't have?

"Let me guess, your father gave you that, too?"

The knot in his stomach loosened slightly. "It was his house, yes." One Kirk had built for his parents ten years before. And then moved into himself after the divorce. They'd already been in Florida by then, and the house had been sitting empty, anyway....

She blinked, her eyes a little cloudy from the late hour, the wine—and maybe something more? Some of the same confusion that was clouding his usually rational and single-focused mind? "And you can afford the upkeep?"

One corner of his mouth turned up. "You afraid I might end up on the street?"

"No." But she was still frowning.

"I can afford the bills."

"Do your parents send you money?"

Kirk lifted a hand to smooth the frown from her forehead, trailing his fingers down the side of her face. Distraction was his only goal.

"I made some money on the sale of the family business," he said. It was more than he wanted to tell her. More than he'd told anyone in his new life. He couldn't seem to lie effectively to this woman.

"So you're independently wealthy."

She hadn't stepped away or removed her face from his touch.

"I can afford to pay my electric bill," he said dismissively, much more interested in the smooth skin beneath his fingertips. It had been a long time since he'd allowed himself the luxury of caressing a woman.

He discounted that night with her in the park, when he'd kissed her but hadn't been able to give in to the need to enjoy a simple touch. The last time had been with Susan. The evening he'd seen her at their daughter's grave...

"Still," she said, her voice soft, growing huskier, "a man should use his talents...."

Kirk kissed her. He hadn't made any kind of conscious decision. Just needed to shut her up.

And to taste her again.

He waited for her to pull back, fully aware of her rules, counting on those rules to protect them both.

Her breasts pressing into his chest didn't feel as if she was pulling back. Nor did the sweet lips opening beneath his. With a vague sense of assurance that she'd stop them soon, Kirk deepened the kiss, his lips playing with hers, tasting, discovering.

She was sweet, with wine—and with her own unique essence. Her tongue was bolder than he'd expected, confident, not at all shy in either advancement or exploration. The intrusion set his blood on fire, making him instantaneously hard.

And if he'd thought she wouldn't notice that reaction, she quickly disabused him of that idea as she pushed her hips against him, fanning a flame spreading quickly out of control.

"Valerie?" He drew back, breath ragged, wondering if he'd have to be the one to prevent a disaster from happening. Though, at the moment, with the wine slowing his brain, he wasn't sure how anything that felt so incredible could be a disaster.

"Mmm?"

Her eyes opened slowly, focusing on him. He waited for reason to dawn. And while she stood there, gazing up at him with a peculiarly peaceful expression on her face, he continued to wait.

He kissed her again before he lost his chance. Just one quick caress... A quick caress that turned into minutes of mutual hunger, of mutual response, inciting something—a feeling—he'd never experienced before.

Kirk knew about passion. The giving of it and the receiving. He knew about desire, about blood that boiled and bodies that consumed. He didn't recognize the compulsive drive pushing him to know this woman. An instinctive perception that he would be changed, and that if he missed this chance, his life would never be what it was meant to be.

Still, he drew back a second time. They had an understanding. Important decisions and choices that had already been made.

Her moan of disappointment cut through him. Laying his forehead against hers, bringing an end to an inexplicable interlude, he forced words he didn't want to speak. "What are we going to do?"

"Well…" She sounded as though she'd been running. "I guess my bed is the most logical choice, but the couch is closer."

The surge of pressure in a groin already swollen to uncomfortable proportions consumed all awareness for a second. And then he was kissing her again. Like a man who was on his way to much more than kisses.

She took his hand, this judge who was also completely woman, soft and sensuous, a mystery and a coming home. She led him through a house he'd yet to see and, eventually, into a bedroom every bit as large and elegantly appointed as his own. Where his wall of windows overlooked the mountain behind him, hers had a view of the city lights.

Not that he gave them more than a cursory glance.

Her bed was king-size, a four-poster of light pine, that stood a foot higher off the ground than normal beds. Just the right height for him to lean her back against it, letting the bed support her while he pressed into her.

"You're wearing too many clothes, Judge Simms," he whispered. He'd used the title without thinking, but knew the distinction was important. He could do this, couldn't *not* do it if he was honest with himself, but he could be under no illusions about who she was. Who *he* was.

While his mind was occupied with the things he couldn't forget, Kirk's hands were just as occupied, removing the lime-green button-down silk blouse Valerie had worn to dinner. A blond curl snagged on the top button as he pulled the blouse off her shoulders. Bending closer to gently free it, he found his lips irrevocably drawn to the indentation between her neck and shoulder blade.

"You're as soft as powder," he said.

"And you, sir, are far too good at this," Valerie answered back, her chuckle turning into a moan as his lips continued across her chest to the opposite side of her neck.

His hands shook as he dropped her blouse on the floor at their feet and ran his palms along her lower back, around to her belly and up to her waist. All the while, his lips were floating across her skin, to her lips, along her neck. He felt as though he was never going to get enough of her. She was exquisite.

When he could stand the anticipation no longer, he moved to the front clasp of her bra, hardly daring to believe he was finally going to see her breasts. To touch and taste them. He'd been trying for weeks to pretend he hadn't noticed them. Or wanted them.

"Hold it." He could hardly suck in breath when he heard Valerie's demand. Didn't she get that it was about half an hour too late?

He stopped anyway, hands at his sides, and stepped back.

For someone who'd just put an end to sublime sensation, she wasn't doing much to help the recovery process. Still spread before him, arms splayed behind her, hips jutting out at the edge of the mattress, she looked more like a wanton than a woman of the court who'd just given a mandate she meant to have followed.

"I might be slightly desperate, but you gotta join me here." Her words didn't make sense.

"Take off your clothes, Kirk, if you're planning to take off mine."

Never had he undressed so fast, or so clumsily. The old Kirk Chandler might very well be alive and well inside him, but it was definitely the new Kirk in this woman's bedroom.

"Better?" he asked, standing before her completely naked, reveling in what had to be the best moment of his life.

Judging by the reaction he was getting, she liked what she saw. Eyes wide, in spite of passion and wine, she stared. Licked her lips. Glanced at his face, and then up and down his body again.

"So, Judge, do I meet your standards?"

"I—" She coughed. Swallowed. "I don't think I had standards," she said shakily, "but if I did, you definitely surpass them."

He pushed her farther back into the bed. Kissed her hard. Long. And unclipped her bra. Then, with his face only an inch from hers, he said, "You kiss like you've had plenty of experience."

His hands covered her breasts, holding them, supporting their weight. Their softness ignited him all over again.

"Believe me, it's surprising me as much as it is you," she said slowly, gasping.

Because her hands and arms were supporting her weight, she still wasn't touching him while he caressed her everywhere. An experience more erotic than he'd ever have guessed.

"Have there been many others besides your husband?"

Her eyes locked on his, filled with smoky desire
and an admiration he knew he didn't deserve but accepted anyway. For the moment.

"One before him."

He pushed his naked hips against the silk of her
panties.

"And afterward?"

"Do we count this?"

Oh, God, if the woman got any sexier he wasn't
going to be able to last.

Still keeping her gaze captive, he hooked a finger
under the top edge of her panties, sliding them off
her hips. "Okay," he answered her. "Sure."

"One."

Her panties on the floor at her feet, Kirk lowered
unsteady hands to her thighs. He intended to explore,
to bring her to the heights beside him. But when her
legs parted at his touch, he had no ability left to carry
out his intentions. He quickly pulled on a condom that
had been in his wallet and then, with a hand on each
of her thighs, he thrust himself inside her, dying a
small death when her tightness took him in, hugged
him, as though that special place had been waiting
just for him.

VALERIE HAD A HARD TIME waiting until four o'clock
Saturday afternoon to drop off the boys' uniforms.
She wanted the excuse to see Kirk again. After all the
other kids had come and gone, she'd invited Kirk to
have burgers with her and the boys, and she didn't

feel a single qualm about doing it. She'd already promised the twins a trip to their favorite gourmet-burger restaurant.

The resiliency of kids—or was it their oblivious self-centeredness?—was something she didn't think she'd ever get used to. She was almost shocked to find that apparently she'd worried for nothing all those months when she'd been so anxious about how her sons would react to their basketball coach joining them in private. Other than a hastily offered "cool," their biggest concern was how soon they were going to get to the restaurant.

Not even the stomachache Blake couldn't quite hide marred the evening. He'd just neglected to take his pill at the sleepover Friday night.

She swore to herself that she wasn't going to assign too much significance to the changes the weekend had brought, but as she lay, relaxed and peaceful in her bed Sunday night, drifting off to sleep, her heart was filled with possibilities.

BY TUESDAY NIGHT, Valerie had finished all her Christmas shopping and had a lot of the wrapping done. She and the boys had gone to her office Christmas party Sunday afternoon, and then she'd spent most of the night wrapping their gifts from Santa Claus. She was on call for emergencies, but she had the next two weeks off as the courts typically shut down over the holidays.

To celebrate the last day of school, she invited Kirk over for dinner. At least that was the excuse she gave everyone. The invitation had nothing to do with the fact that the woman who'd slept with the crossing guard on Friday night was dying to see him. She wouldn't let her obsession with him mean that much.

At least not yet. Whether the boys made a big deal about Kirk's entrance into their lives or not, she knew how vulnerable they were. Brian was much better, miraculously better, but she'd had her warning. She was going to take things very slow where her sons were concerned.

He joked with the boys over dinner, helped with the dishes, evened up the teams for shooting hoops and spent an hour in their room when he went in to say good-night to them.

"What was that all about?" Valerie asked, beside herself with curiosity by the time he emerged. She'd been sitting at the counter in the black sweats and tennis shoes she'd changed into after dinner, writing out her grocery list for the next morning, planning the kinds of cookies she was going to bake, making certain she had everything for Christmas dinner.

Hands in his pockets, Kirk stopped behind the stool where she sat, looking over her shoulder at the list on the counter.

"Basketball, mostly," he said.

"You're evading again."

"It was guy talk, Mom," he told her in a voice a couple of octaves above his own. "And it's Christmastime."

Although she had a pretty strong hunch there'd been more than Christmas to the conversation, Valerie was content to let it go. While part of her needed to know everything that went on in her sons' lives, more of her reveled in the chance to share some of the burden.

"That's quite a list." Valerie tilted her head to the side. He was close, reading over her shoulder. If he leaned down just a little bit farther…

"I make a lot of cookies." The boys couldn't possibly be asleep yet. And even if they were, she wasn't going to have sex with their basketball coach while they were anywhere close.

Not that he'd asked.

She also knew that what they'd done the other night could not be described so callously. Maybe they hadn't made love—she wasn't ready to acknowledge anything so frightening and dangerous—but they'd certainly done more than "have sex."

"You're buying a ham?"

"The boys don't like turkey."

She'd promised herself she wouldn't ask, wouldn't hope. Or impose. But… "What are you doing for Christmas dinner?"

If he said he was—

"Eating out."

"No." Valerie whirled on the stool, looking up at him. "You are not going to a restaurant on Christmas Day. If you're going out anywhere, come here."

"Okay."

"Okay?" If she'd known it was going to be that easy…

"I was hoping you'd ask."

Anything she might have said to that was lost in the touch of his lips against hers. And in the all-consuming need that soared through her the instant he touched her. Four days had been too long.

Apparently for him, too, as his breathing was heavy and uneven when he finally pulled away. "We're going to have to find a way to be alone sometime during the next two weeks, or I might not be responsible for the results," he said with an exaggerated grimace.

Because she was ready to throw everything to the winds in her need to be with him, Valerie didn't dare tell him that the boys were going to be spending the week between Christmas and New Year's with her parents. She was afraid to say anything yet; afraid to make that much of a commitment. The trip had been her parents' Christmas present to her, some time all to herself with no responsibilities. Until recently, she'd been dreading the loneliness.

Now she was dreading what might happen—*would* happen—if she had a week without supervision, even of the twelve-year-old variety.

Especially that kind.

"What's going on with us?" she asked Kirk, her face serious as she gazed at him. In his usual jeans and, tonight, a faded maroon sweater, he stood there, the epitome of everything she wanted in a man.

Or almost. She would've preferred a little more drive to make the most of his God-given talents, but it was such a small thing compared to his work with the kids, his need to make a difference in their lives. To his honesty. His loyalty.

To the fact that he was well known at the coffee shop he frequented many nights a week instead of at a local bar.

It took him so long to answer, she almost wished she could take back the question. She hadn't wanted to ruin the moment.

"I'm not sure," he finally said, his eyebrows drawn as he held her gaze. "With my paternity suit still undecided, I'm still not free. Nor has enough changed for you and the boys. Blake's continued to have stomachaches, and we can't be certain that Brian will hang on to those pounds he gained."

"I know."

"But the companionship is damn nice."

"Yeah."

"So I guess we just take things one day at a time and see how it all plays out."

It was no answer at all. She knew that. And suspected he did, too. But it was the best they had. "Okay."

He backed away a step. "You ready to go for a walk?"

"Sure."

And just like that, she'd made a commitment she knew she couldn't keep.

CHAPTER SEVENTEEN

"I KNOW YOU TOLD ME not to say it again, but I just have to." Valerie's words made Kirk a bit uneasy as they walked slowly through the holiday-lit streets. "Did you see Brian at dinner tonight?" she continued, her hand sliding into his so naturally he wasn't sure which of them had instigated the contact. "He had seconds of everything. And I have you to thank for that."

He'd noticed every bite the boy ate, eager to tell Alicia. This was what his life was about, helping kids. He'd promised his dying daughter that he wouldn't lose sight of himself again. Ever.

That reminded him of another boy who needed his help. Desperately. He'd seen Abraham Billings on Sunday. With the holidays drawing near, the boy was agitated and depressed, and Kirk didn't know how much longer he'd be able to talk the kid into hanging in there. Each time he dropped Abraham off, the boy seemed more depressed. Kirk had to have *something* to give Abraham, some promise he could make that would combat the hopelessness that overwhelmed him.

And about the only place he could get that promise was from Valerie. Juvenile court in Mesa wasn't that big. Valerie had to know the judge on Abraham's case.

If she wasn't the judge herself. But he still didn't think so. He'd made millions reading between the lines of what people said, and while she'd been understandably evasive, protecting the confidentiality of the court, he really didn't believe she'd actually made the decision she'd defended. She'd been a little too detached.

"I've been to see Abraham Billings."

She stopped, dropping his hand. "You what?"

He stood in the street, facing her, noticing that her hair glinted with the reflections of green and blue, red and gold Christmas lights on the houses and in the yards around them. "I've visited Abraham Billings."

"That's what I thought you'd said." She started to walk again, as slowly as before, yet her whole demeanor was different. She was stiff with tension now.

"Valerie, you've just admitted for the umpteenth time that I was right about your own son. Can't you give me the benefit of the doubt about a boy you hardly know?"

Arms wrapped around the velour jacket that matched her sweatpants, she shivered, although the night wasn't cold. "You don't understand."

He might have acknowledged that…if he hadn't been so sure that he *did* understand. Far more than she ever could. He'd been with Abraham, worked with him one-on-one, witnessed his despair, felt the change coming over him. He had the honor of being the only person Abraham even halfway trusted.

"What does Abraham need more than anything?" he asked her.

"Solid ground to stand on."

"And that's exactly what basketball gave him. It's also, believe it or not, what his mother gave him."

"You don't know everything."

"I know that one of his mother's potential tricks beat him up."

She stopped again, stared at him. "He told you that?"

"You want the details?"

He sensed as much as saw the confusion cross her face before she shook her head. Shoulders hunched, she stood there, hugging herself.

"Knowing that, how can you say that boy's mother gave him any kind of security?" she suddenly asked, not hiding her anger.

"The man was a *potential* trick. He'd never met Abraham or been to his home. He'd merely stopped to ask if Abe knew where Carla Billings lived. He was sent on a wild-goose chase, came back loaded for trouble and found Abraham still hanging out where he'd left him. In the end, it was his mother who saved him. She'd been worried when he wasn't home on time, and went to his usual haunts looking for him."

"For God's sake, Chandler! His mother turns tricks right under his nose."

"The situation is not ideal, granted," Kirk said, uncomfortable with that truth. "But there's got to be a better way to deal with this. Abraham feels a very real and strong responsibility to his mother. His identity is, to a great extent, wrapped up in the part he plays as a family member. Not only has he lost basketball, but your court system, this judge you're supporting so adamantly, has even stripped him of his identity.''

''I—'' She stopped, looked at him with a second of stark fear in her eyes.

It was Kirk's turn to feel anger. At her—although he knew she was just doing her job. And mostly at himself for being such a fool. He could hardly believe what he was seeing in her eyes. ''You're his judge,'' he said, incredulous. Hoping she'd deny his words, deny that she'd deceived him. How could he have been so far off the mark?

''I can't comment on that.''

''You are.'' He'd felt warm moments before. Now he was cold.

''I've told you all along I can't comment on that.''

''There I was, telling you about his problems at home and you were using that information against him, weren't you?''

''I have nothing to say to that.''

How could she look him in the eye?

''And the smoking!'' Kirk continued. ''That was a probation violation. Did you write him up for that, too?''

''I can't comment on any of this, Kirk.''

Furious, Kirk stood with hands in his pockets, his jaw tight. Willing himself to breathe, to think, to stop himself before he said something he'd regret.

''No, but that didn't prevent you from fishing for information, did it?''

She turned away then, and he grew numb. As though he stood outside himself looking in.

Damn. Wouldn't half the business world just love this one? He gritted his teeth. The infallible and dangerous, dreaded and revered Kirk Chandler, taken in by a five-foot-five lady judge.

It took him a full two minutes to be able to pry his jaw apart, to remember why the business world—and its opinion of him—didn't matter. To remember that betrayal was his due. To remember his life's purpose.

And to realize that he'd just been given the best chance he'd ever get to help Abraham. He was no longer going through a third party. No, he had the sole decision-maker right there in front of him.

He'd had her beneath him recently, too. Naked. Inviting him inside.

"Abraham needs his mother," he said as calmly as he could. "He's depressed, sinking under the weight of hopelessness. While it might seem somewhat bizarre considering the circumstances, family is everything to that boy. Do whatever you must, put him in whatever programs, give him however many watchdogs, but let him go home, Valerie, or we're going to lose him." She was watching him. Listening. So he continued. "I know you thought the Mortons would be good for him, but their family closeness just makes him feel isolated. Alone. Apart."

She started to walk and, hands in the pockets of his jeans, he kept pace. She was quiet for so long he found it difficult to assess his position. In the world of negotiation, silence usually meant you wanted something you hadn't yet been given. And he'd given everything.

"Do you really care about these things, Kirk?" Her question, when it came, surprised him. "Do you care about *him?*"

"Of course I do."

"Enough to get over yourself and let Abraham have the help he needs?"

Heart sinking, Kirk continued to walk. "Why do I get the feeling you didn't hear a word I just said?"

"I heard you," she said, glancing over at him. "And everything you said just strengthened what I already knew. It's your fault that Abraham's not accepting the help being offered to him."

"My fault!" He didn't know what he'd been expecting. Thanks, maybe, for caring so much. It certainly hadn't been blame. "How do you figure that?"

"Because your presence allows him to hold on to what he had. He has to let go before he'll be able to see what else the world might have to offer him. That's why we remove them so completely from the environment they knew."

Because this was all about saving a twelve-year-old boy, he did his best to listen with an open mind. "I'm sure that works in a lot of cases," he said after careful thought. "But nothing is a hundred percent in life. Nothing. Abraham is an unusual kid. A strange mixture of confusion and good sense, of little boy and mature young man."

"You think Abraham is the only one of his kind?" she asked him, slowing more as they neared her driveway. "We see kids like him often, Kirk. Yes, he thinks life with his mother is everything, but only because it's the only reality he's ever known. If we can get him separated from that reality long enough to realize there's a world of choices before him, he'll be on his way to recovery.''

They weren't going to agree on this. And if he had to help Abraham on his own, so be it. He could handle it. He'd already been handling it. So coming to Valerie hadn't worked; he'd just have to think of something else.

"I'm sorry," she said at the end of the driveway, hesitating as though she didn't want to go in and leave things as they were.

"Don't be." He tried to sound sincere. "While I know you're wrong, I also know you're doing what *you* think is right, which is the very best you can do and all anyone can ever expect."

"You'd be happier with me if I wrote the order in the morning and let him come home."

He almost agreed. And then, the anger losing intensity, had to shake his head. "No, I'm happy with you when you do what you believe is right."

It was the absolute truth. And a new level of awareness for Kirk Chandler.

"You're sure about that?"

"Positive."

Her eyes were shadowed in the moonlight, giving her a vulnerable look as she looked up at him. "You're still coming for Christmas dinner?"

He stared at her for a long time, needing to say no—to the judge. At the same time wanting to say yes to the woman. Another internal battle. Always a battle.

"I wouldn't miss it."

But he was going to see Abraham, too. On Christmas morning, with a letter from the boy's mother and a passenger seat full of the presents Carla had bought for her son. At her son's request he'd called her, made the arrangements. Abraham could tell the Mortons they were from Kirk. What others thought didn't matter. As long as Abraham knew the truth—that his mother loved him. As long as, somehow, he shared this holiday with his family.

"Mom!"

The sound of terror in her son's voice had Valerie racing from the kitchen on Christmas afternoon, leaving the water running in the sinkful of pots and pans. Kirk, who'd been loading the dishwasher, was right beside her.

"Bry? What's wrong?" The boys were in the living room, and never had three rooms seemed so far away.

"Blake's sick, Mom! Hurry!"

Running into the room, she took in everything at once—Blake leaning over the edge of the couch retching, the mess on the floor, the blood, the stark fear in Brian's eyes.

"It's okay, son," she said, ignoring the floor as she sat beside her crying and violently ill son, rubbing his back. 'It's okay, just let it all out. Don't fight it."

"Get us a bucket, a spatula and a clean, cool washcloth, okay, Brian?" Kirk's voice was calm, reassuring, as though boys throwing up blood were an everyday occurrence for him.

"I'd say you overdid it on dessert, Blake, my boy." Down on his haunches, he didn't seem to even notice the stench and the mess at his feet as he took Blake's hand, held on.

"Mom?" Blake was sobbing, his face wet and smeared. Before he could say more, he was seized by another violent spasm. And then another. Until, finally, he seemed to be spent.

Brian stepped forward with the washcloth. "Thanks, Brian." Valerie heard Kirk over her softly spoken reassurances to Blake. Was thankful when, after she pulled her son onto her lap and cradled him against her, Kirk gently wiped his face and hands.

"You're going to be fine," she told Blake over and over. "No big deal." It was the first time she'd ever knowingly lied to her son.

She had no idea whether or not Blake would be fine. And she knew for sure that the amount of blood he'd vomited couldn't possibly be a good thing.

SHE'D CERTAINLY never expected to spend Christmas night at the hospital. Still in shock, Valerie sat in one of the old padded leather armchairs beside Blake's bed, with Kirk occupying the chair next to her. Blake and Brian were side by side on the bed, heads bent over a new handheld video game they'd received for Christmas.

"Guess we should've known Blake was going to be okay when he grabbed that game on the way out," Kirk said softly. A sitcom rerun was playing on the television but the boys seemed to be tuning out everything except each other.

"He just remembers when he broke his arm," Valerie said. "After the initial fright and pain had worn off, his worst memory of the whole thing was waiting for half a day to have the cast put on."

"How old was he?"

"Seven."

"So his father was still alive."

"Yeah." She glanced at the boys, tense, as always, when their father was mentioned. One of Brian's legs hung over the edge of the bed.

"I'm guessing he wasn't there waiting with his son."

That was an understatement. When Thomas had returned home that night, he'd been oblivious to the entire event, having deleted her messages without listening to them.

"Yeah! Get him!" Brian said as Blake maneuvered the game in his hand. He didn't seem to be bothered by the limited movement imposed by the IV attached to his hand. Another hour or two, and they should be able to go home.

"We need to talk about this, guys," Kirk said, slouched in his chair with an ankle over his knee, one elbow resting on the arm of the chair.

Both boys, with apprehension in their identical green eyes, looked up at him, the abandoned game in Blake's hand continuing to emit sound effects.

His head sliding along the back of the chair, Kirk glanced over at Valerie. "Do you mind?"

"No, go ahead." Mind? Didn't he know how much

he'd helped her that day? The strength she'd been able to give to her sons—one while he was subjected to uncomfortable tests and the other while he waited anxiously to find out if his twin was going to be all right—was in large part due to the strength she'd gained from Kirk's calm presence.

From the beginning, he'd treated the entire episode like just another day in sunny Arizona. And in the end, things were going to be as fine as he'd made them seem.

"You heard what the doctor said about the cause of bleeding ulcers," he said, addressing both boys in a voice sterner than she'd ever heard him use.

Two dark curly heads bobbed solemnly.

"He explained that you might have a predisposition to gastric ulcers, but there are certain things that can trigger them or make them worse. Do you understand all that?" Both boys nodded. "The drugs he listed—aspirin and so on—are out. So is heartburn and almost everything else he named." Though his pose was relaxed, Kirk's expression was intent. Looking between him and her boys, Valerie was glad just to sit back, not to carry the burden all by herself for once. She *could* have; she knew that.

But how wonderful that she didn't have to.

"So what does that leave?"

"Worry," Brian said. Blake looked down at the blanket.

"Right." Kirk's forehead wrinkled in a way that had grown endearingly familiar to Valerie. "So what do you think was worrying your brother so much that it made him sick?"

The boys exchanged a glance that brought tears to Valerie's eyes. Their silent communication had always been a source of awe to her. Tonight, even she could hear the message of shared affection, sorrow and blame.

"Me," Brian finally answered. "He was worried about me."

"And Mom," Blake said, peering over at her, his look one of apology, but also of an odd defiance. "She's always doing everything by herself. Just tells us not to worry and she'll take care of it." He met Kirk's eyes. "We're going to be teenagers in another couple of months. And she won't let us help."

The smile on her face didn't falter, but the calm that had settled over her heart after she'd been assured that her son was going to be fine with medication and a carefully watched diet was no longer there.

She'd caused this?

"It's the same with Brian," Blake continued while Brian stared at the game in his brother's hand. "Everyone keeps saying he wasn't eating 'cause he had low self-esteem. Well, how do you think it makes a guy feel to always have his mother taking care of him and never letting him do anything to take care of her? We're the men of the house, but you sure wouldn't know it."

A long speech for anyone, it was even more astonishing coming from Blake.

Kirk's head still rested against the back of the chair, and his gaze turned on Brian. "You agree with your brother?"

With hooded eyes, Brian glanced from one adult to the other. And then nodded.

"So what do you guys think can be done to fix this?"

"I'm going to eat every meal every day for as long as I live," Brian said with such vehemence Valerie almost smiled. In spite of the tears pressing at the backs of her eyes. And then he grinned. "Kind of hard for a guy to feel worthless when his own brother cares so much he gets sick about it."

Valerie did smile then. But they weren't through yet. "And I guess I'm going to be doing less and you guys are going to be doing more," she said, knowing how difficult that would be. She'd been taking care of them single-handedly for twelve years. She'd had to. Giving that up was not going to come easy.

But perhaps it would make their lives easier. In the long run.

"There's another thing bugging me, Mom," Blake said. He looked at his twin and Brian nodded. "They're going to split us up when we go into eighth grade next year," he finished for his brother.

"Yeah," Blake took up. "Mr. McDonald said we have to be on a whole different track from each other."

"It means we won't even be in the same classes." Brian sounded as though he'd been sentenced to life in prison.

Suddenly aware of Kirk beside her, of his tough-love approach to her boys, she smiled at the two of them. "Let's talk about this later," she said. "Everything'll work out. You know it always does."

She'd go see McDonald as soon as school was back in session. She'd ask him to reconsider his decision for next fall, explain why it wasn't a good one.

"You know, if you guys do get separated, it won't be the end of the world," Kirk said lightly. "You'll have that much more to talk about when you meet up again."

"Yeah, but—"

"Nothing is ever going to break the bond that draws you two together," Kirk interrupted. "Unless one or the other of you *chooses* to break it."

He was right about that. But she didn't think her sons should be separated. Especially not now that they were both on the road to recovery.

Let them just be happy and well. It was the only thing in the world she wanted.

As long as she didn't look at the man by her side.

CHAPTER EIGHTEEN

"FAX ME THE PAPERWORK and I'll fly down over the weekend and get him to sign." Cell phone to his ear, Kirk paced around a dining-room table filled with manila folders labeled alphabetically for immediate access.

"It's the day after Christmas, man. I'm taking the rest of the weekend to spend with my sister and her kids."

Yeah, he'd just bet Troy was spending four days with a sister he could barely tolerate for four hours.

"We'll lose the deal if we don't move now," he said. There was an old man dying in a hospital who wanted to know that his eighty-nine-year-old widow wouldn't have to worry about the business he'd run for nearly seventy years. Kirk had found him a buyer.

One who'd called Troy to renege on the deal when his son told him the investment wasn't sound. Kirk knew it was. Knew, too, that he could convince his buyer.

He looked at the table. "And while you're at it, get a flight to Phoenix. I have a week and a half before school starts again and three weeks' worth of work to get through."

"Which we'll knock off before school starts if we

have to stop the clock to do it.'' Troy didn't sound as upset about that as his words might imply.

"If we don't move, we lose," Kirk said softly, his mind on a merger between two family-owned regional hardware chains that were both going under beneath the buying power of the national home-improvement conglomerates that had risen up all over the country. Unless he could find common ground for them. They each had their own terms, seemingly incompatible terms, but Kirk had some ideas.

"We don't move, we lose." Troy's nostalgic tone, more than the words, suddenly registered.

"What?" he asked, frowning as he studied a piece of art his mother had bought years ago; it had never really gone with anything but it continued to grace the walls of this room.

"You're finally back," Troy said.

Kirk immediately launched an adamant denial. Refusing to give voice to the secret fear inside him that his friend and lawyer might be right.

He'd changed. He *had* to have changed. He couldn't face his daughter, or himself, if he was the same man today that he'd been the day he'd received the phone call about Alicia. The call that said she'd been hit by a car and wasn't expected to live. He'd been involved in a multibillion-dollar hostile takeover.

And had signed the deal before he'd let anyone interrupt him with the news.

Those precious hours were the last that Alicia had been conscious.

"V-V-VAL-ERIE?"

Her mind on the report in front of her when she picked up the phone, Valerie quickly focused on her caller.

"Susan?" There'd been so many tearful calls from the other woman two years before.

"Y-yes." The next sentence was so badly garbled with hiccups and whispery sobs that Valerie couldn't decipher the words.

"Calm down, Susan," she said, speaking in the judge's voice she used with kids who were losing control in her courtroom. "I can't help you if I can't understand."

It took the woman a long minute of deep breaths and failed attempts, but finally she managed to get out an entire sentence.

"I've been ordered to take Colton in for a paternity test."

Oh. God. Kirk was getting nowhere with his pursuit and some cold controlling bastard was awarded a test.

"Have you told Alexander about any of this yet?" she asked. When she'd last spoken to Susan, advising her on what to have her lawyer do, she'd practically begged the woman to tell her new husband what was going on.

"No." A couple of ragged breaths followed. And then, "I just couldn't. He's been so good to me. I couldn't tell him I slept with the bastard."

Susan's inability to say her ex-husband's name spoke volumes to Valerie. It was months after Thomas's death before she could allow his name back into her vocabulary. Before that, just thinking his name made her break down.

Detachment was one hell of a coping mechanism.

"Read me the order," she said, letting the subject of Alexander go for now.

She had to wait another five minutes for Susan to get through the whole thing. Or at least enough of it so Valerie could fill in the blanks.

It sounded pretty tightly sealed.

But she couldn't tell Susan that. At least not until she'd taken a look at the order herself. "I'd like to send a courier over for the order and copies of all the other paperwork your lawyer has given you," she said. "Would that be okay with you?"

"O-kayyyyy." The word slurred into another sob.

"I'll send him right now, Susan," Valerie said firmly, sensing how important it was to give the woman something to do. And to get those papers out of her house. "That means you need to have the papers ready. Understand?"

"I do. I-I-I'll have them."

The second she was off the phone, Valerie had Leah arrange for a courier to run by Susan Douglas's house. And left instructions to let her know the second the paperwork arrived.

HER FIRST DAY BACK at work after the Christmas break was extremely busy, and she wasn't back in her office until four o'clock that afternoon.

"It came." Leah met her at the door of their suite and followed Valerie into her office. Nodding, Valerie unzipped her robe and hung it up. Before she sat down, she checked her caller ID. This was the boys' first day back at school, and while Blake had been fine during their quiet vacation at home, just the three of them—plus a few dinners with Kirk, Valerie was still worried about her son.

Releasing a sigh of relief when she saw the blank display, she sank down into her chair, taking the file that Leah handed her.

Opened it.

And felt the blood drain from her face.

"Judge?" Leah's made-up face and twisted light brown hair came into view. Valerie wondered why people thought those ends sticking up like that were attractive. Of course, on Leah, they were. They were part of her elfin charm.

"You okay?" her assistant asked, sitting in the chair across from Valerie. Leah's black slacks had a leopardskin waistband. Which matched the collar on her white silk blouse.

"Have I ever told you how much I like your wardrobe?" she asked.

Leah's eyes narrowed. "No."

Pulling at the collar of her gray flannel dress, Valerie nodded. "Well, I do."

"Thanks."

She glanced at the papers again, and then back up, still nodding. She didn't know what else to do.

"What's wrong?"

What was wrong? Was anything wrong? Valerie wasn't sure. She just felt that nothing was ever going to be right again.

There was no basis for that thought. She wasn't

involved, wasn't committed. She'd had sex. Once. She hadn't even told the man she loved him.

She didn't love him.

She didn't want to love him.

She glanced at the top page again.

It couldn't be. And yet, it made a twisted sort of sense. Kirk had been so reticent about his past. And with a past like his, who wouldn't be?

Leah leaned forward. ''What can I do?''

Looking up, Valerie opened her mouth to tell her there was no reason to do anything. And did something she'd never done at work before. Not even her first day back after Thomas's accident. She started to cry.

''Judge?'' Leah came around to her side of the desk, slid an arm around Valerie's shoulders, gave her a hug. ''Can I get you some water?''

Wiping her eyes, Valerie nodded again. It seemed to be the only thing she could do. ''A bottle of water would be nice,'' she said with a tremulous smile.

He'd tried to change his life, hadn't he? That could be what the crossing guard and coaching stuff was all about. And if that was so, she could hardly blame him for needing to leave his old life behind. For lying to people in the new life he'd created.

After all, he couldn't escape if he brought his sins with him.

Pulling a bottle from the little refrigerator in one corner of Valerie's office, Leah handed it across the desk, reseating herself.

''Tell me what's wrong.''

Valerie glanced down at the report one more time,

and then up at Leah. "You know that crossing guard I told you about?" she asked.

"The one who is the boys' basketball coach?"

"Yeah."

"The one you've been meeting for coffee and late-night walks?"

She wished she'd never told her assistant about that. Thank God Leah didn't know what else Valerie had done with Kirk Chandler.

"He's the man who's claiming to be the father of Susan Douglas's baby."

Eyes wide, Leah gaped at her. "The crossing guard is Susan Douglas's multimillionaire ex-husband?"

"Apparently." She pushed the papers across to her assistant. There was no way the man Susan had described to her was the same man who'd sat with her at the hospital on Christmas night. Or bought dinner for her and the boys two evenings this past week.

He'd lied to her—by omission.

But could she blame him? She'd lied to him, too, by omission. About the Billings case.

Because she was trying to do the right thing. The *good* thing.

And wasn't that what *he* was doing? "By their fruits ye shall know them." A favorite quote of her parents' sprang to mind. By their actions and the results of their actions; that was how people revealed what they really were.

The actions of the Kirk Chandler she knew were generous and compassionate.

It couldn't be the same man.

There had to be an explanation. She was just missing it.

"His having the same name as Susan's ex didn't surprise you?" Leah asked.

"I don't think I ever heard his name from Susan. She reverted to her maiden name when they divorced and apparently had Alicia's changed, too, because the name in the obituary was the same as Susan's. Or maybe that was a mistake." Valerie stared at the papers, unseeing. "She never called him anything but the bastard or him or, once or twice, her ex."

Kirk had lied to her. He'd told her the episode with the woman he'd impregnated had been a one-night stand. Of course, technically, it had been. Susan was engaged to be married at the time.

And Susan. She'd lied, too. In that call right before Christmas, she'd told Valerie that Kirk had threatened her. That he had a violent temper. That she was afraid for her life.

Valerie had told Susan to have her attorney file an order of protection. Looking through the pages Leah had handed back, she saw that it had been done. And that he hadn't requested a hearing to fight the allegation within the allotted ten-day timeframe.

An order of protection against Kirk Chandler? She couldn't imagine it.

Kirk was certain he was Colton's father.

Susan was certain he was not.

And she'd suffered so much already.

Kirk was suffering, too. Although, now that she thought about it, Valerie wasn't so sure anymore. The man must be a consummate liar. A master of evasion.

No wonder he could afford that house of his. He was a barracuda. An immoral, conniving man who'd fathered a little girl he'd never known.

He was just like Thomas.

He was the man she'd fallen in love with.

"I had to identify Thomas's car after the accident." She had no idea where the words came from. Or why. But one look at the compassion on her assistant's face and Valerie couldn't stop the flow.

"I saw the stains on the front of the car—where he'd hit the little girl." She stopped, her sight turned inward to images she usually tried to suppress.

"And the first time I met Susan... After I saw the obituary in the paper, the picture of that child's innocent, smiling face, I went around to Susan's house to offer my condolences, to see if there was anything I could do."

Valerie closed her eyes. "I stood there in Susan's house, seeing this ashen woman surrounded by boxes, the remnants of a life that had ended. The woman was only half-alive herself."

Leah didn't say much, just sat and listened as Valerie relived some of the worst moments of that time in her life.

LATER, in the Mercedes heading home long before she felt ready, Valerie tuned in to her favorite classical station. She hadn't even made it out of the parking lot before her mind was once again stumbling over memories too painful for words.

Where had Kirk Chandler been while his ex-wife was dying inside? Out hunting down deals? People he could force out of business? Susan had said he'd owned an acquisitions firm. That he'd built his reputation on successful hostile takeovers.

That thought led to more memories, things Susan had told her about her ex-husband, how his work had consumed his life, how it had been all about winning. She remembered how she'd thought that Susan's ex-husband and her own had been cast from the same mold.

On the freeway, as she headed from Mesa to Ahwatukee, Kirk's more recent actions took on new meaning. Like his refusal to back down with Abraham. Or Brian, for that matter. Yes, with Brian his approach had worked. But with Abraham? She'd assumed he'd stopped seeing the boy, but had he? Suddenly she didn't think so.

And although the decision to remove Abraham from his home had been extremely difficult, Valerie trusted her judgment on that one. Did guys like Kirk Chandler trust theirs? Or did they just push hard enough to get what they wanted? The man had no scruples. She didn't know a lot about Kirk Chandler the businessman. It had only taken one episode related by Susan to give her a measure of the man. He'd put his own father out of business in a hostile takeover.

Chilled, Valerie remembered the night Kirk had told her about his father's selling of the family business. She understood now the odd note in his voice when he'd told her he'd approved of the sale.

Exiting the freeway, Valerie passed the new mall without a glance. Unscrupulous in business, Kirk

Chandler had also never been a father to Alicia or a husband to Susan. And that about said it all.

He was Thomas all over again. The last thing her boys needed.

Thinking of the twins reminded her of the night Kirk had told her about his son. The fierce need to be a father to the boy hadn't been faked. It couldn't have been.

So could Kirk be that baby's father?

And didn't he have a right to know if he was?

As she sped through town, getting ever closer to home, thoughts of the man she'd known these past months crowded her mind. Whatever he'd been in the past, right now he was nothing more than a crossing guard at an elementary school. Well, that plus playground monitor and lunchroom supervisor. And, of course, a basketball coach.

And he'd been all the father any boy could have hoped for when Blake was so sick on Christmas Day. More of a father than their own had ever been.

It had to be a mistake. She'd make a call first thing in the morning and find out that this was all some horrible coincidence—that there were two men with the same name at the same address involved in a paternity suit. Because that was all her Kirk and Susan's Kirk had in common. A name. An address. And a paternity suit.

By the time she crawled into bed that night with a colossal headache, sick with confusion, Valerie had made one decision. She was going to call Susan Douglas in the morning and recommend that she take

Colton in for a paternity test. It was the only way the woman would ever find any peace.

Because one thing was for sure: Kirk Chandler was not going to give up.

KIRK'S HANDS were clammy and trembling as he started his Vette Wednesday morning after crossing-guard duty. He had an appointment at the hospital in fifteen minutes. For the past hour he'd been replaying the early-morning phone call from his attorney. Susan had agreed to the paternity test.

As early as that afternoon, Kirk might have his son. At least in name. And, knowing Troy, it wouldn't be long after that before he was holding the boy in his arms. He couldn't wait to tell Valerie.

Mostly to keep his thoughts in check, he put in a call to her office on the way to his appointment. She was on the bench, as he'd known she would be, but just hearing her on voice mail calmed him. He didn't leave a message.

This was something he wanted to tell her in person. But he didn't think he'd be able to wait until that evening to share his news.

Test over in minutes, Kirk tried Valerie again, his heart skipping a beat when she answered her phone.

"Hi," he greeted her.

"Kirk, hi." The note of gladness that usually accompanied her greeting wasn't there. Her immediate question explained it. "What's wrong? Is Blake bleeding again? I knew I should've made him stay home an extra week or two. Seventh grade can be pretty stressful—"

"Whoa, slow down," he interrupted with a smile. "I'm just calling to ask you and the boys out to dinner. I have some good news."

"I'm sorry, I can't." Her refusal surprised and disappointed him, not that any negative emotion could last against the elation he was feeling. He'd been given a second chance. "With Blake being sick," she said, "I let things go for too long at home and I'm overwhelmed with chores."

"Can I help?"

"No, the boys have to help. Remember?"

Yeah, and being included in that intimate family memory just added to the glow of this day.

"I could help with their homework while you do other things."

"That's okay. They don't usually have much on Wednesdays except word lists to study. They help each other with that."

"How about a quick trip for ice cream?" She hadn't been this difficult to convince in months. Not that Kirk was deterred by that. Right now, life was as close to perfect as it was ever going to get for him.

"I'm sorry, Kirk, I do want to see you, I need to talk to you, but tonight just isn't good."

Kirk hung up the phone and shook off the sense of foreboding the conversation had given him. Whatever was bothering her he'd just have to fix.

Odd, though, how she'd never asked about his news.

IN SPITE OF HIS CALL to Valerie, Kirk was still buoyed when he left school that afternoon. And, since he couldn't see Valerie and her boys, he knew exactly who he should spend his evening with.

Abraham was delighted to see him, almost too delighted. The boy was outside when Kirk pulled up— and since the visit was unplanned, he couldn't have been waiting for him. Kirk wondered how much time the boy spent out on the street corner, thinking about escape.

"This is so great, Coach," Abraham said, jumping into the car.

"Don't you think you ought to tell Mrs. Morton where you're going?"

"Nah," he said, shaking a head with hair unusually tousled. "They aren't home. Went to some aunt's for dinner, but I didn't want to go."

Pulling slowly away, Kirk glanced at the boy. "They often leave you home alone?"

"I'm not in jail!"

No, but judging by the way he looked, he could have been; all he lacked was the blue cotton pants and short-sleeved shirt. For a boy who'd always been impeccably, if inexpensively, put together, Abraham had fallen apart. His clothes were dirty, the crotch of his pants hanging down to his knees, his shirt looking like he'd slept in it several nights in a row. His hair was longer than normal, unwashed, unkempt.

Over dinner, Kirk's unease only grew. "I can't believe you're really here," the boy said at least four times as they shared a pizza and some soda at a place around the corner from the Mortons'. It wasn't the words that bothered Kirk so much. It was the desperation with which they were uttered.

If the situation didn't improve soon, Abraham was going to do something drastic.

"Come back soon, Coach, okay?" the boy asked as Kirk dropped him off a couple of hours later. They'd shot some hoops at a nearby lighted court and Abraham seemed more relaxed.

"Of course."

"I mean it," Abraham said. He had the door open, but wasn't getting out. There were no lights on in the house, which must have meant the Mortons hadn't returned yet. Kirk didn't understand how it was good for Abraham to be alone at night in a strange house. "Promise you'll be back soon."

"I promise." Kirk gave him the only answer he could. He was coming back, anyway, but as he drove away, he mentally added an extra day a week to the schedule he'd set himself for Billings visits. Apparently spending time with Kirk was the only thing the kid had to hold on to.

AT HOME THAT NIGHT, restless, Kirk thought again about calling Valerie. Maybe she'd finished her chores and they could go for a short walk. Just long enough for him to figure out what was wrong with her. And to share his good news. He got a thrill of anticipation every time he thought about the upcoming days and everything they might bring. Tomorrow, even though it was only a day before the regular floral delivery, he'd take roses to Alicia.

In an effort to focus his energies, he wandered into his dining room, and the projects in various stages waiting for him there. An hour later, consumed by the challenges before him, Kirk caught a glimpse of himself and jumped up from the table, turned off the light and left the room. He was enjoying the work too much.

And it was too late to call Valerie.

He poured a glass of scotch and went out to sit by the pool.

To think about all the things he'd do with his son.

CHAPTER NINETEEN

THURSDAY MORNING, after dropping off the boys, Valerie went in for her appointment with Steve McDonald. Walking quickly, head down, she prayed she could avoid Kirk Chandler. She just wasn't ready to see him yet. Couldn't trust herself to behave appropriately. Partially because she had no idea what that actually entailed.

Screaming at him wasn't something she'd be proud of—but it would sure as hell feel good. Crying was out of the question, but that was what she was afraid she might do. She couldn't remember a time when she'd felt so emotionally fragile.

At least with Thomas, there'd been no illusions of love and support. She'd thought she'd missed those things before, but only now realized that she couldn't miss what she hadn't had. Realized it now that she'd had it—for a few brief, wonderful moments. And missed it already.

''So you see, Mr. McDonald, it's important to the boys that they continue through school together....''

In her navy silk suit, her two-inch heels tucked beneath her, Valerie sat before the principal's desk, eager to be done with this business and get off the school grounds.

She had no idea why Steve McDonald was shaking his head. "We—their counselors and I—don't think that's a good idea, Ms. Simms. Your boys are unusually close, even for twins, and while there are some obvious benefits to that, their closeness also comes with a price. One that can be much higher than you think. The damage such intense interdependence can cause is often greater than the benefits."

What was the man talking about? "Twins share a spiritual connection," she told him. "It's perfectly natural." What kind of counselors did Menlo Ranch employ that they hadn't known something so obvious?

"And being in separate classrooms isn't going to change that," McDonald said, sounding far too much like Kirk Chandler for her peace of mind. "Their identities will have to separate at some point," he said, his hands folded on the desk in front of him. "Unless they marry two women who are willing to live together in the same house and raise their children together, unless they get the same jobs with the same company, it's going to happen."

Of course it would. When they were grown up and—

"Studies show that when the separation comes at an earlier age, twins are far more successful in life and in their relationships."

She opened her mouth, ready to argue her next point, and closed it again. This was déjà vu to an uncomfortable degree. She'd fought Kirk on this very same score. And lost. But Brian had won.

Was it possible that Steve McDonald, like Kirk, could see her boys more clearly than she could?

"Will you at least promise me one thing?" she asked, relaxing back against the seat, her purse in her lap.

"What's that?" The sandy-haired man half squinted at her.

"If the boys aren't thriving after a semester apart, if either of them has a recurrence of the physical problems we've struggled with this year, you'll agree to put them back together."

With one dip of his chin to his chest, McDonald looked at her and smiled. "You've got my word on it."

With that, she'd find a way to be satisfied. She'd worry. But she'd be satisfied.

"I hear both of your sons did quite well on the basketball team this year," McDonald said when she rose to leave.

"They did okay," Valerie told him with a smile. "The games sure were fun to watch."

"Yeah, Menlo Ranch has never even come close to the play-offs before. Kirk Chandler did a great job with them. Not that I'm surprised." He followed her to the closed office door. "He's always had the gift of turning whatever he touches into a success."

Stopping just a couple of feet before the door, Valerie turned. "You sound as if you know him."

"We've been friends all our lives, even roommates in college. I'm actually the reason he's here."

"You are?"

"I'm not sure how much you know about his past,

but since he mentioned having spent Christmas at your house, I guess I can be forgiven for telling you how glad I am to see the change that's come over him these last few months.''

Valerie didn't know what to say. And couldn't walk the few steps it would take to get to the door. ''Oh?''

''Kirk is one of the few men I consider a true friend.''

Steve McDonald seemed like such an ethical man. Yet, if he'd been friends with Kirk his whole life, he must've known him during the past fifteen years.

''He's made some mistakes in his life,'' McDonald continued. ''The man was driven, but had no idea what was driving him.''

Driven to make money, maybe. To win the battle at all costs. Not driven to be a husband or father, though he'd promised to be both.

''After his daughter, Alicia, was killed, Kirk was as determined to kill himself for those mistakes as he'd been to make a success of Chandler Acquisitions to begin with. I offered him the job here to save the life of a friend I value very, very much.''

Valerie said nothing, just waited, needing to hear more even while she didn't want to know as much as she already did.

''Kirk is an immensely determined man. I've always known that he's got what it takes to make a real difference—on a human level, not just business. He's finally figured that out, too, although it took a tragedy....''

Swallowing, Valerie knew she should leave. "He's lucky to have a friend like you."

"How much has he told you about Alicia's death?" McDonald, arms folded across his chest, apparently wasn't ready to let her go.

"Nothing."

"Doesn't surprise me." The principal nodded. "She lived for a full week after she was hit...."

Feeling a little faint, Valerie reminded herself there was no way the man could know that Blake and Brian's father had been behind the wheel of the car that had killed his friend's daughter.

"I went to see her a couple of times, and each time was the same. Alicia in her glass bubble room, so many machines hooked up to her body, her head wrapped in gauze, until you couldn't even recognize the little girl beneath. Surrounded by people, her mother and various other loved ones, by a constant parade of medical personnel." He shook his head. "She was oblivious to the world she was leaving behind."

Valerie couldn't take this. Had already imagined this nightmare so many times.

"And always, in a small waiting room with one small window that had a view of the little girl's bed, sat Kirk. All alone. Staring. I can only imagine the helplessness he must've felt, this powerful man, so filled with determination, finding out that in the end, he was powerless."

Valerie didn't, couldn't, respond.

Steve looked away. "There was no question about

the depth of his grief, though. Even an insensitive klutz like me could feel it.''

She couldn't stop the tears that sprang to her eyes. Didn't even care, at that point, that she couldn't stop them. Steve McDonald was pretty close to tears himself.

''Did you know his ex-wife wouldn't let him in the room to see Alicia?''

When Susan had told her that, Valerie hadn't blamed her....

''The night Alicia died, Susan had finally been led away for a couple of hours' rest. The child could've hung on another week, and Susan hadn't slept at all.'' McDonald paused, peering at Valerie, but she had a feeling he wasn't really seeing her.

''So quietly people barely noticed at first, Kirk slipped inside that room and had an intent conversation with his daughter. I have no idea what he said, but he walked out of that room a changed man. A dying man—until he came to work here.''

KIRK WAS SURPRISED and delighted when there was a message from Valerie on his cell phone Thursday afternoon. She wanted to meet him for coffee at their usual time that night. He left her a message that he'd be there.

And he was, in time to get the private alcove in the back of the coffee shop, and have their drinks ordered and waiting for her. He hadn't yet heard the final results about his son, but was eager to share the good news, anyway.

And to find out what had been bothering her the

night before. Half afraid she'd heard that he'd been to see Abraham again, he had a full artillery planned to convince her to agree with him.

She looked great in a pair of black jeans and a white angora sweater, her feet clad in suede boots with the requisite high heels. She didn't meet his eyes as she sat down—as far from him as she could get on the small love seat.

"I know who you are." The words were ominous. He felt them with a force that was as familiar as it was debilitating. It was the same way he felt every single time he thought of his daughter. Fear, guilt, grief...

"You've always known who I am," he said, attempting to buy time even realizing it was up.

"I know about your past. You're Susan Douglas's ex-husband. Alicia's father. Owner of the now-defunct Chandler Acquisitions."

Walls of ice slid around Kirk. He sat back, leaving his coffee on the table. Hot though it was, it wouldn't thaw him. "You've got good sources."

"My husband, Blake and Brian's father, was the drunk who killed your daughter."

Heart jerking out of rhythm, Kirk stared at her. They were in a coffee shop, for God's sake. You didn't just blurt out something like that.

"He was?"

He couldn't think of anything else to say.

She nodded. And, white and pinched, looked as sick as he felt.

Weren't they just a pair, a mass of mangled emotions, of mistakes and regrets and unfixable pain.

Shock was a good thing. It numbed.

"Small world."

She didn't acknowledge the statement.

"I guess you don't see what you don't want to see," he said a few long seconds later.

Still nothing from her.

"How long have you known?"

Have you been lying to me as long as I've been lying to you? Not that it mattered. It was over.

Just like the rest of his life.

Except Colton. He'd have his son. Which was more than he'd ever dared hope. More than he deserved.

"Since Monday."

Which certainly explained why she'd blown him off the other night.

She hadn't been lying nearly as long as he had.

She'd been married to the man who'd killed Alicia. A man Kirk hated with every part of him. A man he hated almost as much as himself.

Watching Valerie, wondering distantly, if she hated him now as much as he hated himself, he hoped she didn't feel any responsibility for the accident. Even while he knew she did.

He wondered, too, from an even greater distance, how much she regretted sleeping with him.

Rocking forward, her torso leaning over her knees, she stared at the space between their table and the floor. "I'm sorry."

For what? That she'd slept with two bastards? That his daughter was dead? That her husband was?

Sorry their relationship, whatever it was, had ended?

He'd known it was coming. Cosmic justice. He'd fallen for a woman who hated everything his life stood for—the wife of the man who'd taken Alicia's life. Surely something stronger than human will created this twisted, farcical mess of coincidence, this confusion of identities, almost Shakespearean in its dimensions.

Were they laughing now, whoever had arranged this—to punish him?

Had he finally paid what he owed?

Did the bill ever get marked "paid in full?"

"How'd you find out?" It didn't matter; he just didn't know what else to say to fill the suffocating silence.

"I've been advising Susan regarding the paternity case."

He thought he was beyond surprise. Apparently not.

"After the…accident…I saw Ali—your daughter's obituary in the paper." She looked at him over her hunched shoulder. "Her name wasn't Chandler."

"When Susan took her maiden name back, she gave it to Alicia, too. Said it was better that way for school records and such."

"And let me guess, you didn't fight her on it."

"Nope." Which was why even Alicia's headstone bore no part of her father. Other than the roses he kept putting there.

"I saw that picture and couldn't get her out of my mind," she continued after a while in a faraway voice. "Eventually, I went to see Susan, to offer to help her. We kind of became friends. She used to call.

I'd do what I could. What we had in common was horrible, but it was still something in common.''

At least now he understood the complete change in her. Not only had she found him out, but she'd heard it all from the tainted perspective of an emotionally disturbed woman.

''Do you want to hear any of this from my point of view?'' he asked, although he wasn't sure why. What could dragging this out possibly serve? Except to complete his penance and let him move on.

And maybe to help her see that, while he was definitely a bastard, she hadn't slept with the devil himself, which was how Susan would surely have painted him.

''Okay.''

Her tone of voice, her hunched, dejected posture, her expression, were not encouraging. He'd been accused, tried and convicted.

For a crime he'd committed.

Telling himself it was for her sake, he tried anyway. He spared himself nothing as he told her about the years after college, the thrill of finally having a real challenge. The thrill of being in control. Of being the one with power, instead of the one being chained down by the power of others. And then he told her a bit about his life after the accident.

About the night Steve McDonald had stopped by and found him on the third day of a drunk that could eventually have killed him. And how, during the long hours of sobering up, his friend had talked to him and he'd begun to see a way to actually keep the promise he'd made to his dying daughter.

"What promise?"

Kirk leaned forward, elbows on his knees, turning his head to look at her. "That I'd lived my last day for me. That the rest of my life was going to be for others—for kids—who needed my help. That I'd give everything I had over to making sure that other children benefited from the drive and determination that had kept me from her life."

She didn't say anything, but he could sense a softening. And was pathetic enough to let it touch him.

Her silence was unnerving. But he couldn't just walk away and leave her like this.

Yeah, and how much was he kidding himself to think he could walk away at all? Until she sent him out of her life.

He couldn't believe she knew the man, had loved the man who'd killed Alicia.

Couldn't believe he'd never made the connection before. Couldn't believe he wasn't more appalled by it. Except that he knew how Valerie felt about her ex-husband. And he also knew he and that man were alike.

It was probably just the shock, the blessed deadness inside him, but the bitterness, the vile acid, that normally ate him alive when he thought of Thomas Smith was not there.

How could he revile Thomas Smith when he, Kirk Chandler, had hurt his daughter so badly himself?

"So where are you?" he asked.

"I honestly don't know." Her hands clasped in front of her, she glanced at him and then away. "I just keep weighing the evidence over and over."

Always the judge. Which just about killed any chance he might've had. Not that he'd really had any.

"What's the evidence?"

There had to be a way to get up and simply leave. A statement that would allow him to say goodbye. To exit the final scene of this tragedy. He just hadn't found it yet.

"Susan's testimonials over the past two years. And, more recently, Steve McDonald's."

The testimony of an unstable woman. And… "You talked to Steve?"

She nodded, but wasn't forthcoming with any more. Steve would've had only good things to say, Kirk knew that, because Steve was his friend and supporter.

He wondered if Valerie had figured that out—and discounted the testimony.

"There's Alicia's nonexistent father," she continued. "And the hostile takeover of your father's business."

His composure didn't waver. At least on the outside.

"And then there's the man who rescued my sons' health, who's been more of a father to my boys than their own father ever was." She recited her list as though by rote.

So he knew what was in her mind. But not in her heart. Her voice gave nothing away.

She took a deep breath. "There's the man whose wave every morning gave even my worst days a boost." He'd thought she was finished. And braced himself for the other side of that one. "The man

who's making a very fragile woman miserable by in-
sisting on a paternity test that her husband didn't even
know could be necessary. And the man who feels his
responsibility to that child so strongly he can't abandon him, no matter the cost.'' She paused. ''The man
who's learned from his mistakes,'' she said slowly,
''and will go to his grave making sure he doesn't
make the same ones again.''

Glancing over at her, Kirk couldn't help asking,
''Does that mean you might be able to trust me
around your boys at some point in the future? That
you might someday be able to trust me with a long-
term relationship?''

He didn't know where the words had come from.
He wasn't in the market for a long-term relationship.

And the scared look in her eyes was all the answer
he needed.

''I guess the judge has made her judgment,'' he
said. Standing, he walked quietly away.

He'd found his exit line.

ON BREAK between her morning and afternoon calendars on Friday, Valerie picked up the phone to find
Linda James, Abraham Billings's caseworker, along
with his attorney, on the line with a conference call.

''Judge, Abraham Billings is in the hospital.''

''What?'' She sat forward. ''Why?'' Had his
mother been notified yet?

''Took a bottle of pills. Trying to kill himself. We
got to him in time. Pumped his stomach. He's stable
now.''

''I'll write an order for a 72-hour assessment in the

psychiatric ward immediately,'' Valerie said, sick to her stomach. In moments the business was done and the three of them said goodbye.

Still on the line, Valerie wasn't surprised that Linda hadn't hung up, either.

"He left a note," Linda said as soon as the attorney had clicked off. "It's scrambled and hard to read, but the gist of it is that without his mother, or a chance at a basketball scholarship, there's no point in dealing with all the other crap."

"His coach told me that Abraham perked up a lot when he made the team, that basketball could have been a lifesaver," Valerie told her.

"His probation officer said he'd been dealing with episodes at home a little better," Linda agreed. "Handling them without becoming part of them."

Valerie knew Linda well. Respected her. "Do you think that excelling at a sport might've been enough to help Abraham find the solid ground he needed?"

"Sure," the woman said. "Anything's possible." And then, "But you know, Judge, he'd probably have found it with the Mortons, too, if that coach hadn't kept coming by to see him."

So Chandler *had* been visiting Abraham. And he'd done so repeatedly. She'd suspected as much. And was still disappointed to have her suspicion confirmed. The man was as determined and know-it-all as ever.

"There are no easy answers, are there?"

"No, Judge, there sure aren't. Abraham might've made it quicker if he'd been able to stay home and play ball. But he might've ended up dead, too."

"I could have found a way to keep him on that team, even if it meant getting someone to carpool him back to Menlo Ranch."

"You'd have had a hell of a time finding someone willing to do all that driving."

Valerie didn't think so. She knew one man who would have jumped at the chance.

KIRK WAS at the cemetery Friday afternoon, rearranging the baby-pink roses that had been delivered, when his cell phone rang. Recognizing Troy's number, he answered immediately.

"Sorry, pal." Troy's voice was deader than most of the people around him. "Tests came back negative."

"What do you mean, negative?" he asked, turning his back so his gruff tone was away from his daughter's grave. What was Troy talking about?

"I mean you are not the father of Susan's baby."

You are not the father of Susan's baby.

The words reverberated through Kirk after he hung up the phone. Sliding down to his usual seat against the headstone, he took the news calmly. His heart wasn't beating any faster. His breathing was normal. There was no anger raging through him. No veins popping in his neck.

You are not the father of Susan's baby.

He wasn't really surprised. He'd wanted to believe in second chances, but all along, he'd known better. Since watching his baby girl lose her battle with life, while he sat helplessly, unable to do a damn thing to save her, he'd known he was not what fathers were made of. He'd been born without whatever instinct was given to a man that enabled him to be a good father.

He wasn't hero material.

"You knew your old man was a fool all along, didn't you, sweetheart?" he asked softly, pulling at some grass between his feet. "What would I have done with a second chance, anyway? Except fail? The only talents your father has lie in business, little girl. He can succeed there all day long. But don't ever get to hoping he'll succeed at life, you hear me?" His tone grew louder with the intensity of his message to her. "Because you'll just be setting yourself up for disappointment if you do, and I can't bear to disappoint you again, Alicia."

Though he stayed and talked to her long after darkness had fallen and the ground had grown cold, Alicia never said a word.

KIRK WASN'T REALLY surprised to see Valerie's car outside his house that evening. She knew Susan, could easily get his address if she didn't have it already, and would also have heard that Susan's son was not his.

He just wasn't sure if she was there to commiserate. Or to gloat. He couldn't imagine either.

"Where have you been?" she asked, almost like an accusatory wife, as he stopped the Vette in the driveway and climbed out.

"The cemetary," he said before he'd registered the urgency in her tone.

His senses were dulled but not dead. Yet. "What

is it?'' he asked, hurrying over to her. If one of the twins was sick or in trouble...

He'd do whatever it took to wipe that stricken expression from her beautiful face.

''Abraham Billings attempted suicide today. He's in a hospital on the west side. He's conscious, but won't talk to anyone but you.''

Kirk insisted on driving, and on the way to the hospital Valerie gave him the details. By the time he reached the boy's room, he was himself again. Strong. Determined.

''IT'S NOT THAT the Mortons are so bad,'' Abraham told Kirk, talking to him like a desperate kid confiding in a trusted adult. Valerie couldn't help recognizing the positive effect Kirk had on the boy. The trust that had developed between them. Before he saw Kirk, his face had been sullen. Drawn.

It was the only kind of look she'd ever seen in the past. With the exception of the few minutes in her courtroom while they were removing him from his mother.

Carla Billings had been called, and had made a quick trip over. They'd only let her see him for an hour. She'd left eventually, but had adamantly announced she'd be back.

Mrs. Morton had been by the boy's side the entire day, having left only to go down to the cafeteria for a late dinner after Valerie and Kirk arrived.

''It's just that, you know, I miss what I had. You. The team. Every time I see you, I think about the other kids getting you every day at school and I just about go crazy wanting that, too.''

He was nothing more than a sensitive little boy looking for love. And acceptance. And a place to belong.

Kirk wasn't saying much all of a sudden and, looking at his face, Valerie suspected she knew why. He'd just realized he was partially to blame for Abraham's current state. Right before her eyes, he shut down. The energy that pulsated through him with such tangible force slid away; the sparkle of determination in his eyes grew dim.

He didn't give up on the boy, though, telling Valerie more about himself, about his motivations and priorities, in those few minutes than any amount of evidence could have done.

''Let's make a deal, shall we?'' he asked the boy, leaning forward as though the two of them were alone.

''What kind of deal?'' Today's experience appeared to have humbled the boy.

''I'll see to it that you play basketball on a competitive team if you cooperate with your new living conditions. You're going to be in a treatment center for a little while, probably not long, but when you return to the Mortons you're to give them a real chance.''

The boy's eyes shadowed. ''They might not want me back.''

''Oh, they do,'' Mrs. Morton said from the doorway, her plump form bringing cheer into the room.

Kirk stood to give the foster mother the seat next to Abraham. ''What do you say, sport?''

The boy's big brown eyes, peering so trustingly up at Kirk, almost broke Valerie's heart. ''I miss my mom. I need to be home with her.''

Valerie stepped forward then, hoping she wasn't making a mistake. ''Your mom needs some time to herself, Abraham,'' she said softly. ''Time in which she can learn to be the mom to you that she wants to be. This isn't forever, you know. Just long enough to make things right and then you can go home again....''

The boy was frowning, clearly not trusting her.

''It's the best shot you're going to get, son,'' Kirk said sternly.

''I'll think about it,'' Abraham said, clearly not convinced. ''But not unless I get to see my mom.''

''We'll talk about this in court, Abraham,'' Valerie said. ''I'll set a hearing for next week.''

It was the best she could do.

KIRK DIDN'T SAY a word once they left the hospital. Watching for any expression that might cross his face—but didn't—Valerie started to worry about him in earnest. She tried repeatedly to engage him in conversation, but by the time he pulled up at her car parked outside his house, he still hadn't said more than five words.

He expected her to get out before he drove into his garage. She couldn't.

''Just go,'' he said after a long uncomfortable minute.

''You know,'' she said slowly, quietly, ''my husband and I had such incredible dreams when we graduated from law school. We were going to make a real difference, change the world one step at a time. It never occurred to me that we wouldn't. So when the dreams started to disappear, I didn't even see it. I was taking myself so seriously, I'd completely lost perspective. I could no longer see beyond the daily tasks, the routine. And Thomas—after a while Thomas couldn't see beyond the power. And the winning.''

She had no idea where the words were coming from, no conscious plan; she just knew she couldn't leave him like this.

So she talked.

''Every day I go to work and tell myself it's just a job. I tell myself I do my best and no one expects any more of me than that. But it's a huge amount of pressure, you know? Holding the lives of young kids in my hands day after day. Sometimes I wake up in the night in a cold sweat, afraid I might not get one right.''

She sat straight in the seat, both feet on the floor, gazing out the windshield to the darkness beyond.

''You start to play games with yourself to live with that fear, to pretend it isn't there.'' She was putting into words feelings to which she'd never given form. ''Somewhere along the way, I started to see everything in black and white. I stopped looking back. Refused to second-guess myself. My decisions.''

He wasn't moving. He might not even be listening. But neither was he kicking her out.

''My husband said something to me years ago that

I've never forgotten. Something I never understood until the past couple of days. He talked about a very thin line of gray. Describing it as something very few people found—the perfect middle between the spirit of the law and the letter of the law.''

She wasn't sure where she was going with this. Or even if it mattered.

"Go on."

"In the end, he'd been all about the spirit of the law, but it was his own interpretation of that spirit. While I, in contrast, or maybe even in reaction, had grabbed on to the letter of the law with both hands. Then he got in that accident, killed a precious little girl, and I've been afraid to let go of it ever since.''

Her words fell starkly into the intimate interior of the sports car. Kirk's block had only two streetlights, leaving them in almost total darkness.

"I have to trust my judgment," she told him, knowing now that was true. "Hundreds of kids each year, not to mention all the people in this state, count on my judgment. But I also have to trust my heart. Somehow, through all of this, I quit listening to my heart.''

A DISTANT COMPASSION was all he could muster. Kirk listened, not at all surprised she'd found her way. People like Valerie Simms, honorable and naturally ethical people like her, always did.

"Sounds like you've discovered some peace," he finally spoke.

"I think I have." She sounded surprised.

"I'm glad." And he was. Honestly glad.

She turned in her seat and he wished he'd kept his mouth shut, made her uncomfortable enough to leave. "Don't you see, Kirk," she said, "you've been in both places. Where he was. And where I was. Just think how great you'll be when you bring the two together and—"

Holding up his hand, he silenced her. "You're wasting your time," he said unequivocally. He couldn't sit there and listen to her blowing hope into a life that had used up its share. "You're not the only one who's done a bit of self-discovery. I know who I am."

"And who are you?" Her soft words almost hurt.

"Kirk Chandler," he said quickly, before he forgot, even for a second. "The man who lost a daughter I never knew, who spends more time with her now that she's dead than he ever did when she was alive. The man who lost a wife he didn't love enough, who put his own father out of the business he'd built, store by store. The man who, even now, is living a double life—a crossing guard by day, but a businessman at night."

"You're working at night?"

His affirmation was one slow nod.

"Where?"

"Chandler Acquisitions is back in business." Sort of. "Not on as big a scale, certainly, but that might only be a matter of time."

"The same kind of business?" She sounded like she already knew the answer to that. But there was no way she could.

"Not entirely," he told her, compelled, even now,

to sell himself as a decent human being. "I'm working with mergers instead of takeovers."

"And how are you liking that?"

She was hiding her disapproval well. "These new ventures take longer because rather than just going in and grabbing control, it's become a matter of listening. I try to understand the needs of both parties, so I can find them some common ground. It's a more complicated procedure. But I like it."

"Sounds as if you like it a lot."

Yeah, that was exactly what he was afraid of.

"Maybe you just need to look a little deeper into yourself, Chandler," she said, reverting to the sassy tone she'd used when she'd first known him. "Look with your heart."

Did she really think he hadn't already done that? A dozen times in the past twenty-four hours. "Yeah," he said sarcastically. "And what do you see? You meet Susan, a broken woman whom I've just hurt further. And next to her, notice Abraham, a little boy whose difficult life has just been made harder by my certainty that I knew what was best for him."

"You're right, in a sense," she said, and he wondered if that had been her goal. To get him to admit his faults so she could twist the knife a little more. It was no less than he deserved.

"But not the way you think. It's obvious now that Abraham's problems would most likely have been solved more expediently if I'd kept him in basketball."

And that was supposed to make up for the bottle of pills the boy had taken because of Kirk's insistence on dangling in front of him everything he could no longer have?

"And believe it or not, you did Susan a favor, too."

Now *this* had to be good. A stretch even for Valerie.

"Since the day she found out she was pregnant with Colton, she'd been afraid he was yours. Had you not forced the issue, she would've carried that fear in her heart forever, never knowing for sure if the man she'd named on the birth certificate, the man she loved with all her heart, was really her son's father. She also felt guilty for having slept with you and not telling Alexander. As it turned out, he'd suspected all along. Seems he stopped by her house the night you were there."

Kirk didn't know what to make of that. So he made nothing.

"There are still, and probably always will be, shadows in her life, but she's happier today than I've ever known her."

They were the first words Valerie had said that night that eased the ache in Kirk Chandler's soul.

VALERIE TALKED for another half hour. And nothing she said made the light go back on in Kirk's eyes.

"You talk about your intense determination as if it's something dirty," she told him, frustration creeping in. "But look at what it's done for good."

His gaze was blank, turned toward the windshield and the emptiness outside. "You saved my son's life,

Kirk, because you were determined enough to stand up to me. And to him.''

He nodded. And that was all.

She tried a while longer, but eventually realized she wasn't getting anywhere.

''You know,'' she said, climbing out of his car, ''that determination you're so afraid of just might kill any chance you have at a happy life, after all.'' She told him the black-and-white truth, but she told him straight from the heart. ''Because you're using it to punish yourself.'' She sighed in frustration. ''You succeed at whatever you decide to do—and you're succeeding at this.''

ON HIS WAY TO SCHOOL the following Monday morning, Kirk ran through the reasons he was planning to give Steve McDonald for quitting his job. He was going in early enough so the principal would have time to call in a backup guard for Kirk's street corner. There were always custodians eager for the chance to pick up a few extra bucks.

Then Kirk would go home and make arrangements to rent some office space for the paperwork that was now engulfing two rooms in his house. If it wasn't the life he wanted, it was the life he was cut out for. A life he was good at.

Out of habit, he pulled the Vette up to his usual spot in the parking lot across the street from his corner. At that early hour, the street was deserted, but he could easily picture the kids who would soon be crossing there. They'd have all kinds of things to tell him; they always did. And they'd be wondering why he wasn't there.

He didn't like that. Deserting them without warning. It was something Alicia would have expected of him when she was alive. But not, he hoped, what his angel child believed he'd do.

Grabbing the stop sign from the trunk of his car, Kirk donned his vest and took up his post. After lunch was as good a time to quit as any. Steve would be in his office as soon as the noon meal was over. Kirk had met him there many times for a quick meal of their own. Usually something disgusting like leftover cafeteria pizza.

That was one thing he was not going to miss.

The kids were in rare form that morning, rowdier than usual for a Monday morning. Amanda Sue Bates, a young girl who'd barely spoken a word at the beginning of the year, ran up to the corner when her mother dropped her off. "Guess what, Kirk?"

"What?" He couldn't help grinning at her. He figured the huge smile she was wearing must be hurting her face.

"I get to play Dorothy in the *Wizard of Oz!* They called me over the weekend!"

"That's great, Amanda," he said, nodding at a couple of other kids as they joined them at the corner. "Congratulations! Didn't I tell you you'd be good at acting?"

"You said if I wanted the part badly enough I'd get it," she reminded him.

He smiled. Amanda Sue Bates was born to be an

actress, someone who could shine from behind the guise of characters other than her own shy self.

"You'll come see me, won't you?" she asked, hanging back as he stepped off the curb to let the children pass.

"Sure," he told her. One school play in his lifetime couldn't hurt.

He sensed more than saw Valerie's Mercedes pull up across the street. Blake and Brian tumbled out and raced toward him.

"Mom took us up to the weight room on Saturday..." Brian said.

"...and Brian benched two more pounds than me," Blake finished for him.

"And we're both the same weight."

"Mom told us you had a little girl that died," Brian said. The two boys showed no hurry to cross the street and Kirk couldn't quite make himself step off that curb.

"Her name was Alicia," he told them.

"Blake and I think she was a lucky kid," Brian said.

"Because you'd make a great dad, and all," Blake added.

Unless he counted the endless single moments he'd sat and watched his daughter die, Kirk had never believed in a single moment changing an entire life. But as he stared into the two sets of green eyes looking up at him with unmistakable adoration, something irrevocable happened to him. Something stronger than anything he'd ever experienced. In that seemingly incongruous moment, Valerie's boys healed wounds in him he'd never been able to heal himself.

He gave his life for the children. And they, in turn, gave him life. *His* life.

Completely oblivious to the miracle they'd wrought in one broken man's life, the boys messed with each other all the way across the street, Brian punching Blake's arm as they crossed the grass in front of Menlo Ranch.

As he watched them, it occurred to Kirk that what Valerie had said was true. What her husband had also known and not lived by. For years Kirk had been guided by his own ruthless interpretation of moral law, living his life according to a self-serving vision of what was right. Then he'd gone to the opposite extreme, crucifying himself, accepting only the most literal view of redemption. But the spirit of the law sometimes strayed outside the letter of the law. And in the past few moments he'd discovered that very thin line where the two came together in perfect harmony. Looking over, he saw her standing outside her car.

He willed her to walk across the street, not the least bit surprised when she appeared at his side.

There was no time for words. As a matter of fact, he had only about sixty seconds before the next batch of kids showed up on his corner. But looking into her eyes, he knew there was no need for words. And plenty of time for them later. He kissed her, while a giggling group of six junior-high girls witnessed the sealing of his fate.

"Marry me," he whispered as Valerie pulled away.

"Okay."

He nodded. Turned. And stepped off the curb with his sign. Traffic stopped instantly. Obediently. Kirk Chandler expected no less.

VALERIE DROVE to work that morning with a smile on her face. The rest of her life was going to be filled with challenges; she didn't doubt that for a second. A millionaire crossing-guard businessman for a husband was bound to present some tests. As would living with twin teenage boys. But it was also going to be the best life had to bring. Her fiancé was a determined man; he expected no less.

And she trusted his judgment on that.

THE BIRTH PLACE

Enchantment, New Mexico, is home to The Birth Place, a maternity clinic run by the formidable Lydia Kane. The clinic was started years ago—to make sure the people of this secluded mountain town had a safe place to deliver their babies.

But some births are shrouded in secrecy and shame. What happens when a few of those secrets return to haunt The Birth Place?

January 2004

The Homecoming Baby (#1176)
by Kathleen O'Brien

Patrick Torrance is shocked to discover he's adopted. But that's nothing compared to what he feels when he finds out the details of his birth. He's Enchantment's so-called Homecoming Baby—born and abandoned in the girls' room during a high school dance. There are rumors about his parents, and he's determined to find out the truth. Even if he has to use some of Enchantment's residents to get the answers he wants.

Watch for the conclusion to THE BIRTH PLACE:
February 2004,

The Midwife and the Lawman (#1182)
by Marisa Carroll

Available wherever Harlequin Superromance books are sold.

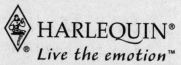

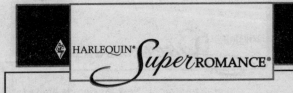

HARLEQUIN *Super*ROMANCE

Crystal Creek
TEXAS

If this is your first visit to
the friendly ranching town
located in the Texas Hill
Country, get ready to meet
some unforgettable people.
If you've been here before,
you'll recognize old friends...
and make some new ones.

Home to Texas
by Bethany Campbell
(Harlequin Superromance #1181)
On sale January 2004

Tara Hastings and her young son have moved to
Crystal Creek to get a fresh start. Tara is excited about
renovating an old ranch, but she needs some help.
She hires Grady McKinney, a man with wanderlust in
his blood, and she gets more than she bargained for
when he befriends her son and steals her heart.

Available wherever Harlequin Superromance books are sold.

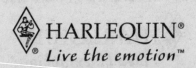

HARLEQUIN®
Live the emotion™

Visit us at www.eHarlequin.com

HSRHTT

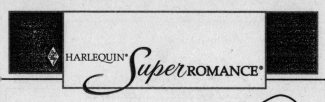

HARLEQUIN *Super*ROMANCE®

The Rancher's Bride
by Barbara McMahon
(Superromance #1179)

On sale January 2004

Brianna Dawson needs to change her life. And for a Madison Avenue ad exec, life doesn't get more different than a cattle ranch in Wyoming. Which is why she gets in her car and drives for a week to accept the proposal of a cowboy she met once a long time ago. What Brianna doesn't know is that the marriage of convenience comes with a serious stipulation—a child by the end of the year.

Getting Married Again
by Melinda Curtis
(Superromance #1187)

On sale February 2004

To Lexie, Jackson's first priority has always been his job. Eight months ago, she surprised him with a divorce—and a final invitation into her bed. Now Jackson has returned from a foreign assignment fighting fires in Russia and Lexie's got a bigger surprise for him—she's pregnant. Will he be here for her this time, just when she needs him the most?

Available wherever Harlequin books are sold.

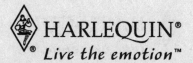

HARLEQUIN®

Live the emotion™

Visit us at www.eHarlequin.com   HSR9MLJ

Forrester Square

LEGACIES · LIES · LOVE ·

*Award-winning author Day Leclaire
brings a highly emotional and
exciting reunion romance story to
Forrester Square in December...*

KEEPING FAITH

by

Day Leclaire

Faith Marshall's dream of a "white-picket" life with
Ethan Dunn disappeared—along with her husband—
when she discovered that he was really a dangerous
mercenary. With Ethan missing in action, Faith found
herself alone, pregnant and struggling to survive.
Now, years later, Ethan turns up alive. Will a family
reunion be possible after so much deception?

*Forrester Square...
Legacies. Lies. Love.*

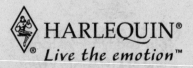

HARLEQUIN®
Live the emotion™

Visit us at www.forrestersquare.com   PHFS5

HARLEQUIN *Super*ROMANCE®

GOING BACK

What if you discovered that all you ever wanted were the things you left behind?

Past, Present and a Future
by Janice Carter
(Harlequin Superromance #1178)

Gil Harper was Clare Morgan's first love. At Twin Falls High School, they were inseparable—until the murder of a classmate tore their world, and their relationship, apart. Now, years later, Clare returns to her hometown, where she is troubled by thoughts of what might have been. What if she and Gil had stayed together? Would they be living happily ever after or would they let past hurts ruin their future together? Clare is finally getting a chance to find out....

Available in January 2004
wherever Harlequin books are sold.

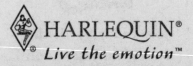

HARLEQUIN®
Live the emotion™